Amber Rose Gill is the winner of *Love Island* 2019, fitness and skincare entrepreneur, and one  television personalities and influe on Instagram, 363k on Twitter YouTube. *Until I Met You* is her Amber's lifelong passion for romantic fiction, and her ambition to see better representation of ethnically diverse characters in the genre. Amber is the face of, and a judge for, the Mills & Boon *Love to Write* competition in search of new romance writers from underrepresented ethnic backgrounds. She lives in London, dreaming of living somewhere warmer and can be found daily on her socials serving up comedic counsel on all things life, love and good vibes.

UNTIL I MET

You

AMBER ROSE GILL

with NADINE GONZALEZ

MILLS & BOON

Mills & Boon
An imprint of HarperCollins*Publishers* Ltd
1 London Bridge Street
London SE1 9GF

www.harpercollins.co.uk

HarperCollins*Publishers*
Macken House, 39/40 Mayor Street Upper
Dublin 1, D01 C9W8, Ireland

This paperback edition 2023

2

First published in Great Britain by Mills & Boon,
an imprint of HarperCollins*Publishers* Ltd 2022

Copyright © Amber Rose Gill 2022

With thanks to Nadine Gonzalez

Amber Rose Gill asserts the moral right to be
identified as the author of this work.
A catalogue record for this book is
available from the British Library.

ISBN: 978-0-00-860861-3

MIX
Paper | Supporting
responsible forestry
FSC™ C007454

This book is produced from independently certified FSC™ paper
to ensure responsible forest management.

For more information visit: www.harpercollins.co.uk/green

This book is set in 11.2/15.5 pt. Bembo

Printed and Bound in the UK using 100% Renewable Electricity at
CPI Group (UK) Ltd, Croydon, CR0 4YY

I dedicate this book to diversity & representation.
Love, after all knows no boundaries. So what better way to
represent than through a love story.

Travel Blog

DRAFT ENTRY #1: GO IT ALONE

Attending a wedding alone. When a man does it, he's going stag. But if he plays it right, the odds of scoring that night are in his favour. What about women? Going doe is dull. But Hollywood loves the scenario. A single girl coercing or cajoling a random guy to avoid humiliation. Mind you, I'm not above these tactics, but such elaborate plots require time and/or money, both of which I'm fresh out of. The wedding is only days away and on my modest salary the most I could possibly offer a man is a free meal and a round of drinks. Besides, this isn't the sort of wedding you can take a stranger to. An intimate affair at a seaside resort in Tobago, the guest list is tighter than a steel drum.

Affirmation: I can do this. I can go it alone. I am whole and valuable all on my own.

CHAPTER ONE

'Ladies and gentlemen, this is the pre-boarding announcement for flight BA209 to Miami, Florida. At this time we ask passenger Samantha Roberts to proceed to the British Airways check-in desk. Passenger Samantha Roberts, please proceed to the check-in desk.'

The insistent monotone roused Samantha from her meditation. She hopped to her feet, grabbed the handle of her carry-on suitcase and made a beeline for the desk. Tall, curvy, with cinnamon brown skin and a head of wild corkscrew curls, she stood out in most crowds. But the Heathrow departure gate was packed. She had to elbow her way to the front of the line.

'Hello! I'm Samantha!' she called out. 'Is something wrong?'

The uniformed airline employee typed as he spoke. 'Ms Roberts?'

'Yes.' She handed over her British passport as proof.

'We see you're travelling alone with a window aisle all to yourself.'

Samantha blushed. *They know. They all know.* Every single person at Gate B12, every pasty, bleary-eyed traveller, knew that she was that sad, sorry girl on her way to a wedding without a date. Not only that, she'd had the nerve to take up an entire aisle just for herself. Before they judged her too harshly, perhaps she should explain. Her ex-boyfriend had booked the seat next to hers. But at the very last minute he cancelled the trip, preferring to throw away an all-expenses-paid holiday in the Caribbean to travelling with her. What could she say? These things happened. Surely, they'd understand.

'We need to accommodate a couple travelling with a small child,' the attendant explained. 'If you'd be gracious enough to give up your window seat, we'll upgrade you to an aisle seat in our first class section. Is that all right?' It was clear he wasn't interested in her answer. Only a fool would pass up a free upgrade. He printed a new boarding pass and handed it to Samantha with a wink. 'Be ready to board when we call first class.'

Samantha returned to the waiting area and dropped into her seat. The upgrade took the sting out of her misery. The trip to Tobago was long and arduous. If she had to go it alone, might as well travel in style.

First stop was a one-night layover in Miami. There she would meet up with her friends, Hugo and Jasmine. All three would fly out to Tobago the next day. Why was she bemoaning her single status if she was travelling in such good company? The answer was simple: all her friends had someone. In fact, this destination wedding was shaping up as a couples' retreat. Jasmine was in a relationship with Jason, a Canadian corporate attorney. Hugo was married to Adrian, a plastic surgeon with such chiselled bone structure and gorgeous mocha skin tone he could have easily gone into modelling instead of medicine. The only other single girl on the guest list, as far as she knew, was Maya, the bride's teenage sister.

Samantha was actually looking forward to the short stay in Miami. She had never been to the city and her friends had a night out planned. Plus it was an opportunity to generate more content for her fledgling travel blog. It didn't change the fact that once she arrived – via first class transatlantic travel – there would be hell to pay.

★★★

In the spring, Samantha had RSVP'd for two for the event of the year: Naomi Reid's Caribbean nuptials. After a mere six months of courtship, Naomi was marrying her 'great love' Anthony Scott, aka 'Fit with Tony', a fitness trainer with an enviable online following. She'd helped choose the bridesmaids' dresses and Timothy, her boyfriend, had booked the flights. He'd been looking forward to it, talked nonstop about fishing and snorkelling. But people change, as seasons do. It was summer now. She and Timothy were through. He'd gone backpacking across Italy with friends, leaving Samantha agonizingly single and without a date for her best friend's wedding.

Samantha pulled out her phone and scrolled through old photos. Not the ones of her and Timothy, cheek-to-cheek, grinning stupidly into the camera – she'd long deleted those. The slightly blurred shots she was swiping through were of her and Naomi on their various trips. They'd grown up together, their identical homes standing side by side in a tidy suburb in Manchester. As girls they'd played with dolls and dreamed of travelling the world in a private jet like Barbie or Wonder Woman, depending on their mood. Although their paths had split after university, with Naomi moving to California to join a graphic design agency and Samantha staying close to home, they'd remained best friends.

Samantha didn't like to compare her life to others', but it was difficult not to draw some parallels. Her closest friend was getting married and settled. She on the other hand had been dumped. OK, fine. She hadn't been dumped exactly. It had been a mutual and cordial see-you-never type of break-up, only Samantha had not seen it coming.

She and Timothy (it was *Timothy*, never Tim or Timmy) had been dating for over two years. Her mother adored him and she'd met his parents. Her friends figured she would be first to go down the aisle. Samantha expected the same and took that responsibility seriously. For months, she hid a stash of bridal magazines under her bed. When Timothy suggested they take a moonlit walk one Sunday night after a light rain, she wasn't expecting him to propose. However, she could tell by his rigid posture that he was nervous and had something important to say. He slipped his hand in hers, mingled their fingers, and met her eyes. 'It's not working,' he said, 'and we both know it.'

Samantha had stared back at his glassy blue irises, wondering if she'd heard him right. Hours later, alone in bed, she replayed the scene in her mind. Every detail was as clear as day, from the shop windows stained with raindrops to the moonlight swirling on the pavement puddles. She heard Timothy's deep voice repeat the words: *It's not working, and we both know it.* She'd withdrawn her hand from his, feeling like a fool.

The man was direct; you had to give him props for that. Samantha sort of admired the straightforward manner in which he'd delivered the final blow. She could use some of that energy now.

Samantha was still actively dealing in half-truths. She hadn't broken the news to any of her friends, not even the bride.

When she turned up in Tobago alone, she'd get the full brunt of their loving concern. Naomi was going to flip. And before she even made her way to the Caribbean island, she had to face the dynamic duo: Hugo and Jasmine.

She should take a page from Timothy's book and deliver the news to them in a sanguine manner. If she broke the news now, they'd have plenty of time to recover from the shock before she arrived. A friendly heads-up text would take care of it.

Samantha closed the photo app and tapped on the WhatsApp icon. After a few swipes, she landed on the extended group chat saved under VEGAS SQUAD, in reference to the trip to Nevada nearly five years ago where she and Naomi had met Jasmine and Hugo. Her thumb hovered over the keyboard. She shouldn't be this nervous. These were her friends, after all. They adored her, but they had the doggedness of unjaded criminal investigators. They wouldn't stop until they got to the truth.

'We are now inviting first class passengers to board at this time.'

Samantha tucked away her phone, and proceeded to the gate. Breaking the news to her friends would certainly be easier while settled in a premium recliner with a warm towel and salted nuts to soothe her anxiety.

CHAPTER TWO

5 July, 7.15 a.m.

SAM'S PHONE TO VEGAS SQUAD (NAOMI, HUGO AND JASMINE)

Sam: This is to inform you that Timothy and I are no longer a couple. Please respect our privacy during this difficult time.

Hugo: What the hell is this?

Jasmine: Thought we banned drunk-texting in the group chat.

Hugo: It's 2 a.m. in Miami. I was dead asleep. This better not be a joke.

Sam: Sorry to wake you. I'm not drunk. This is not a joke.

Hugo: Why do you sound like Buckingham Palace's communication secretary?

Sam: Just trying to be frank.

Hugo: Stop.

Naomi: …

Jasmine: So this is real?

Hugo: OK! I'm up. What happened?

Jasmine: Can't sleep. Always get nervous before a big trip, so don't hold back. Tell us everything.

Sam: Nothing happened. Things fall apart.

Naomi: …

Hugo: Sure it's over, *gata*? Not just a rough patch. We all have bad days.

Jasmine: Couples fight, Sam. You get that, right? It doesn't mean anything.

Sam: Thanks for the insight, but there was no fight. It was a clean break. We both knew it wasn't working.

Hugo: Damn. You two were solid.

Sam: Not really.

Jasmine: What about the wedding? You're still coming, right?

Sam: Just boarded the plane. First class upgrade!!!

Jasmine: Nice!!!!

Hugo: Where were you and Timmy planning to spend the night in Miami?

Sam: At a hotel near the airport.

Hugo: Screw that. Jasmine is staying with Adrian and me. Join us.

Sam: No thanks. I'm fine!

Jasmine: Join us! It'll be fun.

Hugo: We'll take care of you.

Sam: All right. Why not!

Hugo: Good. It's settled! Text me the flight details. I'll meet you at the airport.

Naomi: Nothing is settled! Sam! Are you serious? The wedding is ten days out. TEN DAYS. I can't handle any drama right now!

Jasmine: That's … harsh.

Hugo: It's not like she arranged to get dumped just to give you a stress headache.

Sam: Who said anything about getting dumped?

Naomi: It was going to happen sooner or later. You two had lost your spark. But did it have to happen now? Couldn't you have waited until after the wedding? I gave the caterer a final headcount last week and Timothy was your plus one.

Sam: I was NOT dumped.

Naomi: Makes no difference. You're down a plus one.

Sam: I'm well aware!

Jasmine: Let it go! The food won't go to waste. Someone will eat it.

Naomi: OK … OK … Letting it go. Sorry about you and Timmy, sweetie. I love you like a sister. You know that, right?

Sam: Love you, too. Sorry I messed up your seating chart.

Naomi: No worries. I'll sort it out with the caterer. But no one else gets dumped in the next ten days. Got that?

Hugo: We'll do our best!

Jasmine: OMG

Naomi: Is that really too much to ask?

Sam: OK! Time to switch off mobile phones. Bye for now.

Hugo: See you soon! Going to dive into a bottle of Absolut.

Jasmine: I'm going to cry into a cup of matcha.

Naomi: I'm gutted. I don't know what I'm going to do.

Sam: Well, I'm going to order a mimosa. I could get used to travelling first class.

CHAPTER THREE

The plane had landed smoothly, but the sprint across Miami International Airport left Samantha breathlessly exhilarated. After lockdown, it was such a privilege to travel across country, let alone across the Atlantic.

Samantha was reaching for one of her suitcases as it snaked past on the luggage carousel when Hugo called. True to his word, he had come to meet her. Jasmine was with him, having arrived hours earlier from Montreal.

'What's the hold-up?' Hugo asked impatiently. He was circling the airport perimeter road.

'I'm at baggage claim.'

'Who checks in luggage in this day and age?' he scoffed.

'I do!'

Samantha could never claim to travel light. On an average trip she maxed out the allowed luggage. This time, she'd devoted one suitcase to the various outfits for the pre- and post-wedding events. Her carry-on held her camera equipment and laptop. This trip was going to be fun and productive even if it killed her. She was launching a new travel blog, a dream whose time had come.

'So you'll be out in an hour, then?' Hugo said. 'I'll take another lap around the airport.'

'Can't you pay to park?'

'Can't you get out already?'

'See you in a minute!'

After twenty minutes languishing through customs, Samantha rolled out of the airport. The chilled air gave way to thick humidity. She could feel her hair reacting, each corkscrew curl coiling tighter.

Hugo pulled up to the kerb and hopped out of the truck he'd borrowed for the occasion. Tan and tattooed, with a strong nose and a mop of curly black hair, Hugo was a Miami dream. Jasmine emerged from the passenger side. Petite and pretty, with the golden-brown complexion of sand, she wore her hair in long box braids that spilled down her back. They pulled Samantha into a sloppy hug while a traffic guard blew hard on a whistle, urging them to get a move on. Samantha closed her eyes and lost herself in the embrace. She may not have a great love, but she most definitely had great friends.

★★★

The Vegas Squad came together about five years ago. Naomi was only an intern at the California design firm that ultimately hired her when she was tasked with setting up a booth at a Las Vegas international exposition. They'd booked her a room at one of the grand hotels on the famous strip and Samantha had leaped at the chance to tag along. While Naomi worked, Samantha spent her days lounging by the pool. There she met the Brazilian graphic artist and the French-Canadian illustrator who would turn her life upside down. They were in Vegas for the expo as well, but unlike Naomi, they spent little time in the packed conference halls.

They had a long list of locations and attractions to visit, including a helicopter ride over the Grand Canyon. Samantha had just turned twenty and was still terribly preoccupied with looking cool.

'I'd rather avoid the touristy spots,' she said. She was sitting at the edge of the pool, her feet dangling in the water.

'That's where you and I differ,' Hugo said. He was bobbing along the pool's surface on a swan-shaped raft, sipping a piña colada. 'I'd rather do it all.'

That hot afternoon in Vegas, enveloped by the scent of chlorine and coconut rum, Samantha had an honest to goodness epiphany. A neon light flickered in her mind. Why not do it all? She *was* a tourist. Who exactly was she trying to impress? By playing it cool she was only going to miss out.

From that day on, she joined Hugo and Jasmine on their outings. Nothing was off the table. Selfies with wax figures of celebrities, indoor gondola rides, a dancing fountain show at a quarter to midnight. Once they'd wrangled Naomi free, they got her to join the fun. Somewhere between pool parties at MGM Grand and bottomless cocktails at Vegas Vickie's, the four became friends. On the last night of their stay, they planned a future trip to Mexico. They'd been best buddies and travel partners ever since.

Documenting their adventures in a blog had always been in the back of Samantha's mind, but she'd never acted on it. And as time passed and adulting took its toll, the opportunities for spontaneous travel grew scarce. She and Timothy hardly travelled. He was not one to venture far. A road trip here and there was more his speed. Samantha had shelved the idea until the day Naomi called with news.

'Are you sitting down? Anthony and I are getting married in Tobago and you're all invited!'

Hugo and his husband shared a minuscule condo in the trendy neighbourhood of Brickell. Samantha's luggage joined Jasmine's pile in a space that did not qualify as a guest bedroom. The view from the wraparound balcony more than made up for it, however. After watching the sun set over the bay, they showered, changed, and set out for dinner.

When in Miami, you wore white. That was the unwritten rule. Jasmine had on a white tunic with gold embroidery and a pair of strappy gold sandals. Samantha paired a white cotton mini dress with turquoise mules. Hugo threw a tailored blazer over a plain white T-shirt and kissed his husband goodnight. It was officially ladies' night out. Hugo's pronouns were he/him, but he was definitely one of the girls.

The restaurant was located on a top floor of a glossy boutique hotel only blocks from Hugo's place. He knew everyone from the doorman to the hostess. His popularity helped them score a table on the terrace with glittering views of all Miami had to offer. Samantha and Jasmine ordered mojitos, a traditional Cuban cocktail. Hugo honoured his own heritage with a caipirinha.

The topic of the night was Naomi's flash wedding. Ever since the 'save the date' notice had popped into their inboxes, the wedding had dominated their private news cycle – every email, private text, or group chat had been dedicated to Naomi's mad dash to the altar. Now the time had come to hash it out in person.

If this were a Hollywood production, Naomi would be the star cast in the role of the sophisticated professional who falls for the former jock-turned-fitness professional. They'd met one dreamy California evening in late November. Naomi attended a charity gala and took part in a silent auction. Single women bid on dates or activities with a bevvy of gorgeous single men: firefighters, minor celebrity chefs, and the like. By the end of the night, she'd won a six-week intensive package with Anthony Scott, personal trainer to the stars. In January she booked her first session. At the end of the six-week period, not only was Naomi in the best shape of her life, she was madly in love. Shortly thereafter, she announced their engagement.

It was a lovely story. And yet Samantha had questions: Who does this? Who marries a man within six months of their first encounter? It made no sense.

Jasmine echoed this sentiment, only in French. *'Mais à quoi elle pense?'*

Samantha's French was limited. She didn't have the words in any language to express her confusion. Sensible Naomi wasn't one to rush into any decision, let alone a lifelong commitment.

'The man is hot,' Hugo said. 'That's not even a question.'

'Not at all,' Samantha said.

'But is that any reason to marry him?' Hugo continued.

'Not at all!' Samantha repeated, this time with feeling.

'Do you think she's pregnant?' Jasmine asked.

'No,' Samantha said, happy to confirm this fact. 'I asked her point blank.'

Hugo went back to studying the menu. 'Then I don't get it.'

Jasmine paused a beat. 'Do they have a prenup? I know it's a delicate question.'

Samantha winced. 'I don't know if we can get into that.'

'Oh, we'll get into that,' Hugo said. 'We'll get into *all* of that!'

Samantha was weary. Naomi had pushed back hard when she'd suggested there might be some reason, like a pregnancy, for the rushed wedding. But maybe if the three of them sat her down, expressed their sincere concern, things could go more smoothly.

The drinks arrived. From tropical cocktails they would move on to sushi and poke bowls. Hugo had already put in a dessert order for a chocolate soufflé. Their meal was a mash-up of cultures, just like Miami and, to some extent, themselves.

Samantha, Naomi, Jasmine and Hugo were all a mix of this and that, born into suburbs where immigrant populations overlapped. Naomi's parents were from Trinidad and Tobago, one from each island. Jasmine's mother and father were from Haiti and Canada, respectively. Hugo was Brazilian, born and raised in the outskirts of São Paulo. His estranged father, however, was originally from Germany. Samantha's British family could trace its lineage back to the Victorian era, but her mother was Black, her father white.

'I think we should take Naomi out one night, just us, and have it out,' Samantha proposed.

'You think so?' Jasmine said absently. She was busy snapping a photo of her cocktail glass stuffed with mint leaves.

'Absolutely!' Samantha replied. 'She's our girl and we have to look out for her. I'd want you to do the same for me.'

'Good to know,' Hugo said dryly.

Samantha looked from Hugo to Jasmine. Their expressions were unreadable. She understood that she'd walked into a trap. For a while there she'd been foolish enough to believe her friends intended to respect her boundaries.

Jasmine stirred the ice in her glass with the sugarcane swizzle stick. 'If you broke up with the love of your life and carried on as if nothing had happened, you'd want us to sit you down and get to the bottom of it?'

'If he were the love of my life, sure,' she said. 'Since he's not there's no point.'

'You wanted to marry the man!'

'Not really.'

'You have five Pinterest boards organized by wedding theme!' Jasmine cried.

Samantha tightened her fists under the table. She should have made those damn boards private.

'The point is,' Hugo said, 'you can't drop a bomb on us and not expect to talk about it.'

'There's nothing to talk about. It was the most anticlimactic break-up of all time.'

'That's what shocks me,' he said. 'You two were like couple goals.'

Samantha wasn't buying that. Hugo was happily married and Jasmine was in a solid relationship. There were plenty of #couplegoals to go around.

'You showed more emotion when my cat died,' Jasmine said. 'And Brigitte was very, very old.'

'But she was very, very cute!' Samantha squealed.

Hugo tossed aside the menu. 'This is going nowhere.'

Samantha reached out and squeezed each of their hands. 'Guys, we're together for the first time in God knows how long. Can't we enjoy the night?'

Jasmine fixed Samantha with her feline eyes. 'You wanted an intervention,' she said. '*This* is an intervention.'

'It's been two weeks. I promise, I'm fine!'

'Two whole weeks?' Jasmine said. 'And you're only just telling us now?'

Samantha looked from one to the other once again and gave

up the fight. They were not going to let her squirm away. It seemed that she'd packed quite a bit of emotional baggage for this trip. It was time to offload it.

'You keep saying we were perfect and solid and talk of goals and whatever, but that's not true. We were far from perfect.'

Samantha blamed herself for projecting the perfect couple image to the world. She had never complained about Timothy's annoying habits or called to vent after a fight. So as far as they knew, it had been smooth sailing all the way. How to go about dismantling the myth?

'We had our issues,' she said. 'Logistics played a big part.'

Timothy lived in Sheffield and they only ever saw each other on weekends. Their quasi long-distance relationship made it easy to overlook things. It was exciting at first, of course. During the week, they kept things going via text. On Thursday evenings Samantha rushed home from work, put on a record and tidied up her flat. She made sure to stock up on his favourite beer and crisps. That level of giddy enthusiasm would have been difficult for anyone to sustain. Eventually the anticipation waned. She'd forget to stock up on beer or change her sheets or make a reservation at their favourite Italian restaurant. All too soon they settled into a routine of Netflix on Fridays, Saturdays with friends at some pub or another, and Sunday brunch before he headed back to Sheffield. Thanks to this packed schedule, they managed to avoid meaningful conversation all weekend long.

Samantha stared at her hands as she laid all this out and more. When she dared to look up, Hugo's expression had softened and Jasmine was nodding, encouraging her to go on.

'I'm sad to lose him.' She relived the moment he'd kissed her goodbye. Her cheeks were wet. 'And I hate myself for feeling this way, but with Naomi finding the love of her life and all, it hasn't been easy.'

'This wedding has messed with everyone's head,' Jasmine said. 'Jason keeps hinting that we should be next. I don't even know if I believe in marriage.'

'I got married for the political statement,' Hugo said.

'Yeah?' Jasmine said. 'I thought you got married for the health insurance.'

'That, too,' Hugo said. 'Good thing it's working out.'

They laughed and clinked glasses. Samantha felt unburdened for the first time in weeks. The waiter returned and placed a bowl of edamame at the centre of the table. They all reached in.

'I just wish he hadn't done this so close to the wedding, you know?' Samantha said. 'I might've found another date if I'd had the time to rope one in. I hate that I'm going it alone.'

'You're *not* alone,' Hugo said firmly. 'You have us!'

'Oh, really?' Samantha said. 'Will you slow dance with me when they play Sinatra at the reception?'

'Absolutely,' Jasmine said. 'I'll be your Funny Valentine.'

'Anyway, look at the bright side,' Hugo said.

'Yes?' Samantha asked. An unflappable optimist, Hugo could find the bright side in a total eclipse.

'Your hard work won't go to waste. Go ahead and forward those Pinterest boards to Jasmine. She's obviously next in line.'

'God, no!' Jasmine cried.

Samantha laughed even as her heart was sinking. She'd just been bumped from the happily-ever-after self-service buffet queue, and there was no way she could feel good about that.

CHAPTER FOUR

Naomi's stepdad, Gregory, was filthy rich. This was a detail Samantha had somehow deleted from memory. It all came rushing back in stunning clarity when their car veered off the main road onto a single strip of asphalt lined with tall, skinny palm trees, leading to the beachfront resort in Crown Point, Tobago, their home for the week.

Naomi wasn't born into money. Back when they were neighbours, she was just a normal girl. They attended state school and had no privilege to speak of. Naomi's mother, Amelia, was on her second marriage. She'd divorced Naomi's dad soon after her little sister was born. Then on a trip home to Tobago, Amelia met the true love of her life, an obscenely rich man whose family had come into their fortune with a mobile phone start-up in nearby Venezuela.

Amelia didn't exactly leap for joy when Naomi announced her sudden engagement. She did, however, insist on hosting the wedding. With the recent pandemic still fresh in her mind, she'd decided to spread the guests out in private bungalows over a few acres of land with ocean views. However, it was the view of the surrounding mountains, solid and lush, that left Samantha in awe. She'd stared wide-eyed out the window the moment they pulled away from the airport.

The van drew up to the hotel lobby and she stepped out on wobbly legs. The hotel comprised several newly constructed buildings with white façades and peaked roofs. While Jasmine oversaw the transfer of their luggage, she gathered her bearings. It was the sort of bright, colourful day that only the Caribbean could deliver. Noonday heat pressed down on her. Uniformed attendants rushed to assist, loading their suitcases onto a golf cart under Jasmine's watchful eye. Hugo strode off toward the building marked Main Lobby, his garment bag thrown over his shoulder, wheeling his one suitcase behind him.

'Hey! Wait for us!' Samantha called after him.

'Not my fault you overpacked!' he tossed back.

'Not everyone can get by on two pairs of cargo shorts and a T-shirt, you know.'

As they squabbled, the sliding glass door to the main lobby opened and Naomi emerged, dark cocoa skin gleaming in the sun. She wore a billowy blue dress and espadrilles. A floppy straw hat with 'Princess Bride' embroidered on the wide brim completed her look. And because it had to be said, she was extraordinarily fit. This was no doubt one of the perks of dating a fitness trainer.

Naomi clasped her hands together. 'My people are here!'

All four let out a cry and crashed into each other, eager for a hug.

'I'm so glad you're finally here,' Naomi said. 'Amelia is driving me crazy and Maya is an emotional mess!'

'It's tough for them,' Samantha said. 'You three were so tight.'

'Sam, It's tough for *me!*'

'We're here now, sweetie,' Hugo reassured her. 'And we'll whip everyone into shape. No one is killing my vibe.'

Jasmine pressed her cheek to Naomi's and made a loud kissing sound. 'Congratulations, love! You're glowing! What's your secret?'

'Oh, you know.' Naomi shrugged. 'Fooling around, falling in love.'

Samantha studied Naomi. She did not look like a woman on the verge of making the biggest mistake of her life. She looked calm, rested and her face radiated joy.

'Listen up,' Naomi said. 'Some quick housekeeping issues, then we'll get you settled. First, are Jason and Adrian still scheduled to arrive later today?'

'Nothing's changed,' Jasmine assured her. 'Jason is flying in from Toronto. He'll get here by three.'

'Adrian is done with his last patient and heading to the airport,' added Hugo.

'Perfect. Everyone will be here for dinner.'

Everyone except for Timothy, obviously.

'Is it a formal dinner?' Jasmine asked.

Naomi rested her hand on her chest, the left hand with the two-carat princess cut diamond ring. 'Not too formal.'

Formal or not, Samantha was disappointed. On their first night in Tobago, she'd hoped to catch up with Naomi. It would have been the perfect time to sit down for a chat. Naomi's apparent happiness was no reason to cancel the plan.

'Besides, it's an opportunity for you to meet the boys.'

This particular boy band presumably consisted of the groom, his cousin and best man, and an old college friend.

'Can we get going?' Hugo asked. 'I need to jump in a pool STAT!'

'There is one other thing,' Naomi said. 'It concerns you, Sam.'

'Me?'

'Hey, there!' a woman called out.

They all turned to check out the newcomer. A stunning blonde in a black bikini at the wheel of a golf cart motored toward them. She parked, hopped out, and came skipping close up.

'Everyone, this is Jennifer Carter,' Naomi said. 'My co-worker and my very best friend on the West Coast.'

'Hi! Call me Jen!'

Samantha had heard only good things about Jen, but wasn't sure how she felt about the woman now. There was just something about her. Her hair was too shiny, her smile too bright.

'California has entered the chat room,' Hugo observed.

'Yep!' Jen flashed perfect teeth. 'So what are we talking about? Get me up to speed.'

Hugo obliged. 'Naomi was about to break some bad news to Sam.'

'Oh no, don't worry!' Jen said. 'It's no big deal.'

It irritated Samantha no end that Jen was already in the know. She eyed Naomi expectantly. 'Go on, tell me. What is it?'

'We have a last-minute guest,' Naomi said. 'Since you're alone and no longer need an entire bungalow to yourself, we wondered if you would mind joining Maya.'

Samantha felt a pang of anger. 'You want me to share with messy Maya?'

'It's not like that,' Naomi said. 'We'd upgrade you to a deluxe two-bedroom bungalow, so there'd be plenty of room. You'd never have to deal with her mess.'

We this. *We* that. Which committee had made these decisions?

'It's the party suite,' Jen said. 'It'll be fun. I'd have joined them myself, but I found a last-minute date. I hate going to weddings alone.'

Samantha turned to Naomi and stabbed the air between them with an index finger. 'You said the guest list was on lock!'

'Did I?' Naomi said, once again bringing her left hand to her heart. 'Sorry! I've been such a diva these last few weeks.'

'We forgive you,' Jasmine said.

'Yeah,' Jen said. 'It's chill.'

If it were so chill, why were Samantha's cheeks on fire?

Right then and there, the committee presided over by Naomi and composed of Hugo, Jasmine and Jen decided by unanimous vote that Samantha would share a deluxe two-bedroom bungalow with Maya, and the matter was closed for debate.

There went her fantasies of having an entire oceanside villa to herself – the only tangible benefit of travelling solo. She had hoped to wake up early and record videos for the blog in pristine light, or stay up late and belt out eighties pop ballads while soaking in the tub, or prance around naked if the mood struck her.

Naomi let out a breath, visibly pleased that she'd ticked one unpleasant task off her to-do list. 'Now!' she declared. 'Let's get you all settled and—'

'I'm sorry,' Samantha said. 'But I'm not giving up my bungalow. I need my privacy.'

'Sam!' Naomi said. 'Be reasonable.'

'Sorry. Can't do it.' This was one upgrade that she'd have to pass on.

'Are you sure?' Jen said. 'The party suite is—'

'I think she's sure,' Jasmine said with the urgency of a person attempting to defuse a bomb.

'You heard the girl,' Hugo said, coming to her defence. 'No means no.'

Naomi laughed. 'You're my guest. I want you to be comfortable.'

'Thank you.'

'Can we please get out of the heat now?' Hugo said.

'Yes, sir!' Naomi said playfully. 'Follow me, everyone!'

***

The bungalow was blissfully silent when Samantha crossed the threshold for the first time. She slipped off her trainers and wandered around. The space was all terracotta tile, stucco walls, carved wood furniture, and breathtaking views from every window. The bedroom was serene with a canopy bed swathed in gauzy netting; there were red hibiscus petals sprinkled on the crisp bedding. It had obviously been prepared for a couple.

She flung herself on the mattress, feeling triumphant. She'd had to battle the forces of darkness for this privilege. It had been a while since Samantha was last single, but she didn't remember it being this way. Bumped up to first class or thrown into the party suite, it was all the same. She was expected to step aside and accommodate those with the good taste or plain good sense to travel in pairs. That was BS, utter BS, and she wasn't going to stand for it.

CHAPTER FIVE

With a few hours to kill before dinner with the boys, Samantha swapped her jeans for shorts, grabbed her camera, and set out. Hugo and Jasmine were resting, but she was restless and needed fresh air. The concierge assured her that a fifteen-minute walk in any direction would lead her to a scenic bike trail. She hadn't made it that far when a shop's yellow façade caught her attention. It was a converted gingerbread-style cottage with all the charming touches: wooden filigree details and dormers over jalousie windows. 'Candy's Shop' was painted in cursive over a black-and-white-striped awning. The slim double doors were open wide and secured in place by cinderblock. Samantha snapped a picture and ventured inside.

Candy's Shop was a snack bar, more or less. The menu jotted onto a blackboard had a bit of everything, from tropical fruit juices to ham and cheese sandwiches. A few bistro tables and chairs were scattered about. The countertop was crowded with jars of sweets and boxes of snacks. An older man was at the cash register. He was tall and wiry with reddish-brown skin like tobacco and vivid brown eyes.

'Hello, miss,' he said. 'What can I help you with today?'

Samantha wished she could sample every fruit smoothie,

every sweet treat, but she had a long walk ahead and settled on bottled water, promising herself to return soon with her friends. The man pulled a chilled bottle from a glass-fronted refrigerator and set it on the counter.

'How much?' she asked, reaching into her backpack for some loose notes.

'For a pretty lady like you?' he said, smiling. 'No cost at all.'

A door to a back room swung open and a younger, fitter, taller, broader version of the older man entered the shop. Samantha picked up on a resemblance straight away. Except where the older man was grey and distinguished in a white button-down shirt tucked into pleated trousers, his younger counterpart was overdue for a shave and dressed as if he were about to head out to the gym in a loose T-shirt, sweat pants and trainers. He carried a wooden crate without a hint of strain. Black hair cut to a fade, brown eyes with a steady gaze, smooth brown skin scruffy at the jawline. He was insanely handsome.

'There's no pretty lady discount,' he said, and dropped the crate onto a stack in the corner. 'That'll be four dollars.'

Stunned, Samantha crumpled the crisp new local dollars in her fist. She did not know what to say, so instead she slid him a glance so sharp it could split a papaya in two. Except, he hadn't spared her a glance. He exited the shop by the same door he'd entered.

The older man let out a flow of apologies. 'You'll have to excuse my grandson,' he said. 'He's American.'

The fact that Samantha managed to smile, pay for the water, drop a tip in a jar, and stride out of the shop without knocking over a ladder-back chair was a miracle. She wondered: was there a KICK ME sign pinned to her back? Because it seemed the universe was intent on bruising her backside.

She encountered a trail soon enough. It curved through a wooded area. Samantha walked at a brisk pace, oblivious to the fresh air she'd so craved, the rich red earth under her feet, and the playful birdsong she'd imagined all these weeks leading to this trip. The scenic walk that was meant to calm her only revved her up. She was in a foul mood and the splendours of nature were not enough to relieve it. This week was going to be a nightmare, she just knew it.

The nerve of that guy! So rude! His sweet grandfather was wrong. America wasn't to blame for his attitude. He was an ass, plain and simple. The nerve of Naomi, too, choosing Jen over her! That was what it came down to in the end. She hadn't said it, but it was obvious she had meant to give her bungalow to Jen and her last-minute date. And finally, the nerve of Timothy for dumping her just days before this stupid wedding! None of this would be happening if he'd travelled with her as planned. This was all his fault.

Samantha paused to let out a breath and realized she had no idea where she was. Her brain fogged with anger, she'd forgotten to clock any visual cues. She wasn't lost, just disoriented. The hum of traffic rose from behind a wall of pine trees, so she couldn't be that far away. Earlier, she'd passed a few bikers in neon gear, but also some locals dressed for everyday life. It was clear this wasn't so much a trail as it was a shortcut connecting two neighbourhoods. The question was whether she should push forward or retrace her steps.

Pounding feet and the crunch of dry leaves caught her attention. A jogger was making his way along the trail. Perfect timing. She'd ask for directions and head back to the hotel. Hugo and Jasmine had had the right idea. She should have curled up in bed for a long nap instead of venturing out on her own. Then she saw the jogger clearly. Air buds in his ears, head low, long sure strides, that strong body, that infuriatingly handsome face … Change of plans: she was going to wander in these woods until Naomi sent out a search party. She would sooner die than ask that man for anything.

Samantha pushed her sunglasses up the bridge of her nose and, back rigid, head high, pressed on. He brushed past her, pace steady, without so much as a nod in her direction. She fought the urge to pick up a stick and hurl it at him. Just then, he tossed a glance over his shoulder. Their eyes met. He lost his footing, tripped, fumbled, before landing firmly on his feet with the grace of a cat. Samantha wanted to laugh, so she did. 'Ha!'

He shook it off and ambled toward her. He was just as tall, broad, brown and beautiful as she'd first thought. So he was a real man, not a thirsty single lady traveller mirage.

'Hey,' he said, as he approached, out of breath, sweaty and gleaming in the afternoon sun. 'Glad I ran into you.'

'Can't say the same.'

He'd made her out as a scammer looking to defraud the elderly. At the time, she'd been too stunned, and too distracted by his sculpted arms, to say anything. But things were different now.

'I owe you an apology,' he said.

'Keep it,' she said. 'You didn't hurt my feelings.'

'But I was rude earlier,' he said. 'Besides, my grandfather might not let me back in the shop if I don't at least try to make it right.'

Samantha shrugged. 'Who knows? He might be better off.'

He bit back a smile. 'Look, it wasn't personal. I'm trying to keep the old man in check. He'd give away the house if a pretty girl asked. And you're very, very pretty.'

There was no way to take those words as a compliment. His tone was matter of fact, as if her prettiness was no more remarkable than a yellow dandelion.

'Just FYI: I had every intention of paying and tipping and returning with my friends,' Samantha said.

'I appreciate that,' he said. 'The shop is a start-up. It's early days still.'

What did he mean by start-up? Samantha was a content creator for a reputable financial publication. Essentially, she wrote short blog posts for their website. In her line of work, the term 'start-up' was reserved for companies born online or sprouting in Silicon Valley. Candy's Shop was the definition of a little corner store catering to aimlessly wandering tourists.

'I have to be strict with him,' he said. 'He won't turn a profit this quarter if he keeps giving the inventory away.'

'Or if you keep scaring customers away.'

'That, too.' He folded his arms across his chest and, for the first time ever, really looked at her. 'I'm Roman. Roman Carver.'

'Samantha Roberts.'

'What are you doing here, Samantha?'

'Nothing,' she said breezily. 'Just out for a stroll. If you could point me in the direction of the main road, I'll get on with it.'

'I mean in Tobago. What are you doing here in Tobago?'

'Is that really any of your business?' she snapped.

He backed away, hands up, looking more amused by her outburst than he had a right to be. It made her feel peevish. She hated the feeling.

'I'm a travel blogger,' Samantha blurted.

'Is that right?' he said. 'What's the name of the blog?'

Samantha swatted away an imaginary insect. 'The name?'

He shrugged as if to say, *You heard me.*

She looked around, grasping for an idea. 'The Hidden Path.'

Roman's almond-shaped eyes were framed with thick, arched brows. When he cocked one, questioning, something inside of her came undone.

'The Hidden Path,' he repeated.

'That's what I said.'

'Come on,' he said in a low, teasing voice. 'Confess. There's no blog.'

She would rather eat a worm. 'There's no blog … *yet*. I'm working on it.'

His smile was sunlight, warm and indulgent. Basking in it, she forgot what they were squabbling about.

He pointed past her shoulder. 'Just keep down that path. You'll loop back to where you came from.'

Samantha did her best to sound detached. 'Cool. Thanks.'

He took a step backwards, every taut muscle of his body eager to get moving again. 'Next time you stop by the shop, the bottled water is on me.'

And then he was off.

CHAPTER SIX

At sundown, they gathered on a terrace under a canopy of fairy lights. Although Adrian and Jason had made it in time for dinner, one guest – one of the boys – was alarmingly late. Naomi refused to delay any further and they moved to the table. The seat to Samantha's right remained empty through Amelia's welcome toast. And then *he* walked in.

Clean shaven, sharply dressed, easy and self-assured … he was a lot to take in. If Samantha hadn't been sitting down, she would've fallen to the floor.

Naomi hopped to her feet. 'Roman! You made it. We gave up on you.'

The man had the *nerve* to smile and roll out a smooth, self-deprecating laugh. 'I see that. Sorry.'

Samantha watched him chat with Anthony and bump fists with the best man. Who was this charmer? Where was the grump she'd met earlier today?

'We saved you a seat. You're at the far end next to my friend Samantha.' Naomi pointed at the seat she'd stupidly thought reserved for the ghost of her ex. 'You're in good hands. She's friendly. Sam! Raise a hand so Roman can see you.'

Samantha couldn't raise a finger if she tried. She was paralysed with disbelief. Seriously, what were the godforsaken odds? At any rate, it didn't matter. Roman's gaze narrowed on her. A quick flicker of surprise, a hint of a smirk, and he was back to chatting up Naomi.

When he finally deigned to sit next to her, he murmured a greeting to Jen and her date, and introduced himself to Jasmine, Hugo and their better halves. Then he turned to her: 'Am I really in good hands?'

Samantha toyed with her dinner knife. 'I'd have no trouble wringing your neck, if that's what you mean.'

The corners of his eyes creased with a smile. 'I might enjoy that.'

She had no doubt he would.

Relaxed, unruffled, he addressed the table. 'What are we drinking?'

Answers came from all directions.

'Water.'

'Beer.'

'This rum punch is nice.'

When the server came around, Roman chose a local beer. Samantha reached for her glass of water and sipped past the lump in her throat. 'I'm guessing you're Anthony's mate from uni?'

'I'm his college roommate,' he corrected. 'Don't get fancy.'

She rolled her eyes. 'Do we need an interpreter?'

He considered her a while. 'I think we understand each other.'

God … this was going to be a long night.

'Your name really is Samantha, not a fake name you give out with your fake number?'

'My fake name is Daphne, and I don't give out my number.'

'Never?'

'Not to strangers with bad attitudes.'

'Stranger?' he protested. 'We're past that. You came to my family's shop. You met my grandfather.'

'Is that all it takes?'

He bunched his long, thick brows, not understanding. 'We're in Tobago.'

'Right.'

'My point is, I was straight up with you.'

'A little *too* straight up, if you ask me.'

'You're the one operating under a false identity. You claimed to be a blogger. Remember?'

'It wasn't a lie!' she snapped. 'I'm blogging about this trip. I've taken a ton of pictures.'

Fact check: she'd taken exactly two pictures, both at the airport.

'When can I read it?'

Likely never.

Hugo snapped his fingers to grab Samantha's attention from across the table. 'What's up with you two? Why do you look so tense?'

'Nothing's up,' Samantha said quickly.

'Just getting to know each other,' Roman added.

'Carry on,' Hugo said. 'Roman, Sam is single. How about you?'

'I'm *very* single.'

'Interesting.'

Exasperated, she looked up past the fairy lights, in search of a star to wish upon to start this whole day over.

Roman leaned close and whispered, 'You didn't tell your friends about us.'

'There's no *us*,' she hissed. 'Besides, I forgot all about it. Totally escaped my mind.'

She'd spent the whole afternoon obsessing over it, slicing and editing the reel in her mind. Roman Carver didn't have to know that.

'Not me,' he said. 'It made my day. A pretty lady tells you off … it does something to you.'

There were those stupid words again: pretty lady. But something about the way he said it made her think he meant it this time – not that it mattered. She was absolutely indifferent. She couldn't care less. 'I'm surprised it doesn't happen more often.'

'Oh really?'

His brown eyes sparkled entrancingly. The server chose this moment to return with his beer. He picked up the bottle and poured the frothy amber liquid into a tall, chilled glass. Seconds passed before he could spare her his full attention.

'Samantha?'

'Yes?'

'Don't let me get under your skin.'

'You're not getting under anything!'

Roman's big, rolling laughter filled her ears, followed by the crystal sound of Anthony tapping on his glass for yet another toast. He stood at the head of the table. 'Naomi and I want to thank you all for being here with us. Some of you travelled from very far and we appreciate that. Your support means the world to us. I'm lucky enough to have found my great love and soul mate. That is our wish for all of you.'

Anthony's words prompted applause and much cooing. Naomi was incandescent with a mix of joy and pride. Jen dropped her head on her date's shoulder. Jason pulled Jasmine close and planted a kiss on her temple. Hugo clutched his chest as if his heart might burst.

Roman glanced her way and reminded her to smile. 'You should see your face right now.'

'I *am* smiling,' she said through clenched teeth. 'If I smile any harder I'll pull a muscle.'

'Maybe that's the problem. Try less.'

'*You*'re my problem.'

Dinner was served and the simple shrimp curry with rice and grilled vegetables was so delicious everyone lost the will to chat. By the time dessert was served, Jen's date, a guy named Chris, roped Roman into a convoluted conversation about computers. When they all got up from the table, Samantha pulled Naomi aside. 'I'm exhausted. It's been a long day.'

'Uh huh,' Naomi replied distractedly. 'What do you think about Roman?'

Samantha stiffened. 'Nothing. I think absolutely nothing.'

'He's single, you know.'

'I heard.'

Naomi winked. 'Oh, good.'

'Goodnight, Naomi.'

The plan was to get away as quickly as possible. No one would miss her. With the arrival of Jason and Adrian this afternoon, the couples' retreat had begun in earnest. She was confident in her plan until, out of the corner of her eye, she spotted Roman breaking away from the others and moving in her direction. She darted off the deck toward the path to the bungalows.

'Samantha! Wait up!' he called after her.

She could pretend she hadn't heard him and keep on

marching. Why didn't she want to? Why did her heart flutter with excitement? What was going on with her?

Roman caught up easily. 'Can we talk a minute?'

'Honestly, haven't we talked enough?'

He frowned. 'You still hate me.'

'Hate is a strong word.'

'I'm actually a nice guy.'

'Sure you are.'

'I'm a good friend – just ask Anthony. And I'm pretty laidback once you get to know me.'

Samantha shrugged, unimpressed. 'I'm all those things, too.'

'Why can't we get along?'

She had no answer for that. 'How about we try again tomorrow?'

'Fair. May I walk you to your room.'

'It's not a room. It's a bungalow.'

'All to yourself?'

'Yes. And it's not selfish!'

'Why would it be?' he said. 'I should've taken up Anthony's offer and gotten one for myself.'

'Why didn't you?'

'I'm not a tourist.'

Without realizing, they'd started down the path and walked a long while in silence, side by side, his hands shoved in his pockets and her arms crossed over her chest. Night had fallen. The sea was out there somewhere. She could hear and smell it, the salt air a constant reminder.

After a while, Samantha stopped and looked around. Nothing seemed familiar. The stone-paved path had turned to gravel. Neatly pruned shrubs had given way to soaring palm trees.

The surf was louder. They were nowhere near her bungalow or any other building, for that matter. Had they gone down the wrong path?

'I think we're lost.'

'Hold on. There are lights up ahead.'

Roman charged forward. She followed him and, to her surprise, he pushed aside a palm frond and revealed the view.

The hotel was not on the beach but nestled above it. They'd stumbled upon one of the many outdoor lounges with a privileged view of the ocean rippling in the moonlight. It wasn't a scary, deserted spot where a girl could end up murdered. Far from it. A few other couples were relaxing, lounging on daybeds and sipping cocktails. Paradise found!

Roman turned to her. 'What do you think? Should we stay a while?'

Samantha took off skipping to one of the circular lounge beds, a strong breeze ruffling her hair, and fell onto it, landing on her back, arms flung wide. It was Roman's turn to follow. She heard him mutter, 'Guess we're staying a while.'

'We'd be crazy not to. It's gorgeous out here.'

He approached her, grinning. 'But you were in such a hurry to get away from me.'

'Don't push your luck.' She sat up and drew her knees to her chest. 'This is perfect. I've had such a stressful day.'

He turned sombre. 'Sorry if I made your day more stressful.'

Just when she'd given up hope of ever getting a sincere apology from the man, he delivered.

'Anthony has a lot on his mind,' he continued. 'I don't want him thinking that I'm starting trouble with his bride's best friend.'

Samantha was willing to bet that honour and distinction went to Jen. 'I'm her *oldest* friend. Jen has replaced me in the *best* friend department. I've been demoted.'

'If it's any consolation, Naomi is Anthony's whole world now. There's little room for anyone else.'

'Circle of life,' Samantha mused.

Here they were, two insiders on the outside.

Samantha extended a hand, inviting him onto her lounge bed. There was space enough for two.

CHAPTER SEVEN

As it turned out, you couldn't just skip to one of the reserved lounge beds and not order a drink. An attendant cleared up that misunderstanding.

'I heard the rum punch is nice,' Roman said.

Samantha nodded her approval. They ordered two. When the attendant returned with their umbrella-topped drinks, they clinked glasses.

'Do you like weddings?' he asked.

'I do, and I don't. It's complicated. And you?'

'Me? It's simple. I don't.'

'Not at all?'

'I've got nothing against marriage. Just can't take all the fuss around weddings.'

'With that attitude, you won't make it through the week.'

'Here's what I'm thinking,' Roman said. 'We should forge an alliance, stick together, watch each other's back.'

'Share intelligence?' she suggested.

'Exactly.'

'That might be smart,' she said. 'If we're not careful they'll set us up with any random person.'

'Oh, we'll be careful,' he said.

She liked the smoky quality of his voice. 'All right,' she said. 'We can give it a try.'

'Good. Now tell me what you really think about Anthony and Naomi's getting married five seconds after jumping into bed.'

Samantha covered her mouth. She'd come close to spitting out her cocktail, which would have been a shame because it was quite nice. She went with the simplest explanation. 'It's love! Don't you believe in it?'

He was silent for a bit. 'I think it's great they're so sure.'

'They better be: it's only days away from "I do". But I admit I was sceptical.'

'Not anymore?'

'It's just … they look so happy, ridiculously happy.'

He agreed. 'They make a good couple. I like Naomi. Her people are from Tobago, that's a plus. And Anthony is one of the good ones.'

'Sounds like we're the bad people.'

He nodded. 'Bitter, jaded people.'

'It's obvious they're in love,' she said. 'Why can't we trust they're doing the right thing?'

'Because we know that love isn't always enough.'

Samantha paused to look at him. She tried seeing past the hardened mask of self-confidence. Had he been hurt, too?

'My plan was to come down here and talk some sense into Naomi,' she said.

'Don't you think it's a little late for that?'

'I just want to be sure she knows what she's doing.'

'I'm going to let Anthony take the plunge. If he crashes and burns, so be it. It is what it is.'

'Some friend you are.'

'Don't worry. I'll be there to help pick up the pieces.'

'It's the least you can do.'

'The way I understand it, it's Anthony's fault. It was love at first sight for him. After their third date, he went shopping for the ring.'

'The ring isn't enchanted. Naomi could've said yes, but not yet.'

'There's something about Anthony that makes you think you can walk on water. That's why he's so successful.'

Samantha plucked the paper umbrella out of her drink and gave it a twirl. 'I could use that energy.'

'Enough about them,' he said. 'Want to tell me why you're single?'

'I don't.' She took one last sip from her glass, set it down, and stood. 'Want to walk me back now? I need sleep.'

He sunk his teeth into his lower lip. 'Touchy subject?'

She took a step toward the exit. 'I can go it alone.'

'You'd wander in circles all night.' He set his glass next to hers, untouched. 'Let's go.'

This time Roman didn't leave anything to chance. He asked around for directions to her bungalow. They wandered along the winding path. The resort was quiet; the laughter and music had died down.

'Was it a bad break-up?'

'Let it go, Roman.'

'For the sake of transparency, I should tell you that I know some things.'

Her voice took a sharp tilt. 'What things?'

'Nothing specific. One of the wedding guests cancelled last minute. If I had to guess, he was your guy. Am I wrong?'

'Not anymore. He's off backpacking in Italy and I never want to hear from him again.'

'Let's hope he falls off a cliff.'

'Now that's just mean!' she cried.

'I'll be mean so you don't have to.'

'I appreciate that. Honestly, I don't want to talk about my ex.'

'That works. I don't want to talk about mine. Let's seal the Ex Files shut.' He nudged her forward. 'Have you noticed we're the only single people here?'

'Us and Maya,' Samantha replied. 'Seems like people are pairing up and falling in love left and right.'

'We don't want to be one of those people.'

'We don't? Why not?'

'You're heartbroken, and I don't have the time.'

'Is that why you don't have a date? You didn't have time to find one? Sorry, I don't buy it.'

'I had a date.'

'Where is she?'

He looked away. 'Thought we weren't talking about our exes.'

That was fine with her. 'Just so you know, I'm not heartbroken. Get that out of your head.'

Angry, frustrated, disappointed, yes, she wouldn't deny it. Heartbroken? No. Absolutely not.

'Come on, Samantha,' he said, adopting the sober tone of a pharmacist. 'I've been there. I know the signs.'

'Since you're an expert, what are the signs?'

'You're sulky, moody, cranky, ready to jump down everybody's throat.'

'Not everybody, just yours.'

'I deserve it,' he said. 'And I can handle it. Still, aren't you here to have fun?'

'I'm here to survive this wedding. That's it. That's the goal.'

'I'm up for fun,' he said, wistful. 'It's been one hell of a year.'

Her mind reeled, spinning scenarios in which Roman Carver was living his best life, partying like a rock star. What would that even look like? Could she handle it?

'Well, this was all very illuminating.' She slipped her keycard out of her clutch purse. 'Plus you've managed to get me back to my humble abode. I guess this wasn't a total waste of time.'

He looked up at the bright yellow bungalow with its wraparound veranda and quaint wooden swing. 'It's cute.'

'Cosy, too.'

'I'll leave you here,' he said. 'Will I see you tomorrow?'

'Depends on the wedding itinerary. Are you up to speed?'

'I'm on top of it. I check the website for updates every day,' he said, walking backwards.

'Will you be joining us for sunrise yoga, then?'

'Not even for your beautiful smile.'

'Ha!' She swivelled and rushed up the wooden steps, her smile widening. She didn't make it inside. Her curiosity demanded she ask one last question. 'Hey!' she called after him. 'Would you really let Anthony crash and burn?'

'I love Anthony,' he said. 'But lately he's been so goddamn smug.'

Samantha barked out a laugh. 'You know what? He and Naomi are going to get on fine!'

'I can feel it!' Roman said. 'Go to bed, pretty girl. Goodnight!'

CHAPTER EIGHT

A boy band means drama, and theirs was no exception. Roman filled the role of the quiet drummer. Anthony was the charismatic lead singer that drew in the girls. His cousin, Ted, was the jerk guitarist who was going to screw it all up. Roman had only met the guy a couple of times over the years. Every time, he'd got a bad vibe. So it came as no surprise when he walked in on them at each other's throats.

After leaving the charming Samantha Roberts at her doorstep, he'd made a beeline to Anthony's spot. When the news broke that one of Naomi's friends had been dumped last minute and would be arriving alone, he hadn't cared enough to ask follow-up questions. Now he wanted answers. How serious was that relationship? How badly was she hurt? Was it too soon to make a move? He couldn't imagine a scenario where he wouldn't. He'd been thinking about her all day. Feisty. She *was* feisty. Whenever she glared at him, it just made him want to do things. Except, Anthony was about to land a punch in his cousin's stupid face. Roman pushed the pretty girl out of his mind and rushed to break up the fight.

He blocked Anthony. 'Calm down. He's not worth the trouble.'

Ted turned turnip red. 'You're going to let him talk to me like that?'

Roman pointed out the obvious. 'I'm the only thing standing between you and his fist.'

'You don't think I could take him? I taught that punk how to stand up to bullies.'

'Twenty years ago!' Anthony bellowed.

'And I don't give a crap.'

Roman was thrilled when Anthony told him the wedding would be on his turf, practically in his backyard. He hadn't signed up for this. He'd come to Tobago to reset, get his head straight and his life together. 'What's this about?' he asked Anthony.

Anthony darted a finger at his older cousin. 'He started it.'

This was the level they were playing at; playground warfare. Yet when he looked from Ted to Anthony, he could tell the mood was serious. This was no friendly fall-out between cousins. What had happened? Not one hour ago, they were laughing over dinner. He tried to get an answer from Ted. 'Why are you starting trouble?'

'I'm trying to talk sense into him. That's all.'

Not another person trying to talk sense into Anthony and Naomi, Roman thought wearily. His old college roommate, the most stubborn person Roman knew, had met his match in Naomi. If they wanted to get married, no one and nothing could stop them. 'Man, get over it. It's way too late for that.'

Anthony walked in circles in the tight room. 'And no one wants to hear it!'

Ted ran a hand down his face. 'I'm wasting my breath here.'

'You are,' Roman said. He ought to know better.

'All right. I'm out.'

Ted charged out the door, letting it slam behind him, only it bounced and flung wide open.

Roman looked to Anthony, who was shapeless and deflated on a wicker rocking chair. 'What the hell was that?'

'How much time you got?'

Roman shrugged. 'I'm in no rush.'

'Grab a beer. Shut the door.'

Travel Blog

Title TBD [Still]

DRAFT ENTRY #2: RUN TOWARD ADVENTURE

I may not like to travel light, but I've decided to leave the girl I once was at Heathrow airport. Last night, in Tobago, I was a single girl, sipping cocktails in the moonlight with a fit, funny, infuriating man and loving every minute of it. I swear I did not see that coming. Going forward, that's what I want: a surprise at every turn.

Affirmation: I will run toward adventure.

Even if I fall, bruise a knee, and lose face, I will get up and keep on running.

Welcome to Tobago

To our special guests, friends and family, we want to extend our warmest welcome. Thank you for joining us in beautiful Tobago to celebrate our special day, the start of a new journey. We are honoured to have you.

In your rooms you will find a welcome basket with bottled water, sunscreen, insect repellent, two types of painkillers, antacid, a map of the area, and a disposable camera (for fun).

Read on for the week's events

We took a lot of care in curating exciting events that you will enjoy. We've also left plenty of downtime for you to explore the island on your own terms. We're overjoyed to spend this time with you!

Much love,
Naomi & Anthony

Wedding Week Schedule

For all excursions we will meet in the lobby at the appointed time. Thank you.

Sunday 10 August:
6 a.m. Sunrise Yoga at Hibiscus Terrace (optional)
10 a.m. Argyle Waterfall (climbing gear/bathing suit)

Monday 11 August:
6 a.m. Sunrise Yoga at Hibiscus Terrace (optional)
10 a.m. Cotton Bay (snorkelling)

Tuesday 12 August:
6 a.m. Sunrise Yoga at Hibiscus Terrace (optional)
10 a.m. Nylon Pool (swimming)

Wednesday 13 August:
6 a.m. Sunrise Yoga at Hibiscus Terrace (optional)
10 a.m. Buccoo Bay (mangroves and more snorkelling!)

Thursday 14 August:
6 a.m. Sunrise Yoga at Hibiscus Terrace (optional)
10 a.m. Beach Day at Pigeon Point

Official Wedding Weekend

Friday 15 August:

3 p.m. Rehearsal

5 p.m. Cocktails & Barbecue at the resort (beach cocktail attire)

Saturday 16 August: Wedding Day

10 a.m. Bridesmaids' Bubbly Brunch (Palm Terrace)

4 p.m. Groomsmen's Cigars Lounge (Palm Terrace)

6 p.m. Wedding Ceremony at the Sunset Veranda

7 p.m. Reception at Garden Cove

Sunday 17 August:

7-9 a.m. Continental Breakfast

11.30–2.30 p.m. Departures

CHAPTER NINE

Samantha hoped to catch a minute alone with Naomi at sunrise yoga. But she overslept, arrived fifteen minutes late, and found the small group of early risers flowing through the stages of the sun salutation. There was no instructor, only the commands of an anonymous yogi pouring out through a Bluetooth speaker. Naomi was there, faithful to her bride-to-be aesthetic, in a white halter and matching yoga pants. Amelia sat cross-legged on the mat next to her. Jen and Chris were flowing side by side. Maya was there, groggily going through the motions. Naomi cheerfully waved her over. Samantha grabbed one of the last remaining mats and joined in.

Upward facing dog. Downward facing dog. Was Roman right? *Warrior one. Warrior two.* Was it too late to intervene? While Naomi had never seemed more serene, Samantha was wearing herself out, analysing a matter that was settled. *Hands to heart centre.* Was she meddling? Naomi was an adult and free to make her own choices, after all. *Savasana.* Maybe she ought to give it a rest. Then again, maybe she wasn't quite ready to give up. After all, if the tables were turned, she wouldn't want Naomi to give up on her.

The soft chime of a bell signalled the end of the practice.

Samantha sat up on her mat and took in her surroundings. The Caribbean Sea spread out to the horizon, turning crimson where it touched the rising sun. Much to her surprise, she felt at peace for the first time since arriving on the island. She rolled onto her feet and dusted herself off. *OK,* she thought, hands on her hips. *Let's hope this feeling lasts.*

***

It didn't.

When she returned to the bungalow, her mother called with news. 'I've done it at last, Sam!'

She unlocked her door with her keycard. Alarmed, she asked, 'Done what, exactly?'

Diane had been hinting at renovating her old bedroom for years. She dreamed of turning it into a crafts room of some sort, a haven where she could pursue all her DIY dreams. It was selfish of Sam, who'd officially moved out at nineteen, but she wasn't ready to give up her space quite yet. Where would she sleep at Christmas?

'Submitted my official retirement request.'

'Wow! Congrats, Mum!'

This was exceptional news. Her mother had intended to retire from the hospital where she worked as a nurse as soon as she was eligible yet kept postponing for one reason or another … or maybe just for one reason: money. They weren't rich, and likely would never be. Her mother had been working since she was fifteen. The idea of stopping working altogether was unfathomable. When Samantha had pressed her on the issue of retirement, she said she had to get her affairs in order first.

'Sounds like you're going to die,' Samantha teased. Her mother dipped another biscuit in her tea. 'No difference.'

Her mother was a competent nurse, but she'd entered the profession out of necessity and started her training the year after Samantha was born. The goal was to make enough to afford a house. Her father worked in IT as a support technician. Steady work, but not enough to support a family of three and take on a mortgage. Samantha was five when they moved into the two-bedroom detached house in Manchester that she would forever call home. She quickly bonded with Naomi. They pledged to remain best friends forever. Over the years, when she wasn't blogging on some social media site or another, whipping up homemade concoctions to tame her curly hair, or re-watching her favourite romantic comedies, she was hanging out next door. However, their mothers, Amelia and Diane, had never warmed to each other. To Diane, Amelia was merely the 'diva next door'.

'I did it,' Diane repeated. 'In three weeks I'm free. I can finally relax.'

It was well deserved. Her mother had worked through the pandemic and it had worn her out. She was not in the best of health herself, and would benefit from a slower pace.

'We need to celebrate!' Samantha exclaimed. 'When I get back we'll go out to dinner. I'll make reservations.'

'Or we'll have a quiet night at home. I'll make a cake.'

Samantha poured a glass of water in the kitchen and took it into the bedroom. 'No, we're having a proper dinner party. And you shouldn't have to make your own retirement cake.'

'My chocolate cake is special. Besides, what else will I have to do?'

She flipped on the ceiling fan and flopped onto the bed.

'Please don't tell me you're going to retire just to catch up on your shows.'

'What if I am?' her mother retorted. 'I'm going to bake, drink tea, work on my quilts, and catch up on my shows. When I tire of that, *maybe* I'll join a gym. But that's a big maybe.'

Samantha pinched the bridge of her nose. Her parents embraced a slow and quiet life, resisting excitement in all its forms. They never ventured far from home and refused to spend money on extravagances. They were stable and predictable and she loved that about them. Deep inside, Samantha worried she would turn out just like them. After university, she'd returned to her hometown and secured a job. Her friends had travelled far and wide in pursuit of exciting careers. This bothered her. She didn't want a small, tidy and predictable life. She desperately wanted to break out of her box, chase wild dreams, and crisscross the world. Somehow, she'd fallen into the same patterns that had shaped her early life. Hadn't she picked Timothy because he was safe and steady? Look how well that turned out.

'I insist we go to London and celebrate properly. Invite your friends.'

'My friends are organizing a surprise party in the nurses' lounge, Sam. They don't know that I know, but I know everything.'

'Those are your co-workers, not your friends!'

'When you work my schedule, your co-workers are your friends. Sometimes, they're your family.'

'Fine. It'll be just us three.'

'We'll discuss it when you get back. Now, tell me. How is Naomi? And how are you? Are you having a rough time?'

Her mother wasn't the only expert at dodging difficult

conversations. 'Can't talk now. I'm late for our first outing. Exciting stuff.'

'All right, doll. Send photos! Your dad says hi.'

***

Naomi's stepdad had sprung for an air-conditioned bus to safely chauffeur them to and from their many excursions. The girls filled the front rows. When Roman ruffled Samantha's hair on his way to the back of the bus, all the girls cooed.

'I'm loving this!' Jen squealed. 'It's like a high school field trip.'

Naomi rose to address them. 'Attention, everyone! This will be a short outing. A hike and a swim and we're heading back.'

'What's the rush?' Hugo asked from the very back seat.

'We have high tea with Amelia at four thirty.'

Hugo cupped a hand to his ear. 'Excuse me, what?'

'You heard me.'

Samantha raised a hand. 'Sorry, ma'am. That's not on the schedule.'

'It is now,' Naomi said. 'Any questions?'

Jason cleared his throat before addressing Naomi. 'Could we speed through the hike and take our time at the waterfalls. That's a high priority for me.'

'Noted.'

Hugo's hand shot up. 'This isn't a question. Just like to point out that it is effing hot in Tobago and hot tea may not be *my* cup of tea. Get it?'

Naomi advised him to suck it up. 'We have to be back on time and dressed and ready for high tea at four thirty. End of story.'

'You tell 'em, babe!' Anthony shouted his encouragement. He was seated behind Roman, who asked to be officially excused.

Impatience crept into Naomi's voice. 'Yes, Roman. You are excused for the rest of the day. The tea is to welcome our new guests.'

'Well,' Jen said. 'Chris and I have been here a while so …'

Naomi issued a one-word warning. 'Jen.'

'I don't know what you guys are complaining about,' Jasmine said. 'It sounds lovely.'

'You English and your tea,' Hugo said. 'If she were serving lemonade, I wouldn't have a problem with it.'

'Maybe there'll be an ice tea option,' Jen said. 'What do you think, Naomi?'

Naomi pointedly ignored the question.

'What do we wear?' Jasmine asked.

'Smart resort casual. Any sort of dress will do.'

'No fancy hats?' Hugo asked.

'Screw you guys,' Naomi said. She gave the driver the all-clear.

Samantha was still giggling like a schoolgirl when Naomi slid into the seat beside hers. 'Glad you're in a good mood,' she said. 'Because I've been meaning to talk to you about Roman.'

'What's there to talk about?' Samantha asked, all wide-eyed and innocent.

'I won't mince words,' Naomi said. 'You should make a move on him.'

Samantha knew this was coming, but she bristled anyway. 'Is there any specific reason? Or simply because he's the only single man within arm's reach?'

'Well, he *is* single,' Naomi said. 'He's also smart, fit and financially independent.'

'He's also kind of cocky and cute.'

The last bit was Jen's contribution to the private conversation. She slumped over the back of their bench and popped her head between them. Before Samantha could object to the intrusion, Jasmine did the same. 'Hey. Are we talking about Roman?'

'Uh huh,' Naomi said. 'I think he's a perfect match for our girl. What do you think, Sam? Is he your type?'

'What kind of question is that?' Jen asked. 'He's everybody's type.'

Jasmine burst out laughing. 'He's a Type O universal donor.'

'I need you all to calm down,' Samantha said. 'I'm here for a wedding, *your* wedding, Naomi. I'm not interested in starting anything or stealing your thunder.'

'Darling, you can't possibly,' Naomi said. 'I'm the goddess of thunder.'

Jasmine tucked a long, thin braid behind her ear. 'Please don't let the wedding stop you! Have fun! You only live once.'

'Why do you think I brought Chris?' Jen said. 'It's definitely to start something.'

'Good luck to you,' Jasmine said.

Naomi brought her hands together in prayer. 'Godspeed.'

At a loss, Samantha blurted, 'I'm focused on my blog.'

'You've got a blog?' Naomi asked. 'This is the first I'm hearing of it.'

'Writing about a budding romance is a great way to kickstart a blog,' Jen said. 'I should know. I work mostly with content creators.'

At her wit's end, Samantha exploded. 'Guys, did you forget? I've just got out of a relationship!'

'There is the truth,' Jasmine said. 'I knew it would poke its head out eventually.'

'Sweetie,' Naomi said. 'That was ages ago.'

'That was literally days ago.' She could count the days on one hand, OK, maybe two. 'It's still fresh.'

'Little Timmy is out of the picture,' Naomi said. 'That leaves you wide open for Mr Roman Carver. Make your move.'

'Life is short,' Jasmine said.

'Life is short,' Sam repeated. 'Is that from the Old Testament or the New?'

'Don't be a smartass,' Naomi scolded. 'Jasmine is right. Life is too short to go around moping over men like Timothy.'

'I'm not moping. I'm taking a breath.'

'Between breaths, take a look at Roman,' Jasmine suggested. 'I think he fancies you.'

'You think so?' Naomi was choking with glee. 'Tell me everything.'

'Little things. It's the way he looks at her and laughs at everything she says. Didn't you notice last night?'

How did Jasmine notice any of this? She'd only had eyes for Jason.

'I love this for you,' Jen said.

Jen's enthusiasm and optimism was evergreen. Was this why Naomi liked her so much? Compared to her, Samantha was a black hole of scepticism and doubt.

The bus driver shut the door and fired up the engine. Everyone settled into their seats and nestled air pods into their ears. Naomi tilted her head back and closed her eyes, a smile tugging at her lips. Samantha glanced out the window and then, briefly, over her shoulder. Roman was a few rows back, deep in conversation with Chris. Even so, they locked eyes. Samantha tore her gaze away and willed herself to stare out the window at the lush green scenery and the homes built into the hilly terrain. In the back of her mind an electrical storm had begun.

★★★

A short while later they were in the heart of a nature reserve. Their guide, a stocky man named Jude, paid in advance by the wedding committee, was waiting to greet them at the park entrance. 'Ladies and gentlemen, welcome to the Argyle Waterfalls and Nature Park.'

They were not a large group. Maya and Anthony's cousin Ted and his wife had opted out, no doubt preferring to spend their day at the beach rather than trekking through a jungle for the pleasure of a cool swim, only to trek through the same jungle to get back to the car.

Once they'd filed out of the bus, Naomi drifted to Anthony's side. Everybody stretched and they were off.

'Hey, Jude!' Jason called out to the guide moments later. 'How far to the waterfalls?'

'Not far. A fifteen-minute walk,' Jude said. 'Will you swim?'

'Try and stop me.'

'There are three levels,' Jude explained. 'The first basin is nice and shallow. Guests like to climb to the higher levels, but you do so at your own risk.'

'Understood.'

Samantha was entranced by the lush green forest. Jude pointed out each bird and each tree, providing a brief history of fauna and flora alike. Samantha paid attention. A Trinidad motmot bird spotted on a branch was a national symbol and featured predominantly on the local five-dollar note. The rubber trees were imported from Brazil. The teak trees were protected under government law. The trumpet tree bloomed bright yellow for one month out of every year. It was all fascinating stuff, but Samantha gradually tuned Jude out and tuned in on Roman. He followed in his casual way, hands stuffed in the pockets of well-worn cargo shorts, a baseball cap pulled down over his eyes. Every now and then he asked a question. He told Jude it had been a while since he'd visited the park. He used to come often as a kid when he spent his summers at his grandparents' house. He'd been meaning to come out to the waterfalls for a swim, but had never got around to it.

'You should make the time. The waterfall is excellent to relieve stress,' Jude said. 'You'll feel ten years younger.'

Roman clapped the older man on the back. 'No doubt.'

Samantha snapped a photo of a motmot bird, but made sure Roman was in the frame.

★★★

'We are approaching the waterfall!' Jude announced even though the sound of the rushing water made it obvious. They were making their way down wide, long steps embedded into rock. A bright yellow sign advised the use of the handrail. Jude echoed this message: 'Watch your step! Slippery!' Despite all that, Samantha slipped and fell on her bum, coming very close to taking Jasmine down with her.

'AHHUGH!'

Jasmine screamed. 'Jesus! Are you OK?'

Everyone had stopped in their tracks and swivelled to face her. Naomi cried, 'Sam! Don't you dare break a hip!'

Roman took the stairs by twos to get to her. He held out both hands for Samantha to grab and gently, so gently, raised her off the cold, hard, slippery, moss-covered rock. Samantha was embarrassed to her core. After reassuring Jude that she was not in peril or pain, they continued.

The group divided into pairs to complete the descent with Samantha and Roman at the end of the line. Roman slipped an arm around her waist – for balance.

'How do you feel?' he asked.

She felt stupid and foolish, but that didn't take away the pleasure of having Roman at her side, his solid body pressed against hers. The feeling was heightened by the birdsong, sunlight streaming through the trees, and a sudden breeze sprinkled with droplets from the waterfall. And then she snapped out of it. 'I'm fine. Thanks.'

'What would you do without me?' he asked.

Samantha leaned into him even as she pushed away his comment. 'Somebody has a hero complex.'

'It's your sneakers,' he said. 'Those are for powerwalking in the park.'

She glanced down at her trainers. They were the slip-on variety. 'Sorry. I left my hiking boots at home.'

Admittedly Samantha hadn't been in the best headspace when she packed for the trip. She'd tossed random items into her suitcase, ignoring the list Naomi had forwarded weeks in advance. For this hike through a nature reserve, she was wearing a loose T-shirt, fitted cycling shorts, a bucket hat, and trainers with absolutely zero grip. Jude explained that it had rained the night before and boots would have been a preferable choice. Jen, Chris, Naomi and Anthony were suitably attired because, naturally, 'they hike all the time back in LA.'

Finally, they made it to the waterfalls. Water cascaded down the mountainside, splitting in different directions in an argyle pattern, filling a pool below.

'Here we are, ladies and gentlemen!' Jude exclaimed. 'Three levels, three pools. The highest point is 450 feet above sea level. Tobago is under sea level at the moment.'

They stood in awe. A minute later, they stripped down to the swimsuits worn beneath their clothes, eager to dive in – all except Samantha, who had some questions.

'How deep is it?' she asked Jude.

'The lowest level is eighteen feet,' he said. 'The higher levels are shallow. You'll use that rope there to climb, but at your own risk.'

'Uh huh.'

'Come on, Sam!' Anthony said, ever the encouraging coach. 'I know you're a city girl, but don't be scared. You can do it.'

Samantha had not grown up climbing trees or swinging from vines. She'd played roughhouse in padded rooms and got her adrenaline rush from climbing jungle gyms and diving into ball pits. Jumping into a waterfall sat well outside her realm of experience.

Hugo and Adrian were the first to leap, hollering something about freedom on their way down. Meanwhile, Roman had stripped off his T-shirt and rolled it into a ball. From his broad shoulders to his narrow waist and every rippling ab in between, he was more beautiful than she'd ever imagined. There was a tattoo of a thorny black rose on his right shoulder and the ace of spades on his back. She had no desire to jump into a shallow pool and every desire to touch him, to explore the ink work and feel the grain of his tight skin. Her inner Jude cautioned that she would do so at her own peril.

Anthony was concerned with Naomi's welfare. 'Stay here,' he said. 'Sit on a rock and let the water flow down your back.'

Naomi was outraged. 'Like a mermaid? I don't think so.'

'For safety.'

'Don't be ridiculous. I've done this hundreds of times.'

'No, you haven't.'

'Trust me. I'm an island girl at heart. I can do this.'

Jen and Chris had no safety concerns whatsoever. They took off over the cliff, arms extended high.

'Woo hoo! Awesome!' Jen cried.

'Freaking awesome!' Chris echoed.

Anthony and Naomi followed, leaping hand in hand. Jasmine asked Samantha to record a quick video as she and Jason took the leap. And then they were two.

'What are you waiting for?' Anthony called out to them. 'Get in here. It's great.'

Samantha squirmed in her bustier bikini top that was designed for lounging in the sun at best.

Roman took her aside. 'We can stay here, do some bird-watching.'

It was a really sweet offer and her heart broke a little. 'Don't be silly. Go on. Jump. I'll be right in.'

'Samantha …' He took a step closer to her. 'How about we do this together.'

Her first instinct was to say no, to repeat her affirmation. *I can go it alone.* But she didn't want to, and as it turned out, she didn't have to.

'I could totally do this on my own,' she said. 'But I wouldn't want to leave you hanging, not with everyone watching.'

'Thanks,' he said with a grin. 'Can't tell you how much that means to me.'

'You're welcome.'

'OK … ready?'

Samantha nodded.

Roman held out his hand. 'Let's go for it.'

And they did. Together.

Travel Blog

Title TBD [Note to Self: Work on title]

DRAFT ENTRY #3: DARE TO FLY

Travel is a time for leisure, no argument here. It's for lazy days lounging in the sun and indulgent nights. Tapas dinners and jugs of wine. It's for naps, naps and more naps. However, it can also be a time for pushing boundaries, stepping out of cosy comfort zones and taking risks. You may discover that you're braver than you thought.

I jumped off a cliff today. Let that sink in.

Your girl jumped off a cliff!!!

I dived several metres down into a natural pool. I scaled the side of a mountain, with the aid of a threadbare rope, and sat at the top tier of a waterfall while spring water massaged my back. I did it all in the company of some very cool people. And guess what? I feel ten years younger. I feel free. Not only that, I've realized that I can do scary things.

It wasn't easy. For a split second, while standing at the cliff's edge and staring into the churning waters below, I felt faint.

The trip to the Argyle Waterfalls had been high on my list.

I'd dreamed of standing under a gentle cascading stream, looking amazing in designer swimwear. I never for one moment imagined I'd be leaping into an abyss. It took the gentle nudging of a new friend to get me going; that was a welcome surprise. But in the end I did it! I flew! It was freaking awesome.

CHAPTER TEN

Back at her bungalow later that day, just as it started to rain, Samantha set up a mini workstation in the living area. The coffee table made for a decent desk. She set up her laptop, a mini mood board with clippings from travel magazines, and set the mood by lighting a candle and arranging the crystals she'd brought for clarity and good energy. After staring at the blank screen for a while, she typed a piece about the power of facing her fears. It wasn't groundbreaking stuff. She doubted anyone would be interested. But *she* broke ground today. Not a minor thing.

Samantha reached for her camera and scrolled through the images of the day. The best moments were missing. After she'd fallen on her arse – a low point – she'd lost interest in taking photos, mainly because the man featured in just about every single frame had been by her side. She didn't want to attribute her new-found bravery to Roman. That was the opposite of girl power. Or maybe she should. What harm was there in acknowledging that she'd been inspired and encouraged by a new friend?

Wow. She and Roman were friends. How in hell did that happen?

Samantha flashed back to the moment when Roman helped her to her feet. The image was stored away in the hard drive of her mind. The waterfall framed his silhouette. She'd begun to think of him as 'The American'. It wasn't until that moment that she saw him as an American boy who'd spent his summers in the Caribbean while his friends went to baseball camp or whatever. Although he'd mentioned not having time to visit the natural park, he seemed very much at ease there. When he joined her on the long trek down the stone steps, she felt safer. And when he extended his hand to hers, she reached for it without hesitation. She trusted him.

A knock on her door roused Samantha from her dream state. She was surprised to find Naomi on the veranda, still in the flowery dress she'd worn to high tea. She had a bag of plantain crisps and two bottles of local soda. 'Want to help me cheat on my diet?'

'How can you still eat after we've stuffed ourselves for one straight hour?'

High tea with Amelia wasn't the stuffy event they'd feared it would be. While ice tea was not an option at the resort's Indian tearoom, prosecco was. If Amelia, their host, was less than impressed by her ragtag guests in rumpled sundresses, wet hair, and thong sandals, she didn't let it show. Once they'd finished up the masala sandwiches and lamb samosas, they moved on to sweets and the mood soared. All in all, they'd had a great time.

'I worked up at appetite at the waterfall,' Naomi said.

They sat on the wooden swing. It took a while for Samantha to relax. Was this a spontaneous visit or an item on Naomi's to-do list? *Spend quality time with bridesmaids. Check!*

Naomi, on the other hand, looked very relaxed. 'Let's get this swing moving.'

At her count, they kicked back and jerked forward until

they eased into a steady rocking motion. They gazed out at the garden. A fine drizzle was turning everything soggy. The rich scent of earth enveloped them.

Naomi sighed. 'This weather ...'

'Are you worried it'll rain on Saturday?'

'Not really,' Naomi answered. 'It's the wet season, so I knew there was a chance. They'll set up a tent in case it does. Anyway, look at this!' She swept her arm. 'Like a watercolour painting ...'

Samantha agreed. The waterlogged yellow and pink bougainvillea flowers were more vibrant when glistening wet. But she doubted any bride would welcome rain on her special big day. She had to credit Naomi for taking it in stride.

Naomi was older than Samantha, but she'd never been so aware of the age gap until now. Her friend had changed, matured. She was still a drama queen, but beneath the theatrics she was calmer than Samantha remembered. Was this the effect of morning yoga, all that hiking in LA, or just Anthony?

Speaking of Anthony, this was the opportunity she'd been waiting for. Her chance to talk to her friend without Jen running interference, the chance to get it all off her chest. Before she had a chance to say a word, Naomi spoke up first. 'There are a few things I'd like to chat about.'

'Oh?' Samantha gulped down her cherry red soda. How typical was this? She wasted time spinning in circles, choosing her words. Naomi aired her every grievance without hesitation.

'Let's start with Jen,' Naomi continued.

'I am *not* giving up my bungalow for Jen and Chris to—'

'Don't worry about that. We've got them sorted. I don't know if you've noticed, but Anthony's cousin moved out this morning.'

'The best man?'

Naomi popped a crisp into her mouth. 'He and his wife moved to an Airbnb in town.'

'Is something wrong?'

Naomi wiped her greasy fingers on a paper napkin. 'He needed more room.'

That made no sense, but she was glad for Jen and Chris. 'I guess it worked out.'

'All's well that ends well,' Naomi said breezily. 'Now about Jen. Sam, tell me, are you jealous?'

'What?'

'Are. You. Jealous.'

Samantha took another gulp of soda and considered her answer. A mature person would deny this. 'Absolutely, I am! It's been all about Jen since the moment I arrived.'

'Well, now you know how I feel.'

'What does that mean?'

'It's been all about Hugo and Jasmine since the moment you met them in Vegas.'

'That's not true! We're all friends.'

'They're *your* friends, Sam,' Naomi insisted. 'You met them and fell in love. I've been tagging along ever since. Don't get me wrong; I think they're great. But it was just you and me before them.'

Samantha's grip tightened on the soda bottle. She'd never seen it that way. It was true that Naomi had been busy at the convention when Samantha met Hugo and Jasmine by the hotel pool. Later that night, they went out for drinks and had a blast. But Naomi hadn't wanted to go. She was tired from work and had to wake up early the next morning. So, really, Samantha had had to drag Naomi along. 'I never knew you felt that way.'

'Never mind.' Naomi waved away her concerns. 'I love them both. They're fun and quirky and a little crazy … like Jen. But she'll never replace you.'

'Promise?'

'Of course!' Naomi wrapped an arm around her shoulders and squeezed. 'You stayed up all night to watch horror movies with me. Jen never would.'

Samantha laughed and wiped at the tears in her eyes. Naomi was more than a friend; she was family, a bossy big sister, and she loved her.

'Anything else you wanted to chat about?'

'Oh, yes. Roman.'

'Oh, please, don't start!'

'I might have come on too strong earlier on the bus and for that I apologize.'

'Well, thanks. You did lay it on pretty thick.'

'I just think he's a solid guy,' Naomi said. 'He's the reason Anthony and I got together – one reason, anyway. The day we met, I told Anthony I was from Tobago and he mentioned his best mate had just relocated there. Then he did that thing we hate and rattled off all the Trini foods he loved. Next thing you know we were in bed.'

'You're not at all hard to get.'

'The man loved okra and rice. That's worth something.'

'Apparently.'

'You two seem to get along great at the waterfalls. Why not take a chance?'

Roman Carver was a cliff she simply didn't want to jump off. She was just beginning to feel like herself again. 'Sorry. I don't want to waste my time.'

'That's not how time works,' Naomi said, munching gleefully on a crisp. 'It passes you by no matter what you do. What if I had written Anthony off as a waste of time?'

'I get it!' Samantha cried. 'You and Anthony are #couplegoals forever until the end of time!'

'Just until the end of the week. We'll be an old married couple by August.'

'Since you brought up Anthony, there's something I'd like to ask you.'

'Yes?'

'Do you think …' Again, the words died in her mouth. She couldn't do it. She couldn't be the one to dampen Naomi's mood. Mistake or not, her friend was on an adventure of a lifetime. Samantha's one job was to cheer as she leaped off the cliff. Woo hoo!

'Do I think what?'

She went with the first thing that came to mind. 'I was wondering, do you think you'll take his last name.'

'I'm Naomi Reid for life, but when you factor in kids it's different. I'll add a hyphen. Naomi Reid-Scott. That's sounds all right.'

'Kids? How soon do you plan on having those?'

The future Mrs Naomi Reid-Scott glanced at her. 'Soon. We want a large family.'

'You do?'

'Yes,' she said. 'Anthony is an only child. The age gap between Maya and me is so great, I feel like her aunt sometimes.'

'Her cool aunt.'

'Of course.'

Samantha didn't have siblings. She'd wanted a little brother.

Her parents had tried, failed and given up. In the end, she'd been allowed a puppy. This didn't mean she wanted to rush out and have children, though.

'Can't you just imagine me with a squad of kids?' Naomi asked.

'Not really.'

'Oh, come on! It's been a dream of mine for ages. When we played with dolls, I always got the mini van … and the private jet.'

'I always got the helicopter. I want to go places!'

'And I want to carpool my kids to and from school, ballet and tennis, and fly them to England in style over winter break.'

Clearly, Samantha didn't know as much about Naomi as she'd thought. 'This chat has been very eye-opening.'

Naomi clapped. 'Good! Because there's one more thing.'

'What now?'

'I wondered if you could give a little speech at the rehearsal dinner.'

The rehearsal dinner was actually a rehearsal barbecue. Anthony had insisted on a low-key, informal gathering before the main event.

'My aunt Donna is the maid of honour and she'll bore us all to tears on the wedding day. It's OK. I've made peace with that. But the night before is just for us. My mother is taking the older folks out for a proper dinner. We get to chill by the beach. What do you say?'

Samantha was at a loss for words. She hopped off the swing and onto Naomi's lap, pulling her into a hug. 'Let go of me!' Naomi cried.

'Never! I'll never let go!'

'It was a simple yes or no question. You're taking it too far.' Samantha kissed her cheek. 'You know I love you, right?'

'Aww … I love you, too.' Naomi allowed herself to be hugged for a second more before shaking her off. 'Get away! You're crushing the bride.'

Travel Blog

Title TBD [Still...Come on Sam]

DRAFT ENTRY #4: FOOLS RUSH IN

I started this blog ranting about my best friend's wedding. Let's pick up from there and start again.

My oldest and dearest friend is marrying a man she won at a charity auction a few months ago. (For all intents and purposes, she will be known only as 'The Princess Bride[1].') If it sounds outrageous, that's because it is. I won't lie: I was properly scandalized. But we've had time to talk and I'm seeing things differently. I am maybe coming around. They claim it was a case of love at first sight. Who's to say that isn't love in its purest form?

I don't want to be a fool in love. Nobody does. But I don't want to be so foolish as to not recognize love when it walks right up to you and calls you by name.

---

1   Names have been changed to protect the innocent.

CHAPTER ELEVEN

Next morning, they set out for a day of snorkelling at Cotton Bay. They met at the usual spot outside the main lobby. Just as the bus came around, Anthony made an announcement. 'Roman can't make it! His old man has a health issue.'

Samantha was about to board the bus. Crippling disappointment kept her from taking another step. 'Is he OK?'

'The old man? I'm sure he's fine.'

Anthony's response did nothing to reassure her. 'Should we check on Roman before we head out?'

'I'm sure he's fine, too.'

Samantha swapped her beach bag from one shoulder to the other. The idea of going off to the beach, of leaving Roman to deal with his issues on his own, didn't sit well with her. That wasn't how you treated a friend.

'Hey, guys!' she called after the group. 'I think I'll stay behind.'

Naomi whipped around. 'Are *you* feeling OK?'

'I'm fine. I'll check on Roman. He might need help at the shop.'

'Or company,' Anthony suggested. 'He might need company.'

Samantha caught Naomi's sly smile and ignored it. 'Go on. I'll catch up with you all when you get back.'

A moment later, the bus pulled out with her friends waving

and cheering and making fools of themselves. After a slow count to ten, she set out on foot to Candy's Shop.

***

Roman was behind the counter, sipping coffee from a paper cup and scrolling his phone. He was unshaven yet fresh in a light blue T-shirt and faded jeans. 'How can I help?' he asked without looking up.

'A bottled water, please.'

His eyes cut to her as equal parts shock and amusement brought out their sparkle. 'Pretty lady … I didn't expect to see you today.'

'I heard about your grandfather. Is he OK?'

Now Roman just looked confused. 'He's fine. He went into town to pick up a new pair of glasses.'

Samantha could have died from embarrassment. 'Is that all?'

'Why? What did Anthony tell you?'

'Nothing. Just that your granddad had a health issue … a health crisis, I believe.'

'Anthony blows everything out of proportion,' Roman said. 'He doesn't go often into town, so I told him I'd watch the shop.'

'That's good of you.'

'I'm a great grandson.'

She dropped her hefty beach bag on the floor and took a seat at the lunch counter. 'I hate to admit it, but it's sort of endearing.'

He went over to the same glass-fronted refrigerator as last time and returned with an extra-large bottle of water. 'On the house.'

Samantha pulled out a ten-dollar note. 'No way.'

The note stayed on the counter where she put it.

'Where's the rest of the gang?' he asked.

'On their way to a fun-filled day of snorkelling.'

'You stayed behind?'

Samantha struggled with the bottle cap. 'I thought you might need help dealing with your grandfather's health crisis.'

He took the bottle from her and twisted the cap loose. 'You ditched your closest, dearest friends for me?'

She snatched the bottle from him. 'That's *not* what I did.'

'That's what it boils down to.'

'I don't need this,' she said. 'Remind me never to do anything thoughtful for you again. Goodbye.'

'What? You'd leave me in my time of crisis?'

Samantha lost it. 'Roman! For the last time—'

He cut her off with a torrent of laughter. She would have been irritated if she didn't love his laugh so much.

'Come on,' he teased. 'Let me enjoy this. It's not every day a pretty lady rushes to my rescue. Honestly, I don't know how to act.'

She should have got on the damn bus. 'Whatever,' she huffed. 'I could be snorkelling right now.'

Roman leaned on the counter, propped his chin in his hand. 'You like me.'

Samantha turned away from him and made a big show of checking her phone for messages. There were none. She let out her most melodramatic sigh.

'It's more than that,' he said. 'You *care*.'

That was too much. 'When will you get it in your head that I'm a caring, loving, selfless, stellar human being?'

'Oh, I get it.'

She'd done it; she'd let him get under her skin. Here she was, hot and bothered and breathing fire. Meanwhile, he was supremely cool, his elbows on the counter, a wry little smile creeping to his eyes. She paused for a breath and pulled herself together. 'Are you quite done? Because we're not going around in circles like this all day.'

'You're right about that,' he said, looking past her shoulder. A customer had wandered in. In his mid-thirties, wearing a Harvard T-shirt and Bermuda shorts, an expensive-looking camera dangling from his neck, he was the picture-perfect tourist.

'Need help?' Roman asked.

'Just looking. Thanks.' After browsing a long while, he purchased a bag of crisps. 'Where do you keep the candy?' he asked. Roman stared blankly at him. The guy may be a financial maverick, but customer service was not in his skill set.

'The sign says "Candy's Shop",' the tourist said. 'I thought I might find liquorice or something.'

'My grandmother's name is Candace. This is *Candy's* Shop.'

This was news to Samantha. 'I'd made that same assumption. When I came in the first time, I thought you sold sweets ... or something.'

Roman's eyes cut to her. 'You want liquorice, too?'

There was no proper way to respond to that except to smirk. 'I'd take a chocolate bar, if you had it.'

The tourist backed out of the shop, hands raised over his head. 'Didn't mean to start anything. Have a nice day, you two!'

Once he was gone, Roman opened a drawer, pulled out a miniature chocolate bar and tossed it her way. It was one of her favourites, chock full of caramel and peanuts. 'Thanks,' she said. 'But you've scared yet another customer away. Just admit you're no good at this.'

'It's not my life's calling. I'll tell you that.'

Samantha slid onto a barstool. 'What *is* your calling?'

'That's what I'm here in Tobago to figure out.'

'You don't live here permanently?'

'No, I couldn't,' he said. 'The slow pace would kill me. I'm on sabbatical.'

'From what?'

He shifted, looking increasingly uncomfortable. 'Money peddling on Wall Street.'

'Oh? Was that your official title?'

'Pretty much.'

'You're a long way from Wall Street.'

'I know it.'

'What's the plan?' she asked.

'A bit of freelancing.'

'Back in New York?'

'I'm consulting, so it's anywhere with Wi-Fi,' he said. 'For now the focus is to help my grandfather get his new business off the ground. He put a lot of money into renovating his old store when this resort opened up last spring.'

'To draw hapless tourists like me.'

'Tourists like you keep so many businesses afloat; you have no idea. I've worked with a few, helping to improve their discover-ability online. They can't depend on word of mouth anymore and some haven't kept up with the times.'

She wouldn't admit it, but she was properly impressed. His story was inspiring: leaving his job, starting a business, waking up in paradise every day. That was the dream.

A group of women pulled up in a car and rushed into the shop. Wearing nothing but Spandex, they looked like escapees from a yoga retreat. They marvelled at the cute décor. A few whipped out phones and started snapping pictures. Two approached the counter.

Roman greeted them in typical Roman fashion. 'If you're looking for candy, you've come to the wrong place.'

Samantha buried her face in her hands. She had to hand it to the man. He never missed an opportunity to be a world-class smart-arse. Fortunately, these ladies were his type of people.

'If you've got beer and chips, you're good.'

One approached a display case loaded with fat golden empanadas. 'We'll have some of these, too.'

Without prompting, Samantha hopped off the barstool and helped Roman behind the counter. She found a pair of tongs and the white paper bags for the empanadas. Roman grabbed the beer and the women loaded the counter with bags of plantain crisps. Meanwhile they plotted. 'The patties are for now. The snacks are for later. We'll stash them in our suitcases.'

They were definitely escapees from a yoga retreat. Samantha asked them to tag Candy's Shop on any photos posted online and waved goodbye as they pulled out in their rental car. 'Namaste!'

They worked like this for the rest of the day. She took care of the customers, selling sandwiches, empanadas, soft drinks, and bottled water to a steady clientele of tourists on their way to or heading back from various excursions. Roman oversaw a delivery, organized the storage room, and restocked shelves. They stole a moment to eat after the lunch-hour crowd emptied out.

At the end of the day, Roman counted the cash at the till drawer and let out a low whistle. 'We work well together.'

'You're a businessman and I'm a business writer,' Samantha said. 'I think we can run a little shop.'

He sorted the notes into piles and locked them away. 'It's like we're made for each other.'

All day she felt like a ball of wool caught between the paws of an incredibly naughty cat. Roman was toying with her and having fun with it.

'Roman Carver, you're a flirt. Good thing I'm immune.'

'I hope not,' he said. 'I have something in mind.'

She was curious, if nothing else. 'What is it?'

He rounded the counter. 'You're here for just a few days.'

'I'm aware.'

'Want to have fun?'

'I don't know what you mean.'

'I think you do.'

She absolutely did, and she could see, in vivid detail, all the many splendid ways she and Roman could take full advantage of this limited time. The 'yes' was at the tip of her tongue. Naturally, she said no.

'Scared?'

'Please!' she scoffed. 'I'm not interested.'

'I think you are.'

Someone had to set this man straight. The burden fell upon her shoulders. 'You're not irresistible, Roman.'

'But you are, Samantha.'

The shop was quiet except for a song playing low on the radio. The air was static around them. Roman was still as a cat. He watched and waited. Finally, he asked, 'Want to think about it?'

Fortunately, her closest, dearest friends came to her rescue, saving her from answering. They pulled up in the bus and filed into the shop making wild and outrageous demands. 'Where's Sam?' 'Release her at once!' 'Free Sam!'

Wet hair, tanned skin, in flip–flops that left sand on the floor Roman had just swept, they were a wild crew.

Naomi approached Roman. 'How's your grandfather?'

'He's fine. There was no crisis.'

'Good to hear,' she said. 'I like him. He gives me free stuff.'

'There'll be none of that!' Samantha intervened. 'Buy your snacks and support the local economy.'

'In that case, I'll take a dozen of these,' Jason said, admiring the assortment of pastries. 'I want to do my part.'

Jen and Chris purchased cans of coconut water. Jasmine stocked up on tins of ginger tea all the while painting an image of Cotton Bay. 'Guys, you missed out. It was breathtaking.'

Anthony eyed them with interest. 'You two spent the day here? Alone? With no adult supervision? How did that go?'

'I don't know what I'd do if it weren't for Sam,' Roman replied.

Anthony grinned, obviously pleased with himself. 'I bet!'

'Ready to clock out?' Hugo asked. 'Tonight is sheet masks and Chardonnay.'

This declaration was greeted with an ear-piercing cry from all the girls. Sheet masks and Chardonnay was a timeworn tradition. It had started in Las Vegas and continued on every single one of their trips; Samantha couldn't miss out.

She removed her apron and, without giving it too much thought, went over to give Roman a hug. It felt right. Hugging him, touching him, finishing his sentences, all of that felt natural now. He hugged her back, pinning her to him with an arm around her waist. The casual and friendly hug confirmed something she'd suspected. To be held by Roman, to feel him and breathe him, was a brief stay in heaven.

'See you tomorrow?' She was suddenly anxious she would not see him again soon enough for her liking.

He didn't answer, not with words, anyway. His eyes told her

he would not let her down again. So much about Roman was in the things he left unsaid.

★★★

Roman swept the sand his friends had dragged into the shop and locked up for the night. The spare apron Samantha had used was folded neatly on the counter. He smiled as he tossed it into a basket, along with his, for tomorrow's laundry. He could not stop smiling.

Samantha had thought nothing of skipping out on an excursion with her friends to spend the day at the shop with him – a gesture that touched him in ways he hadn't dared show. Not only that, she'd made it fun. She never once complained about the steady stream of work and filled the few moments of downtime with chatter and laughter.

Roman reached for his keys and phone, both stashed behind the counter. He had a string of unread messages from Anthony.

A's phone: Dude, listen up. I'm loving you and Sam.
A's phone: What do you think? She's great, right?
A's phone: This is a good thing. I know it.
A's phone: Don't blow your chance!

Sam was more than great. She was a stellar human being with a big, generous heart. She looked after her friends, and by some strange twist of fate, he was lucky enough to count himself among them. He didn't need anyone telling him how good it could be between them. He'd got a glimpse of that from the brief hug they'd shared. Feisty Samantha turned him on in every possible way. If he had the slightest chance with her, he was not dumb enough to blow it.

Jen was new to sheet masks and Chardonnay night. She arrived with a bottle of expensive tequila purchased duty free at LAX. When Samantha greeted her at the door to Hugo's bungalow, her eyes fell to the bottle and she raised a questioning brow.

'I thought we could do shots,' Jen said.

Clearly, she'd misunderstood. This girls' night in centred on self-care, quiet conversation and aromatherapy courtesy of Jasmine, all in the soft glow of candlelight. Conceived in Vegas, after three consecutive all-nighters, the session had been necessary to prevent physical and mental breakdown. Holed up in Hugo's hotel room, they'd got to know each other pretty well that night. It was one of Samantha's fondest memories.

Hugo came to the door. Samantha stepped aside, leaving him the burden of explaining all this to Jen. He didn't. Instead, he reached for the bottle. 'Yes, and thanks,' he said. 'Come in. It's a party now.'

He went straight to the kitchen and splashed tequila into paper cups.

All right, then. So much for that.

'None for me,' Naomi said from her bed of throw pillows on the floor. 'I'm on a strict diet.'

Samantha balked. 'Since when? You ate everything in sight yesterday.'

'Which is why I have to cut back if I want to fit in my dress,' she replied.

Jasmine lit a stalk of incense. 'Don't argue with the bride. She can do what she wants.'

Naomi raised two long, manicured fingers in the air. 'Thanks, babe.'

Jen had brought salt and limes, as well. She helped Hugo distribute the cups and proposed a toast. 'May the next sheet masks and Chardonnay night be held at my house in Los Angeles. You're all invited.'

As far as toasts went, this one was unconventional. Samantha needed more information. 'Are you saying your house in LA can accommodate us all?'

Naomi caught Samantha's eye and nodded. Samantha mouthed the word *wow*.

'Watch out,' Hugo said. 'Don't think we won't take you up on it.'

The evening went off the rails after that. Although it wasn't very late, Jasmine proposed a late-night swim. 'It's a crime to be cooped up inside when it's so gorgeous outside.'

And so, they all went back to their respective bungalows to change, and took the bottle of tequila to the pool where Adrian, Chris and Jason so happened to be hanging out. Naomi sent a message to Anthony and very soon he was diving backwards into the pool. Sickly solitude wormed its way into Samantha's heart. There was the general malaise of being the only single girl in this field of couples, most all of them frolicking in the water, plus the sting of missing Roman.

She itched to call him, even though she had no idea where he lived or how long it would take him to get here on such short notice. She didn't even have his number. She missed him when she threw back another tequila shot, and when she pretended to laugh at Adrian's jokes or feigned interest in Jason's stories, and especially when she sunk into the warm waters of the pool to escape them all.

Travel Blog

Title TBD [Note to Self: Wish I could magic a title!]

DRAFT ENTRY #5: BELIEVE IN MAGIC

The Nylon Pool is a sandbank in the sea. Nature lovers are drawn to its beauty, the white coral sand and schools of tropical fish. Dreamers come seeking its magical powers. They say swimming in the pool reverses the effects of ageing by ten years. Others swear that couples who kiss under its waters will be blessed with a lifetime of happiness. I believe in magic, but none of this stuff applies to me. I don't want to look like my thirteen-year-old self ever again, so I'll gladly pass on the anti-ageing stuff for now. I'd sign up for a guaranteed lifetime of happiness, but it's only granted to couples.

CHAPTER TWELVE

Early Tuesday morning, they boarded the boat at Pigeon Point. The sea was choppy, the wooden boat rocked. While her friends admired the fresh day and clear turquoise waters, Samantha had her head between her knees, overcome with queasiness. She didn't complain. The destination was worth a little nausea.

As a local, Roman had negotiated a fair price to reserve the boat for the morning. After a moment chatting with the captain, he crossed the deck with his sure stride, making his way toward her, cotton shirt flapping in the wind, Wayfarer sunglasses catching a glint of sun, brown skin gleaming like bronze. He was as fresh as the day itself, yet the corners of his mouth tilted down with concern. 'Naomi sends crackers.'

He handed her a sleeve of their favourite water biscuits. How did she get her hands on this stuff?

'Thanks.'

'She's seasick, too.'

'Is she?' Samantha looked past him. Naomi was locked in Anthony's arms and looked great.

He hunched low and cupped her face in his hands. 'Now what can *I* do to make it better?'

This time when her stomach bottomed it had nothing to do

with the motion of the sea. Samantha was used to his laidback demeanour. Who knew he could be this tender and attentive? By the looks of it, her friends were just as intrigued. Naomi watched from the cocoon of her fiancé's arms. Hugo caught her eye and winked. Jen gave her two enthusiastic thumbs up. Jasmine gave her a break, only because the bank of coral reef visible through the glass-bottom boat had her transfixed.

'I heard there was a wild party last night,' Roman said.

'It was pretty wild,' she admitted. 'I would've called you but I don't have your number.'

He traced a finger along her hairline, catching the stray curls and moving them out of her eyes. 'Are you trying to get my number?'

Samantha's face warmed. 'No, I—'

'All you have to do is ask,' he said.

'That wasn't what I—'

'You don't strike me as someone who has trouble asking for what she wants. Am I wrong about that?'

He was toying with her again. 'You could have asked for mine.'

'Give me your phone.'

Samantha took this as a dare. She slipped her phone out of the back pocket of her denim shorts, opened a new contact page, and handed it to him. He gave her a smile before he took it from her, typed in his contact information and, as an added bonus, told her which apps he used for international calls and texts. Samantha watched his fingers move over the screen. This might be a small step for some. For her, it was a giant leap. If he was in her contacts, he was in her life.

'So,' he returned the phone, 'do you think we could go for a late-night swim sometime?'

She clutched the phone in her hand. 'Let's stick to daylight.'

Jason made his way toward them and sat down on the bench next to her. He was slathered in sunscreen. His curly brown hair was still wet and glistening from a morning swim. 'Sammy, it's been a while since we chatted.'

'How goes it, Jason?'

'Great. Exceptional. Perfect. And you?'

Her gut twisted with nausea. She took a deep breath. 'Perfect. Never better.'

'Good, good.' He scratched his head. 'Thought I might run something by you.'

She nodded. 'I'm listening.'

'You're one of Jasmine's closest friends,' he said evenly.

'I like to think so.'

'If I could get your support, it would mean so much to me.'

'Would you like me to go?' Roman asked.

'No. It's cool.' He did not look cool at all. 'I'd like your opinion on this, too.'

'Jason, just come out with it!' Samantha cried. 'You're scaring me.'

'I'm going to ask Jas to marry me.'

'Seriously?'

A new wave of nausea slammed through her. She gripped Roman's arm to keep balanced. He pulled her tight and whispered, 'The word you're looking for is *congratulations*.'

Jason went pale underneath his mask of sunscreen. 'That wasn't the reaction I was hoping for.'

Samantha realized she'd blurted her innermost thoughts out loud. 'I meant it in a good way.'

'But you said it in a horrified way.' Jason's mouth flattened with worry. 'Do you think it's a bad idea?'

'No!' She reached out and gave his shoulder a reassuring squeeze. 'It's a fabulous idea. You caught me off guard. That's all.'

'I love her. I want to marry her.'

'That makes perfect sense.'

'What about you, man?' Jason searched Roman's face. 'What do you think?'

Roman stiffened beside her. She wondered what had got to him. Was it the mention of love, marriage – or a combination of both?

'I think you two have something special. And you're very lucky.'

Samantha had braced herself for sarcasm, derision – or a combination of both. Anything but earnestness.

'Adrian helped me pick out the ring. Do you guys want to see it?'

'You have it with you?' Samantha asked, puzzled.

He padded the zippered pocket of his shorts. 'Right here.'

He'd brought an expensive piece of jewellery on a boat excursion. Did he not trust the hotel safe? What if they went down like the *Titanic*? 'That's risky, don't you think? What if you lose it at sea?'

'I'll need it to … you know … *pop* the question.'

'Wait …' Samantha swallowed hard. 'You're going to propose *today*?'

He nodded. 'At the Nylon Pool.'

'But why? What's the hurry? We've only been here a couple of days. You can take a breath.'

'I agree,' Roman said. 'Relax. You're in Tobago. You haven't had your first ginger beer. There's no rush.'

'As tempting as that sounds, I can't afford to wait,' he said. 'It has to be today. According to the schedule, there won't be another opportunity to return to the Nylon Pool.'

Samantha was more confused than ever. 'So what? It's not the only pool on the island. I promise you there are others.'

'It has to be this one. I don't want to get down on one knee at a random beach.'

'Why?' she and Roman asked in unison.

'They say if you kiss under the water—'

Samantha covered her eyes with her hands and groaned. 'I know what they say.'

'If that were true, none of my cousins would be divorced,' Roman said. 'Pretty sure it's something they made up to attract visitors like you.'

'I get it,' Jason said. 'But Jas loves that kind of stuff.'

He had a point. On this trip more than ever, Jasmine seemed fascinated with the natural world, its beauty and mythology. While some women dreamed of proposals atop the Eifel Tower, she would appreciate this much more.

Jason looked to Samantha, then Roman. 'You think it's corny.'

'Absolutely,' Samantha said. 'But just the right amount of corny.'

Roman approved. 'Why the hell not? Go for it.'

'Thanks, guys.' Jason sighed, relieved. He went on to describe in some detail a vintage diamond ring with ruby accents. 'It's really beautiful.'

Samantha reassured him. 'She'll like the ring because she loves you.'

'The thing is …' Jason looked about worriedly. 'Lately, every time the topic of marriage comes up, she's been ambivalent. I can't get a reaction from her.'

Samantha distinctively remembered Jasmine saying she didn't believe in marriage, or something to that effect. She couldn't tell Jason that. His water blue eyes were brimming with love, excitement, and hope. It wasn't her place to break his heart. That would be up to Jasmine. However, she could tell Roman, which she did as soon as Jason went away and was well out of earshot.

'Well,' Roman said dryly. 'That was triggering.'

'Why is that?'

'No reason.'

'Should I have told him about Jasmine's views on marriage? Maybe I should tell him.'

'No,' he said. 'He's got a ring in his pocket. He has to see this through.'

'OK. But if this doesn't work out, it's all hands on deck. I'll give Jasmine a shoulder to cry on. You make sure Jason doesn't drown in the magic pool.'

'It's shallow. He couldn't if he tried.' He brushed a corkscrew curl away from her eyes and asked, 'Feeling better, pretty lady?'

She was no longer feeling nauseous. However, she was feeling a whole lot of other things. 'I feel great.'

With so much fun in store, how could she not?

The sun was high when they arrived at the Nylon Pool. All they had to do was leap off the boat into the shallow blue waters. This time, Samantha did not need a pep talk or a life coach. She joined her girlfriends at the edge of the deck. They dived in together in an unsynchronized fashion. Another glass-bottom boat pulled away, and they had the pool to themselves. Jen and Jasmine marvelled at the clarity of the water. Naomi exfoliated her limbs with fistfuls of coral sand. Samantha floated on her back and closed her eyes to the limitless sky. It made her feel small. That morning at sunrise, the voiceover yogi had left them with a mantra that kept tugging at her mind: *Your future does not have to mirror your past.*

Samantha craved change. Her break-up with Timothy only sharpened the craving. Her flailing love life didn't mean her career couldn't soar. She had stumbled into her line of work by luck of the draw. Desperate to start earning a living after graduation, she'd applied for a slew of jobs and accepted the first offer. The work was steady, the pay fine. She couldn't even complain about her boss and co-workers. They were decent people and had always treated her well. Some had worked at the publication for decades and the newcomers hoped to replace the senior cadre as they marched off toward retirement. Samantha couldn't fault them. It was a safe plan, a solid plan. However, she secretly yearned for more.

Samantha hadn't confided in anyone except her mother, who'd advised her not to do anything rash. Timothy would not have understood. He had a temporary position. Each year, his employment status depended on the renewal of a grant. He envied her salaried position and paid time off. The last thing she'd wanted was to whine to him about her growing dissatisfaction. She thought of Roman. Was quitting a high-paying job in New York City to start a virtual consulting firm while chilling in the Caribbean a rash move? If so, could she do something similar?

Her moment of self-reflection came to an abrupt end once the guys plunged into the tranquil waters, disrupting the peace. Samantha straightened up and wiped water from her eyes. Hugo was headed her way. The tropical climate suited her friend. His complexion had deepened to a golden brown. He wore nothing but swimming trunks, sunglasses and designer slides. Sometimes he slipped on a tropical shirt, but not often.

He called out to her. 'Hey, bestie, what's up?'

'Just soaking up the sun.'

'You heard what's going down, right?'

'Not sure what you're talking about?'

'Don't be cagey. I'm talking about Jason's proposing to Jas in these enchanted waters.'

'Shh! What if she hears?' Samantha whipped around to make sure no one had overheard. She spotted Jasmine at the far end of the pool, hanging out with Jen and Chris. All three were attempting tree poses in waist-high water.

'What's the protocol?' Hugo asked. 'Are we cool with this or what?'

'We play it cool, obviously. We can't do or say anything to tip Jasmine off.'

Hugo's expression clouded. 'That's not what I meant. I specifically remember Jas saying she didn't believe—'

'I know what she said!' Samantha said. 'But this is her

moment. Whatever happens, they'll work it out. We have to trust the universe.'

'The universe is such a bitch. How we gonna trust *her*?'

Samantha dissolved into laughter. Hugo splashed her with water and took off to join Adrian.

Roman waded his way toward her and she instinctively reached out to him. She was feeling too good to play it cool.

'Are you all right?' he asked.

'What do you mean?'

'You looked preoccupied earlier. Am I wrong?'

He wasn't wrong. 'How could you tell?'

He dragged a finger along her jawline from her chin to her earlobe.

'It was just a feeling.'

Samantha had to steel herself. This man was giving her all the feels. 'I have a question. Was it tough leaving your job to start out on your own?'

Roman took his time, considering his words. 'It was one of the toughest things I ever did. If anyone tells you different, they're lying.'

'What prompted you to do it?'

His gaze skidded along the water's glistening surface. 'For reasons I don't want to get into right now, it was time for me to leave my firm. I'd been growing bored with the work for a while.'

'Bored? On Wall Street?'

Maybe she'd bought into the stereotype, but she imagined there was never a dull moment at the centre of the financial world.

'I worked the tech division. Which may sound cool. At

the end of the day, my job was to approve financing for apps invented by Ivy League grads that did little or nothing to help anyone. Most ended up losing money which should've been better spent elsewhere.'

Samantha understood completely. What the world needed now was love, not another dating app that put love on an algorithm.

'Why do you ask?' he said.

'Maybe I'm bored with work, too.'

'Don't do anything rash.'

'Now you sound like my mother.'

'It's true,' he said. 'Make a plan, *then* do something rash.'

'That makes sense.'

A manta ray swirled around Samantha's legs and skimmed her calves. She screeched in surprise, lost balance, and very nearly toppled over in the water. Roman caught her just in time. He circled his arms around her waist and drew her to him.

'Come here, you,' he said. 'Let me hold you steady.'

That was how she found herself nestled against Roman's hard chest, with the sun on her back, the sea breeze in her hair, and manta rays circling around her legs. Life couldn't be more perfect.

A peaceful silence prevailed among them. Anthony rubbed sand on Naomi's back. Hugo and Adrian were snapping photos with Adrian's state-of-the-art camera. Jen and Chris were following a school of tropical fish. Roman held her close, she relaxed in his arms. He smelled like sunscreen and sea salt.

Out of the corner of her eye Samantha spotted Jasmine and Jason in the distance. He sank down to one knee in the water and held up a ring. The diamond caught the sunlight and twinkled. Samantha leaned into Roman and held her breath.

Jasmine never looked more beautiful in a white bikini. Her long braids were tossed over one shoulder. She pressed her hands to her cheeks and stared down at Jason. The universe was more than kind. Jasmine nodded yes and let Jason slip the ring on her finger. They embraced and together slipped under the water's surface in a kiss that would seal their happiness for all time.

Naomi gasped, drawing everyone's attention to the couple. At first, no one made a move. Then, abruptly, everyone cheered. Adrian rushed forward with his camera. Samantha couldn't move. She was busy wiping away the tears that kept springing to her eyes. Roman tucked a finger under her chin and turned her face to his. 'Sam … don't cry.'

'I can't help it. Don't tease me.'

'I wouldn't.'

Maybe the waters were enchanted. There was no other way to explain the miracle unfolding. Roman raised her chin with a finger. She arched forward, wind in her hair, wanting, eager, open to whatever this was or turned out to be. Samantha circled her arms around his neck and drew him to her. While no one was watching, he kissed her and she, longingly, kissed him back.

★★★

That night, they were a rowdy crowd at dinner. To celebrate Jasmine and Jason's engagement, they left the hotel and went out for seafood. Jasmine wore cut flowers in her hair. Over dessert Naomi proposed a toast. 'To J and J who found magic in T and T! We wish you a lifetime of happiness.'

They raised beer bottles and various rum cocktails.

'Hear! Hear!'

'Cheers!'

'I'll drink to that!'

Samantha clinked glasses with Roman. When their eyes met and a current raced through her, she reminded herself that they didn't have a lifetime of happiness ahead. Their paths would split at the end of the week. No matter how good their kiss had been, how magical the moment, she couldn't let it go to her head. Frustrated, she rose from the table and excused herself. 'Just popping into the ladies' room.'

Jen grabbed her handbag. 'I'll come with.'

Samantha's heart sank. She had hoped to lock herself in a bathroom stall and wallow for a bit. Now she would have to be nice, keep up the chitchat, and keep on pretending to be a girl out with a gorgeous guy, having the time of her life.

Jen proved her wrong. She was quiet on their way to the restroom, quiet while they entered the stalls, and quieter still while they washed and dried their hands. Samantha studied her reflection in the mirror and fluffed her curls. Jen rummaged through her handbag and produced a tube of lipstick. The silence dragged on. Samantha felt compelled to say something.

'Everything all right, Jen?'

'I'm fine,' she said. 'It's just … we're here for a wedding and now there's this beyond-romantic proposal … I'm going to lose it. You know?'

'I know! Right?'

Samantha couldn't hold back. She burst out laughing. Jen laughed, too. At last, they'd found common ground!

'I don't mean to be a bitch about it.' Jen leaned on the vanity, struggling to regain her composure. 'I'm happy for them. I swear I am. They're such a cute couple—'

'Jen, I get it,' Samantha said. 'They're a wonderful couple and I couldn't be happier for them. But I think I've reached my limit.'

'At least you have Roman,' Jen said. 'I saw you two steal a kiss at the pool. I'm pretty sure we all did. You'll probably get roasted in the morning. Tonight we're celebrating the happy couple.'

The teasing didn't bother her; that was inevitable. 'We're just having fun. There's nothing much to it.'

That was the problem, she realized. There wasn't much to what she and Roman were doing. A fling, that was all. She wanted more from life, work that mattered and relationships that offered more than just fun.

'I wouldn't be so sure. I see the way he looks at you when you slip and fall, when you laugh, when you're pissed, when you're seasick, or when you're just existing.'

'I wouldn't read too much into that,' Samantha said. 'How about you? How are things with Chris?'

'Chris doesn't look at me like Roman looks at you. That tells you all you need to know.'

There was so much frustration laced in Jen's words, it made Samantha wonder where the upbeat California girl had gone. 'Have you known him long?'

'Best friends since high school,' Jen replied. 'I can't get him to see me any other way.'

'I guess it's hard to break out of those roles.'

'This is the first time we've travelled, just us two. I mean without our usual crew. I was hoping this trip, this wedding, could shift things.' Jen swiped on lipstick with a trembling hand and slipped the tube into her purse. 'Sorry. I'm ranting. I don't mean to kill the mood.'

'It's fine,' Samantha said. 'Is that why you wanted my bungalow?'

'Naomi had us in separate rooms. I needed a sexy spot to seduce my best friend.'

'Understood. Naomi says you're sorted now.'

'We are, thanks to the best man up and leaving. Am I the only one who thinks that's weird?'

Jen exited the bathroom. Samantha followed, lost in thought. Come to think of it, it *was* weird. Why had he left? Why didn't he come around anymore?

They were approaching the table. Chris was deep in conversation with Hugo and Roman. He looked up and Samantha could swear she'd caught a twinkle in his green eyes. She grabbed Jen by the arm and dragged her to a corner.

'What is it?' Jen grimaced. 'Do I have lipstick on my teeth?'

'No, you're fine. Actually, you're more than fine. You're *fire*. But you might be wrong about Chris.'

'You're sweet, Sam, but I'm not wrong. I've given that man so many chances, dropped so many hints.'

'Listen, we're here for a finite amount of time. Dropping hints is not going to cut it. Be direct.' Samantha winced and borrowed Roman's line. 'You don't strike me as someone who has trouble asking for what she wants.'

Jen took a moment to absorb the advice. Then she straightened her shoulders and tossed a lock of flat-ironed hair. 'You're right. What have I gained by playing it safe? Nothing.'

'And just so you know, he doesn't look at you like an old friend. I see a spark there. He never leaves your side.'

'That's because you're an intimidating bunch.'

'Can't be helped,' Samantha said with a grin. 'Now let's head back before they think we're lost.'

★★★

Samantha felt lighter when she returned to the table. Jen was a smart, confident, fun-loving woman and yet she was stuck in limbo with the guy she fancied. Meanwhile, Roman had made it clear to everyone how he felt about her. No guessing games required. There was something to that.

'Hey,' she whispered. 'Just so you know, they're going to drag us tomorrow for kissing at the Nylon Pool.'

'Tomorrow?' He grabbed the back of her chair and dragged her closer to him. 'Kiss me now. Let's get ahead of the story.'

'I like how you think.' She gathered a fistful of his soft cotton T-shirt and pulled him in for a kiss. The table erupted in cheers.

REVISED

Wedding Week Schedule

Wednesday 13 August:

6 a.m. Sunrise Yoga at Hibiscus Terrace (optional)

~~10 a.m. Buccoo Bay (mangroves and more snorkelling!)~~

10.45 a.m. Dolly's Bridal Boutique Final Fitting

CHAPTER THIRTEEN

To quote Naomi, Amelia put her foot down. She insisted her daughter quit crisscrossing the island with her friends and get serious about finalizing the wedding plans. There were linens and place settings to select, a cake topper and keepsakes to approve. The final fittings and touch-ups of the bridal gown and bridesmaids' dresses, all purchased in London and already touched up, could not be postponed another day. The outing to Buccoo Bay was cancelled. Instead, the ladies were headed into town.

Samantha welcomed the break. She loved swimming and snorkelling and all the rest, but she was eager to venture into the capital and explore the city streets. She was the first to join Naomi and her mother in the hotel lobby. Jasmine and Jen arrived soon thereafter. Finally, Maya made a sluggish entrance. The valet attendant brought around Amelia's SUV and they all piled in. Amelia took the wheel and slowed to a stop at the guard gate. Naomi pointed out a black saloon waiting for security clearance. 'That's Roman!'

Samantha perked up in the third row of the SUV. She couldn't even hide her excitement.

'Mum, stop,' Naomi said. 'He probably didn't read the revised wedding schedule.'

Samantha had to agree. There was a fair chance Roman wasn't starting his day checking for updates on the Naomi and Anthony wedding website.

Amelia flashed her headlights. The black saloon pulled over to the side of the cobblestone road. Naomi addressed Samantha in the rear-view mirror. 'Sam, go and tell him we won't be snorkelling today. He can find Anthony at the pool, if he'd still like a swim.'

Maya raised her hand. 'I've got a question. Why do the guys get to lounge by the pool and we have to go pick out table linens?'

Amelia shot her down with a look. 'Haven't you lounged enough?'

Samantha climbed out of the vehicle, happy to escape the tempest that was brewing. Roman had lowered the tinted driver's window and called out to her. 'Where are you off to?'

'Change of plans: The girls are going to do girl things. The lads are lounging by the pool.'

'What qualifies as girl things?'

'Picking out cloth napkins. It's more complicated than it sounds.'

'I don't get to see you in a bathing suit today?'

'Afraid not.'

Earlier, when Naomi had informed her via text of the change in itinerary, her first thought had been of Roman. While Naomi had a lifetime of bliss ahead, she had only a precious few days and didn't want to waste them.

'Want to hang out later?' he asked. 'I'll take you somewhere off the tourist trail. It'll be good material for your blog.'

Was this his roundabout way of asking her out on a date? Why did this simple invitation make her irrationally happy? Could she stop grinning like a fool for five seconds? The moment called for nonchalance. 'I guess … I'll bring my camera.'

'I'll pick you up at seven.'

'That should work.' Amelia, or possibly Naomi, tapped on the car horn to get Samantha's attention. The SUV stood idle on the side of the road leading off the hotel grounds, yet everyone inside was actively straining to catch a look at them. 'They're getting restless. I should go.'

'I can't imagine Maya is up for this,' Roman said. 'Tell her I'll help her escape.'

'I would, but I need you alive for tonight's date.' He moved to grab her waist, but she jumped out of reach. 'It is a date, right?'

'It's whatever you want,' he called after her. 'And nothing could keep me from it.'

She blew him a kiss and, heart skipping, raced back to the waiting car.

★★★

Far from their quiet seaside retreat, the city centre was chaos and Dolly's Bridal Boutique was at the heart of it. Amelia parked kerbside and, before leading them inside the salmon-coloured shop, promised to treat them to lunch if they behaved. Shockingly, Jasmine was the first to misbehave. She tugged at Samantha's arm and pulled her aside. 'Let's hang outside a while. We don't get out of the resort much, I want to soak all this in.'

Of them all, Jasmine was the eco-traveller. She scheduled visits to forests and reefs, any type of nature reserve she could find. When they visited a city, she was determined to get a feel for its 'vibe' outside the tourist-designated areas. One of the best experiences Samantha had had in Mexico was an afternoon following Jasmine about in a local marketplace. So if she wanted to hang outside, where it was hot, instead of inside an air-conditioned shop, Samantha wouldn't argue. She would, however, insist they find a spot in the shade.

Jasmine didn't waste time. 'You're warming up to Roman. I love this for you. Stepping outside your box, trying new things.'

A dimple popped in Jasmine's cheek whenever she was being cheeky. 'Flirting with a hot guy is hardly brave new world type stuff.'

'At least you admit he's hot.'

'Fine! I admit it. Roman Carver is insanely sexy. Happy now?'

Jasmine threw her hands up in exultation. 'Yes! I am! Thank you! I thought Timothy cut out a part of your brain.'

Samantha refused to stand in the dismal shade of the shop's awning, breathing in the exhaust from every motorbike that sped by, only to talk about Timothy. 'You got engaged. Now *that's* a big deal.'

'It just hasn't sunk in yet.' She held out her hand to show off the ring. On her slender finger, it was more beautiful than Jason had described. 'I'm still in shock.'

'You had us worried for a while,' Samantha said. 'I recall you saying you didn't believe in marriage.'

'I don't know what I believe in, to be honest.'

The light in Jasmine's eyes flickered out. Samantha wished she hadn't said anything. The last thing she wanted was to introduce doubt. Jasmine was happy with the choice she'd made, even if it was in contradiction to a loosely drawn belief system.

'If you believe Jason loves you, you're all set.'

'This has more to do with my mother than Jason,' Jasmine said. 'She's a devout Catholic and vehemently opposed to "living in sin".'

Samantha nodded gravely. 'She fears you've lost your virtue.'

That brought a smile to Jasmine's lips and a brief reappearance of the dimple. 'God knows I lost my virtue a while ago.'

'Isn't there some sort of penance you could do? A few Hail Marys could sort that out.'

'Tell her that,' Jasmine said. 'The last time I visited, we bickered the whole time. It was Christmas and I wanted to pack up and leave. We haven't talked much since then. I couldn't tell Jason because that would put a strain on our relationship, and I tell Jason *everything*. It's been a stressful few months.'

Jasmine had never mentioned any of this. 'You could have talked to us.'

'Want to know the fastest way to kill any vibe?' Jasmine asked. 'Bring up your Catholic mother over brunch with your friends.'

'But we're not your brunch buddies. We're your actual friends. You should feel comfortable enough to tell us when you're going through a difficult time.'

Jasmine shot her a look, as if to say, *You're the least qualified person to lecture anyone on the need for transparency in relationships.*

'Fine,' Samantha huffed. 'We can all do better in that department.'

'I'll tell you this,' Jasmine said. 'When Jason got down on one knee in the middle of the sea, none of that mattered. The answer was clear to me. I love him. He loves me. We're going to be happy.'

'Of course you are.'

'I haven't told my parents yet,' Jasmine mumbled. 'My mom is going to be thrilled, and I don't want to give her the satisfaction.'

'Enjoy your trip. You can tell her when you get back,' Samantha said. 'What's a few more days of spiritual anguish in the greater scheme of things?'

'Just a drop in the ocean of time.'

They were both laughing now.

'Where will this magical wedding take place?' Samantha asked. 'Beneath a Yucatan pyramid? Amidst the Greek ruins?'

'Most likely in Montreal next July,' she said. 'It'll be easier on my parents, and I'd like to show my friends around my city for a change. Have you ever been?'

'To Canada? Never.'

Jasmine wrapped one of her braids around her finger, looking a little nervous. 'Would you like to come and be my bridesmaid?'

Ah! So this was what Jasmine wanted to ask her all along. 'Absolutely, I would!'

'You sure? It's a tight turnaround from this gig. Naomi hasn't put you off the job?'

'Are you crazy? I live for this stuff. Besides, Naomi has been surprisingly chill, so far. I trust you'll be the world's coolest bride.'

'Don't worry,' Jasmine said. 'When it's your turn to walk down the aisle we'll bend over backwards to make it special. Just name your spot and we'll be there in peach satin dresses and matching shoes.'

'If you put me in a peach satin dress, I swear—'

'Come on! I wouldn't do that to you! You're my *friend*, not some distant cousin I'm trying to humiliate.'

'May I have a plus one?'

'Making plans for you and Roman already?'

'No,' Samantha said flatly. Who knew where Roman would

be in one year's time? However warm and safe and tingly she felt with Roman, this flirtation had an expiration date. It ended the day after Naomi's wedding with a big kiss goodbye at the airport gate, if that. 'But if I'll have to pay for a date, I should start saving now.'

'My money's on Roman,' Jasmine said. 'Fifty bucks you show up with him. Canadian dollars, naturally.'

'Really? You only just met him?'

Jasmine offered a one-shoulder shrug. 'I have a good feeling.'

Samantha had a feeling her friends had lost their collective minds. She could anticipate this type of frilly logic from Naomi, but expected more from level-headed Jasmine.

'Life doesn't always follow a predictable path, Sam. Remember how concerned we were for Naomi and Anthony just a short while ago? Now I can't imagine a more perfect couple.'

'Apples and oranges. Roman and I are having fun, not falling in love.'

Jasmine's dimple taunted her. 'If you say so.'

★★★

The afternoon unfolded in a predictable fashion, with Maya playing the role of the disgruntled little sister to a T. She hated her dress. The hemline was too long or the waistline too high. Either way, Samantha wasn't paying too close attention. She scrolled through social media while the nineteen-year-old railed on.

'I realize it's Naomi's big special day,' Maya said. 'But I want to look cute in the photos.'

'It's an empire waist,' Amelia said. 'It's classic and chic.'

'It's *Little Women* chic. That's not the look I'm going for.'

Naomi stepped out of the fitting room in a strapless lace gown with a mermaid train. There was no doubt in anyone's mind that she had achieved the look that she was going for: goddess of thunder meets Caribbean queen meets elegant bride. Maya gasped, Amelia cried, and Samantha, Jasmine and Jen snapped photos. The shop owner popped open a bottle of champagne and as everyone toasted the bride Samantha soaked in the moment. It was undeniably true that Naomi's chance encounter with Anthony had changed all their lives. Jasmine was taking a bold leap, Hugo was enjoying a well-deserved break, and Samantha was slowly and surely climbing out of a rut.

Naomi returned to the dressing room. After a while, she popped her head through a crack in the door and summoned Samantha. 'You! Come in here.'

Samantha's heart sank. What had she done? Was she in trouble? Who did she have to be nice to now? Jasmine wished her luck as she slinked toward the back of the bridal shop. She found Naomi seated on a tufted banquette in her shapewear.

'You rang, ma'am?'

'Jen says you gave her one of your famous pep talks,' Naomi said. 'I'm proud of you. That shows growth.'

Samantha relaxed. 'It was nothing. And you're right about her. She's not half bad.'

'Told you!' Naomi said, beaming. There was nothing she liked more than being right. 'Looks like I was right about Roman, too. You two are a perfect match.'

Samantha's smile faltered. Everyone was so quick to celebrate this thing with Roman. Sadly, she couldn't join in. 'It's no big deal. We're just having fun.' She bit her lip to keep from launching into the same refrain. She could downplay it with the others, but not Naomi. 'I like him. I really do.'

'Aw! That's so sweet!'

'Sure, but I don't want to like him too much.'

'OK …'

'Come Sunday, all of this magically comes to an end.'

'Um … Sure. I see your point. On the other hand, you don't want to miss out. If you like him and you're having fun, why overthink it? You'll look back at this time when you were young and free and you met this great guy on a once-in-a-lifetime trip.'

Samantha nodded. The champagne had already given her a headache. 'We're going to hang out later tonight.'

'I like the sound of that!' She counted on her fingers. 'Let's see … Jen asked Chris out to dinner. Our newly engaged couple might want some quiet time. Maybe tonight we can all spread out and do our own thing.'

Samantha could only imagine how stressful this week was for Naomi. She felt responsible for everyone's wellbeing. She and Anthony must want some quiet time, too.

'Are you stressed?' she asked.

'To the core,' Naomi replied. 'Amelia isn't making it any easier. But it'll go by fast and at the end of the day I'll always remember the time when all my friends flew down to this tiny island in the Caribbean to support us. You've made our dream come true.'

Samantha's core turned into mush. She joined Naomi on the banquette. 'I have to say this. For a while I worried you two were making a mistake. Rushing it. I don't anymore.'

'Oh, Sam! Where's my little friend who used to run toward adventure. You're so cautious now.'

Samantha shrugged. 'It's different now. I'm adulting.'

Naomi rolled her eyes at that. 'We're allowed to make some mistakes. What's the worst that can happen?'

She could think of a million things, not least of which was heartache. 'We can get our hearts broken.'

'That is what Tobago is for! Come back anytime, rest, have some cocoa tea. You'll be ready to get back out there and break some hearts of your own.'

★★★

It was raining when they left the shop a half hour later. The Chinese restaurant across the street was the only practical option. They were offered a large round table by the window. Samantha drizzled pickled Scotch Bonnet pepper sauce on a chicken wing drenched in a soy and ginger sauce. She watched a group of school-aged kids race from one storefront awning to the next, trying to stay dry. They were laughing, making a game of it. Their brown faces were glossy with raindrops and sweat. The rain let up just as fast as it had started and the kids took off, running toward adventure.

Travel Blog

Title TBD [Note to Self: Work on this!!]

DRAFT ENTRY #6: YOU ARE WHAT YOU SEEK

'You're so cautious now.'

My friend struck a nerve with that one. I can't say it didn't bother me. I have to admit that I'm not quite the adventure-seeker I dreamed of becoming. The track record is clear: time and again I've settled for comfort and security over uncertainty and risk. Bottom line, I've talked a big game and not delivered. Fear has kept me in a tight cocoon.

The question is: what am I going to do about it?

CHAPTER FOURTEEN

'Ready?'

Roman showed up on time, looking smart in a black T-shirt and jeans. He smelled good, too. Samantha was a mess – tank top, shorts, flip-flops, hair piled on top of her head. She stepped aside to let him in. 'Absolutely. Just give me a minute.'

He strode past her and paused at the entry of the sitting room, taking in her mini office set-up: laptop, journals, the camera that she wouldn't take with her on tonight's outing, the candle and the crystals.

'Were you busy?' he asked.

'I was working on a blog post. You know … the blog that exists only in my head.'

'"The Hidden Path" …'

'Uh huh.'

'It exists in your computer hard drive. That's a start.' He approached the coffee table and pointed to the stones: tiger's eye and citrine, for motivation and creativity, plus her favourite pink quartz. 'And what's all this?'

'Those keep me productive.'

'May I see your work?'

That simple request sent her spiralling. She crossed the room and slammed the laptop shut. 'Absolutely not!'

Roman took a seat on the couch. His gaze swept over her and she just knew he was about to say something devastatingly accurate. 'You're afraid of letting people see your work. That's why you haven't published yet.'

'It's not ready,' she said, defensive, ignoring the fact that she'd just written a post about conquering her fears.

'People will have to read it.'

'I'm aware of that.'

'Why not start with me?'

'You'll make fun of it.'

A crease deepened between his brows. 'I won't.'

'All right.' She clutched the laptop to her chest and plopped down on the coffee table, facing him, her legs crossed between his parted knees. 'Tell me one thing that scares you.'

'Excuse me?'

'You want to read my private thoughts. You need to share something with me.'

'You scare me.'

'I'm serious, Roman.'

'You scare me, Samantha.' His voice was low and he sounded very serious. 'The way you make me feel scares me. I haven't felt that in a while.'

The laptop slipped from her grip and landed on her lap. She looked at it a while and handed it to him.

He hesitated. 'Are you sure?'

She was sure of one thing: it was time she started doing the things that scared her. Opening up to others was top of that list.

As it turned out, 'opening up' was the quickest way to shut a door between her and Roman. She'd left him to read while she got dressed. During the short drive to the venue, he complimented her writing, noted that the blog had less to do with travel and more to do with her life and relationships, and then he went quiet, leaving her to stew in anxiety the rest of the way.

For their date, Roman had chosen a courtyard bar and grill featuring a live Soca band. The outdoor space was enclosed with tall bamboo and the laidback patrons swayed to the music while drinking beer straight from the bottle. She and Roman sat at a rickety wooden table, a flickering votive candle and bottles of lager between them. Before he could withdraw from her any further, she asked him for his hand.

Roman pulled away. 'In marriage?'

'Don't be ridiculous!'

'I don't know. There's a lot of that going on.'

'Just give me your hand.'

He reluctantly complied. She traced her fingers over the bold, dark lines. 'Your lifeline is short.'

He laced his fingers with hers. 'What the hell … They say only the good die young.'

'It doesn't mean what you think,' she said. 'You'll live an independent life.'

He offered his palm for further inspection. 'What else is in store for me?'

'Let's see …' She ran an index finger along the more prominent creases. The vertical line running along the centre was not one of them. 'Your fate line is not as bold as the others.'

'None of this sounds good, Sam.'

'It means you're the master of your fate. Outside forces won't influence your choices so much.'

'I wish that were true,' he said. 'Lately, it feels like nothing is in my control.'

'Want to talk about it?'

He shook his head. The movement was so slight she nearly missed it. 'Tell me about my love life. How do you predict that'll go?'

'Most guys ask about money.'

'I know how to make money,' he said. 'I don't know how to make a relationship work.'

'Welcome to a very select club, my friend.' She traced the topmost horizontal line that started just below his middle finger and split in two. 'You should know, I don't predict anything. It's all in the lines.'

'Well?' he said.

'You have a restless heart.'

'You should feel it now.'

'Again, not what I meant!' she said. 'The line is deep, which suggests interpersonal relationships matter to you. But you'll likely have multiple lovers or friendships.'

'Before I die at thirty-five?'

'In a blaze of glory!'

The band started up again. He stood and extended the hand that had revealed so much and yet so little. 'Come dance with me.'

On the dance floor, he pulled her close and whispered, 'What about your heart line?'

'What about it?'

His hand slid down her back. 'How many hearts have you broken?'

'None, by my count.'

'I guess there's still time.'

Samantha was convinced nothing short of a wrecking ball could shatter this man's heart. 'I'm not a heartbreaker, Roman.'

'No, you're a sweetheart.'

He pressed a kiss to her temple, a polite, friendly kiss. She didn't like it.

***

An hour later, Roman drove her back to the resort and walked her to her door. They lingered there a while. Roman's eyes looked black in the darkness, his features sharp. It was not yet midnight and Samantha did not want the night to end.

'Would you like to come in … for water?' she offered.

Water was the official beverage of the Friend Zone, which was somehow where she found herself.

'No, thank you.'

Roman took a step back and leaned against one of the porch columns. He was studying her again, in that serious way.

Samantha took a step forward. 'Do you hate the blog posts? I admit it's not my finest work.'

'Like I could hate anything you do.'

'What is it, then? I know something's wrong.'

'I thought you were writing about travel and Tobago, Cotton Bay and the Nylon Pool.'

'Well, I never actually made it to Cotton Bay.'

'You know what I mean,' he said. 'It's about you and your feelings and all the things you struggle with.'

'You think it's too sentimental? Too touchy feely?'

'It's raw and honest.'

'It made you uncomfortable.'

Roman shook his head. 'It made me see that your break-up bothers you way more than you let on.'

She couldn't deny it. 'But it's for the best. If he had made the trip, we would have spent our time arguing or actively avoiding an argument – that was more our style. I have no regrets. And it's not like I'm broken or anything. I'm fine.'

Had Timothy bothered to come, she would have been trapped in this bungalow with him, trying to decode his many moods. She and Roman would have never had a chance to get to know one another.

'Maybe I'm the broken one,' he said, almost to himself.

He was fine right up until the moment he read her blogs. All that whining about not having a date must have led him to think she was still hooked on Timothy.

'Samantha.'

'Yes?'

'Would you like to be my date for a wedding I have to attend this Saturday?'

Caught off guard, Samantha laughed. 'It's a little last minute, don't you think?'

'You'd be doing me a favour,' he said. 'I don't want to go it alone.'

Her words from his mouth. Samantha planted a kiss at the corner of his mouth. 'I'd love to be your date.'

He caught her chin and kissed her deeply. 'Maybe I'll come in for water.'

She slipped away from him. 'Too late. That offer expired.'

'Smart call.' He headed down the steps. The gravel crunched under his feet as he made his way toward his car. 'Goodnight, pretty girl!'

REVISED
Wedding Week Schedule

Thursday 14 August:

6 a.m. Sunrise Yoga at Hibiscus Terrace (optional)

SLEEP IN

10 a.m. Beach Day at Pigeon Point

CHAPTER FIFTEEN

Samantha hadn't checked the website for updates. At 6 a.m., she rolled out of bed, slipped on cycling shorts and ambled out to sunrise yoga. The deck was deserted, but she spotted Jen curled up in a lounge chair by the pool. She waved Samantha over. 'Class is cancelled.'

That was disappointing. After a restless night, she'd been looking forward to yoga. The daily practice helped clear her mind. Today, she had a lot of thoughts looping around her head on a carousel. They went from smart to smutty. Should she rethink the travel blog format? Should she tie Roman to the four-poster bed tonight?

She dropped down onto the chair next to Jen's. 'Are we the only ones who didn't get the memo?'

'Guess so. All the happy couples are sleeping in.'

Samantha studied Jen. Her blonde hair was gathered in a long, thin braid. Her face was still creased with sleep. It was safe to assume that she and Chris didn't count themselves among the happy couple contingent.

'So … how did it go last night? Naomi mentioned you and Chris were going out to dinner.'

'It did not go well. Chris and I hit a wall. It's more complicated than I thought.'

'More complicated than he's just not that into you?' Samantha asked.

'He's into me,' Jen said. 'He made it clear. He doesn't trust me. That's the issue.'

'I don't believe it.'

Chris wouldn't have travelled to a tiny tropical island just to be her wedding date if he didn't trust her. All that said, trust was a tricky thing. You had to earn it and work hard to keep it. There was no way to preserve a friendship without it.

'It's true.' Jen's tone was flat. 'Way back when we were neighbours and went to the same high school—'

'Back when he was shy and you had a thing for bad boys?' Samantha teased.

'That's pretty accurate,' Jen said. 'Chris had a crush on me, and I was too busy being the Hottie of Sunny Springs High to care.'

'That's not so unusual.' The shy guy carrying a torch for the hot girl was the plot or subplot of every teen flick, book, mini series, or holiday special. 'That's no reason not to trust you.'

Jen's jaw tightened. 'I told him we were better off as friends. Then I turned out to be a terrible friend. I dragged him to parties and ditched him by the end of the night. I only hung out with him when I was bored and would break our plans last minute.'

'You were … what? Sixteen?' Samantha asked. 'He can't hold you accountable for poor choices made before you were old enough to vote.'

'*I* was sixteen,' Jen said. 'He was fourteen. Chris is younger than me, by two years. His genius is the only reason we were in the same grade. He's a math whiz and transferred into our school for advanced classes. The age gap doesn't make much of a difference today. Back then, those two years might as well have been ten. He was a textbook nerd, painfully shy and awkward. My mom kept telling me to be careful with him. I wasn't. I was embarrassed to be seen with him.'

Samantha tried in vain to picture Chris as a little genius. With his soft-spoken demeanour, easy smile, and mop of chestnut hair he wore loose or in a bun, it was easy to dismiss him as the quintessential hipster. She never guessed there might be a sharp mind behind those moss-green eyes. On the other hand, Jen's pretty features told the whole story. She was hurting. Samantha wondered if she would ever forgive the girl she was at sixteen.

'Chris isn't a kid anymore,' Samantha said. 'Ask if he's willing to give you a second chance. If the answer is no, maybe you should move on.'

'I asked him last night,' Jen said.

Samantha leaned forward, fully invested now. 'What did he say?'

'He said I shouldn't "settle" for him. He doesn't think he's my type. I don't even have a type. I go through phases, sure. But Chris has always been the one I turn to when things go sour. He's always been my person. He calms me down. I draw him out of his shell. We balance each other out. I know how rare that is and I can appreciate it now.'

'I have a tough question for you,' Samantha said.

'Go ahead,' Jen said. 'I don't mind.'

Even with the green light, Samantha hesitated.

'It's OK,' Jen said. 'I dumped all this on you. It's only fair you should get to ask questions.'

'All right.' Samantha straightened up. 'In your heart of hearts, do you see a future with Chris, or are you merely trying to make up for the past?'

Samantha didn't doubt that Jen loved Chris. But as Roman had smartly pointed out, sometimes love isn't enough.

Jen kept her gaze fixed on the pool. It was long and narrow. The water was a sparkling blue and the surrounding palm trees cast long shadows on its glossy surface. To be miserable in paradise was a unique form of punishment.

'Both,' Jen replied. 'He's grown into the man I want to have a life with. That doesn't take away the guilt. I feel bad all the time. It doesn't go away. I've learned my lesson. Now I work twice as hard to be a good friend. But I'll tell you what, it's draining.'

Jen fanned her face with her hands as if to clear the air. Samantha studied her a while. So this was the person behind the performance, the not-so-sunny side of Jen. She preferred this person. Samantha may not be able to help her patch up her romantic life, but when it came to friendships, she was more than qualified to give informed advice. 'I was jealous of you and Naomi, of how close you two are. She was my best friend and now she's yours.'

'Oh, God, Sam! Don't say that! If you only knew how much she cares about you. You're like the sister she deserves. Not that Maya isn't lovely, but you know ...'

'I know.' Maya had entered a bratty phase at age ten and never outgrew it. 'My point is: you can relax. Naomi is sold on you. She thinks you're amazing. Despite everything, Chris is still in your life. Give yourself a break.'

'You're right,' Jen said. 'I am pretty great.'

Samantha settled back on the lounge chair. 'Now *that's* the Jen I know.'

'I promised myself that if Chris didn't come round on this trip, I'd give him up,' Jen said. 'It'll break my heart, but I'll do it. I can't drag this on forever. It's not healthy.'

'You should have kissed him at the Nylon Pool. That would've fixed it.'

That got Jen to laugh, a sorry little laugh that ended with another sigh. 'You're a good listener.'

'Why, thank you!'

'I'm sorry about Naomi. I don't want to steal your friend.'

'You can't,' Samantha said. 'She's stuck with me. Besides, California is her home now. I can't always be there. She's going to need someone to binge-watch television and drink cheap wine.'

Jen teared up. 'I'm always down for that.'

'You two are up early! What are you plotting?'

That was Hugo. He had never once participated in morning yoga, preferring to start his day with a few laps in the pool. This morning, his grumpy expression clashed with his sunny Hawaiian print swim trunks.

Jen quickly brushed a tear away. 'Hey there, handsome!'

'What's up with you?' Samantha asked. 'Didn't you sleep well?'

'Nope.'

He fell onto the lounge chair on Jen's right and blew a kiss Samantha's way. Then, in typical Hugo style, he blurted out a surprise. 'Adrian wants to sell our condo.'

'No!' Samantha cried. 'I love your flat.'

The memory of that night in Miami was clear in her mind:

she, Hugo and Jasmine on the balcony watching the sunset over the bay. It seemed like a lifetime ago.

'So do I,' Hugo said. 'Adrian wants to buy a house in Weston to shorten his commute.'

'You don't sound happy about that,' Jen said.

'Do you see me in a gated community in Weston?' Hugo asked.

'Depends,' Jen said. 'Where is Weston?'

'Smack in the middle of the rich mom suburbs.'

Samantha hated the idea. 'Increasingly, I picture you as a beach bum.'

Hugo pointed at her. 'That's why we're friends.'

'I like Adrian,' Jen said. 'But don't let him pressure you. Trust me, I'm a product of the suburbs. You don't want to be there if you don't really want to.'

'I know exactly what you mean.'

Samantha had questions. Hugo and Adrian hadn't rushed into marriage like Naomi and Anthony. She would've thought they'd had the basics figured out. 'Hadn't you guys agreed on those types of things before you settled down?'

'There's no such thing as settling down,' Hugo said. 'You just wake up one day and there you are.'

She went back to staring at the water. One thing was clear: none of them had anything figured out.

Jen balled up a small towel and tossed it at her. 'I meant to ask how *your* date went last night. I hope you had a better time than Chris and I.'

'We got to know each other better.'

Jen wasn't satisfied. 'Is that all you have to say?'

'There's not much more to say.'

'We want the juicy details,' Hugo insisted.

Samantha balled up Jen's towel and tossed it at him. 'We click. The chemistry is there, but it's like we're on a seesaw. When I warm up, he cools down.'

'You two are exhausting!' Naomi came up from behind, startling them all. She wore a floral kaftan and large sunglasses. She gestured for Samantha to scoot over and joined her on the lounge chair. 'You're overthinking this. Just get it on, already.'

Samantha gladly made room for her. It was like old times, when they hung out in each other's bedrooms, gossiping for hours. Still, she kept her tone stern. 'Sorry my dating life isn't spicy enough for you.'

'Don't apologize, darling,' Hugo said. 'Just get on with it. Make your move.'

'I see what's going on here,' Samantha said. 'You're locked into relationships and living vicariously through me.'

Jen wagged a finger. 'I'm not locked into anything and I'm very much invested in this. You've only got a few days left. Take your shot.'

They heard the click–clack sound of Jasmine's sandals on the steps leading to the pool deck before she emerged amid the potted palm trees. She ambled along, yawning all the way. 'I woke up to make tea and saw you all from my window and was struck with FOMO.'

'Same here,' Naomi said.

'You two should go back to bed,' Jen said. 'This is a gripe session.'

Jasmine sat cross-legged at the edge of the pool, the water rippling behind her. 'I've nothing to contribute. I'm literally on cloud nine. But every session needs a moderator, right? Let's start.'

'Awesome!' Naomi exclaimed. 'A recap! I came late and missed the good stuff. Catch me up.'

'Who wants to go first?' Jasmine asked.

Hugo raised his hand. 'Adrian wants to move to the 'burbs.'

'Noooo!' Jasmine and Naomi cried in unison.

'Oh yes,' Hugo said.

'Tell him he has to put that up for a vote,' Jasmine said. 'Now, what about you, Sam? Want to go next?'

Samantha wanted to be a good sport, but overall, she was in a good place. 'Roman asked me to be his date for the wedding. So you can put away your sad, pitying looks for the next person who gets dumped.'

Naomi's response was quick. 'You admit you got dumped, then?'

'I admit nothing.'

Samantha's sudden reversal of luck confirmed all of Jasmine's convenient theories on life. 'See? You just never know. Always err on the side of optimism.'

'But there is one thing. We are teetering on the edge of the Friend Zone. It may well be a platonic date.'

'Oh God …' Jen groaned. 'Those are the worst.'

'Maybe not,' Jasmine said. 'Why force it? My advice is to let it flow. Friendship lasts longer than any fling.'

'You may be right,' Hugo said. 'Adrian and I started out as friends.'

'She's wrong!' Jen cried, clearly exasperated. 'Friendship is a total waste of time!'

'Jen,' Jasmine said. 'Is there something you'd like to share?'

'Chris doesn't trust that my feelings are genuine. Since I'm twenty-nine and single, he thinks I'm settling. We will never be anything more than friends.'

The shocking revelation was Jen's age. Samantha blurted, 'You're twenty-nine? You don't look a day older than nineteen.'

'Thanks, guys,' Jen said. 'But high school was a long time ago.'

'She's a branch manager,' Naomi said, putting Jen's age in context.

'DM me your skin care regime,' Hugo said.

'I drink a ton of water.'

'That's not going to cut it, darling,' Naomi said. 'We need details.'

Hugo agreed. 'Product names, preferred tools, routines, etc.'

'We'll follow up on that later. Someone add Jen to our group chat,' Jasmine said. 'As for Chris, he has some issues to resolve. I suggest you give him space.'

Jen nodded. 'I think so, too.'

'Is that it?' Jasmine asked. 'Have we covered everything?'

Naomi shyly raised a hand. Everyone turned to her. She cleared her throat. 'I may have something to gripe about.'

'Is it the wedding?' Samantha asked. 'Do you need help?'

Come to think of it, she hadn't lifted a finger to help out all this time. Since arriving in Tobago, Samantha had focused on her feelings and her fledgling blog.

'Is it the missing best man?' Jen asked.

'Oh, yeah,' Hugo said. 'Where is that guy? His wife was nice.'

Naomi slipped off her sunglasses. Without the stylish accessory, she looked worried.

Jasmine encouraged her to say more. 'Go on. This is a safe space.'

'Anthony and Ted are on the outs.'

'Is that why he's staying off campus, so to speak?' Jen asked.

The answer was evident. 'They had a row the first night and he left the next day. He's gone.'

'Gone … as in *gone*?' Hugo asked. 'I thought he and his girlfriend found an Airbnb in the capital.'

'I thought that was strange,' Jen said. 'This place is amazing. Why leave? I didn't press it because I needed the bungalow to seduce Chris. We all know how that turned out.'

'They stayed at the Airbnb until they could arrange a flight back to Florida.'

Samantha instinctively wrapped her arms around Naomi's slender shoulders and squeezed. 'You've been keeping all of this from us?'

'I want you to have a good time,' Naomi said. 'And to leave here with good memories.'

This time they all cried out as one. 'Don't be dumb!' Hugo exclaimed. 'We're having a blast.'

'The time of our lives, truly,' Samantha said. 'Look at us! We're in paradise.'

'Girl, we can handle a little drama,' Jasmine said. 'You don't have to hide from us.'

As ever, Samantha had questions. 'What was the row about?'

Naomi pressed her lips together. She looked uncomfortable. 'I'd rather not say.'

'It's between them,' Jasmine said. 'We don't have to get into that.'

'Thanks,' Naomi said. 'I'd prefer not to.'

Hugo offered to stand in as the best man in a pinch. Naomi thanked him and turned down the offer. 'His uncles arrive on Friday. He'll have plenty of candidates to choose from.'

'That's pretty shitty of Ted,' Jen said. 'Imagine your best man walking out on you. No one deserves that.'

Naomi folded her arms and fell silent. Jasmine and Samantha exchanged looks. 'All right!' Jasmine said brightly. 'I think this has been a productive session. Should we chant "om" three times?'

Hugo shut that down. 'Yoga was cancelled.'

'OK.' Jasmine chuckled. 'Let's at least set intentions for the rest of the week.'

'I *intend* to get married,' Naomi said. 'That's it.'

'I intend to dance my ass off at your wedding,' Hugo said.

'And I intend to follow your advice,' Jen said.

'How about you, Sammy?' Jasmine asked.

'I intend to go with the proverbial flow.'

'Good plan.'

Maya arrived and, judging by the look on her face, she was in quite a mood, as well.

Jen greeted her first. 'Morning, sunshine!'

Maya rolled her eyes. 'Give it a rest. It's 7 a.m. How are you all so damn chipper?'

CHAPTER SIXTEEN

A mysterious man on a motorcycle was waiting outside Samantha's bungalow. She ran to him. 'Hey there, handsome stranger!'

He looked up from his phone, his smile bright like the morning sun. 'I thought you were asleep in there. I was going to text you.'

Feeling playful, she whispered, 'I was at a secret meeting of the inner circle.'

'How did that go?'

'We added Jen to the group chat.'

'That sounds like official business,' Roman said. 'What else did you discuss?'

'The departure of Ted Rivera. Did you know the best man is gone?'

Samantha wondered if Ted's abrupt and unexplained departure was the first sign of trouble in paradise.

If Roman knew anything about it, he gave nothing away. 'I noticed,' he said.

'More room on the bus for us, I guess.'

'Speaking of the bus,' Roman said, 'I can't ride out with you to Pigeon Point. I have to handle a family matter. I'll join you there later.'

'Thanks for letting me know,' she said. 'I might have rushed to your rescue again, knowing me and my big, generous heart.'

'That's why I came here to tell you in person,' he said. 'I know you just can't help yourself. You're too good and we don't deserve you.'

'Thank you for finally acknowledging it.'

'Ride with me?'

Samantha took a step back and considered the motorcycle he was straddling. It could only be described as vintage. 'On that thing? Where did you get it?'

'It's my cousin's bike.'

'How many cousins do you have?'

'A lot,' he said. 'I can't remember half their names.'

Hands on her hips, Samantha eyed Roman this time. 'You *can* ride this thing, right?'

'Just hop on. We won't go far.'

Samantha said a quick prayer and climbed aboard. Roman offered her a helmet and helped her with the strap. 'Hold me tight,' he said, as if she wouldn't be clinging to him for dear life, and they took off.

They left the resort grounds. It was early still and the surrounding neighbourhood was calm. With the fresh morning mountain air in their faces, they sped along the winding roads, slowing down only for a red hen and her chicks. Samantha loosened her grip on Roman's waist and simply enjoyed the feel of his strong body. She pressed her cheek to his wide back and closed her eyes, which only made her dizzy, so she opened her eyes and took it all in.

As promised, Roman had her back in time to get ready for the outing. 'I'll see you later,' he said.

She slid off the bike and handed him the helmet. She shook out her curls. 'By the way, the answer is yes.'

He looked at her quizzically. 'What's the question?'

'You asked if I wanted to have fun. The answer is yes.'

His eyes narrowed. 'Yeah … I remember saying something along those lines.'

'Once more for the cheap seats, the answer is yes.'

'Sorry, pretty girl. That offer expired.'

'Really? When?'

'Last night,' he said. 'If you're still interested, the terms have changed.'

'That's convenient.'

Roman kickstarted the bike's motor. 'Be ready for negotiations later today.'

Samantha watched him ride off, wondering how one man could be so devastatingly charming and yet so utterly frustrating.

Travel Blog

Tentative Title: The Group Chat
[Note to Self: Maybe... Maybe not...]

DRAFT ENTRY #7: THE BFF MAINTENANCE PLAN

My friends and I mainly keep in touch via group chat. I live in England and they are dispersed across North America. The chat is often aggravating, yet it keeps our connection fresh. It's a constant stream, yet sometimes I worry it will dry out. When we talk in person, there's a special kind of chemistry. We're more open and honest, more generous, too. We've widened the circle to include new members. I get to see sides of them I hadn't guessed at. I want to make the most of this time together. I've devised an action plan:

1. Work on making the Princess Bride's path to the altar a smooth one and resist cluttering it with my insecurities and doubts. Fight anyone who gets in her way.

2   Get to know California Girl. She's going through a tough time and needs support.

3.   Hang out with the original Vegas Squad. Who knows when we'll all be together again?

4.   Talk to the American.[2] Let him know that I have more than enough friends. I want more.

---

2   More on him later.

CHAPTER SEVENTEEN

Pigeon Point beach fulfilled the promise Tobago made to its visitors in postcards and ads. A stretch of white sand faded into deep turquoise waters. After the cancelled snorkelling trip and much drama, the beach day they deserved finally arrived.

Naomi rented out a covered cabana that served as home base. Right away, though, Anthony, Hugo, Chris, Jason and Jen took off paddleboarding.

Samantha took that to heart. Tomorrow marked the official start of the wedding weekend. Anthony's family was expected to arrive in the morning. The rehearsal was scheduled in the afternoon. Afterwards, Amelia was hosting an elegant dinner for Anthony's parents and uncles. The rest of them would set out to No Man's Land for a sunset barbecue. They would be expected to show up on time for these scheduled events, well dressed and well behaved, or suffer Amelia's wrath. This was their last opportunity to just hang out and have fun.

While the others enjoyed watersports, Samantha, Naomi, Jasmine, Maya and friends lounged under lime-green umbrellas, sipped coconut water straight from coconuts, raced along the shore, their bare feet sinking into the soft sand, clear water lapping around their ankles, and posed for a million photos that would later be posted on social media. This was their idea of a fun beach day, and they would not be judged for it.

Samantha missed Roman. She couldn't help checking the time or glancing around to catch his arrival. Eventually, she asked Naomi if she'd heard from him and she said only that he was on his way. 'Since his grandmother had the stroke, she needs more help at home.'

Naomi said it as if it were common knowledge. Samantha assumed he'd stayed behind to help out at the shop, like last time. 'I didn't know. He never talks about his grandparents.'

Naomi didn't think it was a big deal. 'Did you tell him about your nana and her last hip replacement?'

Somehow that wasn't the same thing. Her nana was having a grand time in her assisted living facility. This painted Roman in a new light. He'd left Wall Street to help out his ageing grandparents in their time of need. He could have been anywhere, doing anything, yet he chose to be here.

'Speaking of Roman, there's something I'd like to say.'

Samantha's heart rate ticked up. All this time, she was holding her breath, waiting for some startling revelation that would pull her out of her dream. Roman was too perfect, absolutely too good to be true. Something had to be wrong with him and Naomi was going to reveal it now. Only she didn't want to know. What good would it do? They had a few days together. She wanted to enjoy it.

'Anthony thinks I've been pushing you too hard. He asked me to back off and give you two space.'

Oh? Samantha hadn't expected that. 'Anthony said that?'

'He did.'

'And you're going to do it?'

'What can I say?' She wiggled her toes in the sand. 'He makes me a better person.'

'Anthony's a miracle worker? Can he turn water into wine?'

'Shut up. He's going to ease up on Roman, too.'

Roman would no doubt appreciate that, but it made no difference in the end. Samantha wondered if she should tell Naomi that neither she nor her perfect fiancé had anything to do with her and Roman getting together. They'd found each other on their own and didn't need a hype team to get them across the finish line. In the end, she decided against it. It was easier to let Naomi be Naomi, rather than rein her in. Anthony would figure that out soon enough.

***

Anthony and the others returned in time for lunch. They were about to sit down to grilled fresh fish and chips when Roman arrived. He'd checked three restaurants before tracking them down. Samantha had expected him to show up looking worn out, run down, stressed or any combination of the above. One third of his obligations would have worn her thin. Caring for ageing grandparents was no joke. But he arrived looking better than he had a right to be under any circumstances. He looked fresh in his usual tight, white T-shirt, standard sunglasses and sexy smile. His grandmother had nothing to do with him being late. His uncle's truck had rolled over into a ditch. He entertained the guys with all the details of the truck rescue. But first, he came around to hug Samantha, fluff her hair, and steal one of her chips. After lunch, he stole her away.

'Hey, pretty lady. Want to go for a walk?'

They headed out to the jetty, walking side by side, but not hand in hand, like she would have liked. Still, with the sea spread out all around them, Samantha had the lightheaded feeling of walking on water.

He pointed down to the wooden planks. 'When I was a kid, I snagged a toe on a loose nail and had to get stitches and a tetanus shot. I still have the scar.'

Samantha made a mental note to look for that scar later. Now she had questions. 'Why don't you tell me anything?'

Roman looked genuinely confused. 'I just told you a funny story from my childhood.'

There was nothing funny about tetanus. 'You tell me anecdotes, but not the stuff that matters. Like your grandmother, for example.'

'I'm pretty sure I told you about her. Her name is Candace. Remember that whole thing?'

She lowered her voice even though they were pretty much alone out on their end of the jetty. 'You didn't say anything about her health issues.'

Roman sputtered a response. 'Sure, she had some issues. Still does. I mean, she's not the same since the stroke, but she's better now. Stable.'

Samantha felt terrible. It was clear that she'd touched upon a sore spot. Roman didn't want to talk about his grandmother's health on a sunny beach day. Could she blame him? 'I'm sorry. It's not important.'

'I wasn't hiding it from you. It didn't come up, that's all.'

Samantha was confronted with the truth. The way she felt had nothing to do with his grandmother. Her frustration stemmed from something else. 'I'm getting "maybe" vibes from you.'

He cocked his head. 'Explain.'

She spelled it out. 'Mixed signals, Roman. Like *maybe* you don't want this. *Maybe* you're just not that into me. Whatever the case, it's fine. I just need to know.'

He stepped away, astonished. 'You think that I – Roman Carver, of sound mind and body – for some reason, don't want *this*?'

The sea breeze had picked up, making a mess of her hair. Samantha stood her ground. 'Am I wrong?'

'You couldn't be more wrong,' he said. 'How do you get through life with that kind of wrong thinking?'

'What is it, then?'

'Reading your blog posts changed things.'

'I knew it!' she cried. 'You think I'm a train wreck.'

'No, Sam … I think you're fun and smart and complicated and loving. It's changed how I see you, how I feel, and I had to hit pause and sort myself out.'

Samantha turned away and stared out at the sea. He thought her fun and smart and complicated? She felt the same about him. There was no use putting a casual spin on it. She liked him and he liked her. It was as simple as that. However, it was worth noting that she was booked on a 2 p.m. flight out of Tobago on Sunday. Hitting pause right now might not be the way to go, but she was willing to do it.

She was about to tell him all of this when he smirked and said, 'Just how badly do you want me?'

Samantha tried to shove him into the sea. He yanked her to him. 'I'll take you down with me!'

They laughed and held each other tight. 'I don't want to get stuck in the Friend Zone,' she said. 'If that makes sense.'

Exploring her feelings for Roman scared her to death, but something inside her dared her to take the leap.

He gently gathered her curls in one hand and brought his mouth to her ear. He whispered, 'Come home with me today and I'll show you how good a friend I can be.'

She shivered in the afternoon heat. 'I can't wait.'

'Let's go,' he said.

It was her turn to hit pause. 'Can't. I've booked a steel drum lesson at three.'

'Damn.' He pressed his forehead to hers. 'And I should probably spend time with Anthony. Show him I care.'

That reminded her, she had some intel to share. 'There's been a development on that front. Anthony has vowed to butt out of our affairs.'

'Oh, yeah?' He pulled her tighter. She melted into his chest. 'Anthony should focus on his wedding vows.'

'I agree.'

He looked past her shoulder at the shoreline. 'They're watching, you know.'

'I bet they are.'

'Let's give them something to see.'

Samantha rose onto her tiptoes. They shared another laugh before he kissed her. This kiss was different from the others, slow and sweet and full of promise. She ran her hands over his cropped hair, slid them down his back. She tasted him and breathed him in, all her senses awake. They were at the very edge of the jetty with the sea all around. She was faintly aware of swimmers splashing in the distance, seagulls crying overhead, and the tumble of the waves, but she was highly attuned to Roman's heartbeat and every sound that escaped his throat. She couldn't wait for them to be alone.

He pulled away and sought her eyes. 'I'm weary of starting things that I can't follow through. Does *that* make sense?'

It made all the sense in the world. 'I'm the same,' she said. 'Naomi says I should just live in the moment.'

'Those two can't stay out of our business, can they?'

'It's embarrassing. Do you think they sit up all night talking about us?'

'I'd bet money on it.'

She laughed, loving his uncanny ability to flip the mood with just a word or two.

Roman cupped her face. 'So pretty,' he whispered.

Adrian came running down the jetty, clapping to get their attention. 'Wrap it up, you two! We've got snorkelling and steel drum lessons in five!'

★★★

Samantha did all right with the steel drums. Chris, the only other one of their clan to sign up for a lesson, did far better. It wasn't her fault. Her thoughts were scattered. Her brain kept skipping ahead, she was eager to leave. She'd frolicked in the sun, skipped in the sand, bonded with her friends, and posed for one hundred photos. It was time to go. She and Roman would be driving back together. They were going to stop by the place he rented just blocks from his grandparents' home. She would finally get a glimpse at his interior world.

After the lesson, she and Chris stopped to pick up fresh coconut water and made their way back to the cabana.

'You did really well back there,' Samantha said.

'It's just the way my mind works,' Chris said. 'I can pick up rhythm and patterns easily.'

She realized that he was apologizing for his proficiency. 'That's awesome. Do you play an instrument?'

'I play a few.'

'A few!'

'How about you?'

'Not even one,' she said. 'In school I got to bang the cymbals. That about sums it up.'

'Still requires pacing and timing.'

'You're too kind.'

This was the most she'd talked to Chris this entire trip. They were a small group, yet rowdy. She'd catch him chatting or laughing with Jen or Roman, but for the most part he kept quiet and to himself. She hadn't made much of an effort, either.

'What do you do for a living?' she asked.

'I'm a mathematician.'

'That's impressive. I don't think I ever met one in real life.'

'I develop software mostly,' he said. 'What about you?'

'I write content for *The Financial Files*. It's a business publication.'

'I know what it is,' he said. 'It's Britain's version of *The Wall Street Journal*.'

'Something like that.'

'In that case, have you heard of Trident Data Corp?'

'I have, actually.'

Samantha had written a profile of the start-up not long ago, after it closed a Series E funding. The company was valued at one billion dollars.

'That's me.'

'You work for Trident Data? That's cool.'

'I *am* Trident Data.'

'You …? How?'

He chuckled. 'I get that a lot.'

'But wait! I did my research. The CEO of Trident is …' Her voice dropped. 'CJ Miller.'

Chris's grin widened. Clearly, he was enjoying this. 'Christian James Miller is a mouthful. Everybody calls me Chris.'

The unassuming and otherwise unremarkable Chris was a multimillionaire?

'Technically, I'm on sabbatical. Burnout is a real thing. Jen never mentioned it?'

'Jen is very protective of you.'

Chris's open expression closed. They walked in silence for a bit before he said, 'Mind if I pick your brain for a minute?'

'I'm no mathematician, but go ahead.'

They'd instinctively slowed to a stop. Chris tapped his coconut to the beat that he'd just mastered on the steel drums. He was nervous.

'What is it?' Samantha asked.

'Do you think I'm an asshole for not giving Jen a second chance?'

'I'm not sure I know what you're talking about,' Samantha stammered.

'It's OK. I know you know a little bit about it.'

Even so, it wasn't her place to give him advice. 'I can't tell you what to do.'

'That's not what I asked. Just tell me what you think.'

Samantha took a sip of coconut water for electrolytes and courage and dived in. 'I think it's a shame you two can't figure something out. You look comfortable together. That's rare.'

Chris squinted toward the horizon. The sun was low and the sea had turned silver. A breeze ruffled his curls.

'Do you forgive her for the way she behaved in high school?' Samantha asked.

If he couldn't forgive her, there was nothing left to talk about. He should just move on.

'Oh, yeah ...' he said. 'I don't think there's anything to forgive. We were all little shits back then. Keep in mind, we were the offspring of CEOs and the products of new money. It was a horror show.'

That certainly painted Jen in a different light. Was everyone filthy rich? 'So, what's the problem?'

'I don't think I'd let anyone in. I've been in lockdown mode my whole adult life. I can build a great company, but I can't establish lasting relationships.'

'I think you're selling yourself short. How long have you known Jen?'

'On and off, eighteen years. We went our separate ways for college and reconnected in Los Angeles.'

Samantha relaxed. They were now in her area of expertise. 'That sounds like a sturdy, long-term friendship to me. You've weathered a few storms and are still together.'

He blinked, deep in thought. She noticed his lashes were blond and nearly invisible. 'That's why I'm scared of messing up and losing her.'

Samantha's heart ached. How could she tell him that if he didn't make a move, he risked losing her, anyway?

She tugged his arm and got them moving again. 'Talk to her. Share all your fears.'

'I did.'

'Try again. I don't think she quite understood.'

Jen's takeaway was that Chris didn't trust her when in fact he didn't trust himself. Roman was the same, taking unnecessary precautions, weary of rocking the boat. Who were they trying to protect?

Chris brought his straw to his lips and took a long sip. 'This is nothing like the crap we buy in cans.'

Samantha took a long refreshing sip. 'It's the real deal.'

'Jen is the real deal,' he said. 'The time is right. I just thought it would get easier, you know?'

'It gets harder, I think.'

'Shit,' he murmured. 'Why does it have to feel like … I don't know—'

'Leaping off a cliff?' she offered.

'Exactly.'

'I can tell you about the first and only time I jumped off a cliff,' Samantha said.

He nudged her in the ribs with a pointy elbow. 'I think I was there and witnessed the whole thing.'

She grinned, remembering the day she'd slipped on the wet stone steps, landed on her bum and made a scene. 'I can tell you this: it wasn't as scary as I thought.'

'I could use a good thrill right about now. It's been a long time. Too long.'

Samantha mimed clobbering him over the head with her coconut. Who knew Chris could be so cheeky?

'Race you back?' he said.

He had to be kidding. 'Not on your life. I'm drained.'

They talked freely to the end. The fun and games were over the moment they returned to the cabana. Naomi was in full drill sergeant mode. 'What took you guys so long? It's going to rain. Gather your things. Let's go!'

There was no trace of rain anywhere, but Samantha knew better than to contradict Naomi. She collected her beach towel and the trendy basket bag she'd bought for the trip. She was ready. 'I'm going to ride back with Roman, keep him company.'

Naomi was distracted, too busy packing the coolers. 'If you're looking for Roman, he's giving Anthony a hand loading the bus.'

Roman was actually right by her side. He'd crept up from behind and wrapped his arms around her waist. Warmth spread all over. No one had ever held her like this; tight, protective. It felt like home.

'Let's escape,' he whispered.

'I should say goodbye to the others.'

'No, you shouldn't. Let's get out of here before it's too late.'

They compromised. Samantha tapped Naomi's shoulder and blew her a kiss goodbye. They took off straight away, racing toward the park's exit. It was funny how re-energized she felt. Roman led her to a dusty red jeep. This vehicle, the motorcycle, and the black saloon belonged to his cousin, a mechanic. He borrowed them at will. It was a reminder that he wasn't rooted in Tobago. Everything was transient and temporary.

He tossed her bag onto the back seat, helped her in, and they sped off. Despite the humidity, the sky was silvery blue. The road ahead was long, narrow and sinewy. The radio was on low. Every cell in Samantha's body hummed in anticipation. She was more than a little frustrated when he pulled to the side of the road.

'We have to do this the right way,' he said. 'Let's buy snacks.'

A roadside stall sold a variety of goodies, made of coconut, rice, chocolate, and ripe plantains. It looked so delectable.

Samantha picked a rice cake from the stack. 'Is this sweet or savoury?'

'You tell me.'

Roman took it from her, unwrapped it, broke off a piece and gave her a taste. She savoured the honey sweetness. 'Mmm … it is.'

He leaned in and kissed her, tasted her. 'Not as sweet as you.'

Samantha closed her eyes. This was the moment she'd relive again and again in the days, weeks and months to come. When their trail of texts had gone cold and she didn't know where in the world Roman was, she'd relive this kiss.

The vendor cleared her throat. 'You two lovebirds best be buying something!'

Roman broke away, laughing. Samantha stood rooted in place. That laugh did things to her, moved through her, loosened and swept away every last bit of doubt. She'd follow it wherever it led.

CHAPTER EIGHTEEN

The little blue house was nestled in a hill surrounded with bougainvillea and thick mango trees. They went around the back. A black cat curled on the porch slunk away. 'Is that yours?' Samantha asked.

Roman unlocked an iron door. 'It belongs to the house.'

'What's her name?'

'Cat.'

They entered a kitchen with black-and-white-chequered floors. A wooden table was pushed into a corner loaded with two laptops, battery chargers, headphones and stacks of worn notebooks. 'Here's where I work.' She followed him through a sitting room with wood floors, sparse furnishing and white-washed walls. It was nice and neat, with no personal clutter whatsoever. They walked straight through and down a short hall to his bedroom. The door was ajar and he pushed it open. 'Here's where I do everything else.'

An unmade bed, a rattan chair stacked with books, a few gadgets and toiletries set up on a dresser, his clothes and shoes organized in an open wardrobe. She wanted to go on snooping, but Roman shut the door and leaned against it. All the air rushed from the room.

'You don't have much. Is your New York life in storage?'

'We're going to discuss logistics now?'

'I want to get to know you. Is that wrong?'

He rested his head on the door, studied her through lowered lashes. She couldn't see his eyes. She couldn't read him. Samantha realized that she might never know Roman, not in any real way. That should have turned her off. Instead, it turned her on.

In the past, when she'd stumbled into bed with a guy, it was always a quasi-mistake. Poor timing, bad chemistry, wrong setting. None of those elements were at play now.

'Come here and get to know me,' he said.

Samantha plucked out the clip holding her wind-tossed hair in place. Her tangled mass of curls tumbled to her shoulders. In the stillness of the room, she heard his breath catch.

'You're so damn beautiful,' he murmured.

Her hair was fried and frizzy, damaged by saltwater and chlorine, her complexion had turned copper-brown in the sun, and her face likely showed her lack of sleep. Even so, she felt beautiful. Time with her friends and all that morning yoga had her thinking clearly for once. She felt like herself again, no longer reeling from a break-up and broken up over having to attend a wedding alone. One by one, her closest friends were pairing off and settling down. They had life sorted out. Good for them. She, on the other hand, was in the eye of the storm. Everything was in flux. There was power in this moment, and she was the one wielding it.

Roman pushed away from the door and cut the distance between them. He dug his hands in her hair and angled her face to his. Their kiss was deep and hard and impatient. His touch opened spaces inside of her, every last hidden cave, leaving her nowhere to hide. He had her, not the person she pretended to be, bubbly and bright, but the sharp and the brittle. All the jagged edges that she'd made smooth to please others, he held in his palms with no questions, no complaints. She thought back to all the times Timothy would jokingly say, 'You're too much.' It got to the point where she suspected it was no longer a joke. She'd been too much for him to manage. To make herself more manageable she'd toned herself down, held her tongue and scaled back her dreams.

She was not too much for Roman.

He was not too much for her.

He walked her backwards and they stumbled onto the bed. Roman covered her with his body and only then did Samantha's world tilt.

'I've dreamed about this,' he said.

She raked her fingers through his stubble. 'How did it go?'

'You were shy.'

'Ha!' She tossed her head back and laughed. 'You must have been dreaming about some other curly-haired girl.'

'I'm lying. You were feisty as hell.'

So was he. Roman tugged at her clothes. He stripped off her tank top and peeled her denim shorts down over her hips. 'Sorry I didn't make the bed this morning.'

She inhaled the sheets, which carried his scent. 'Sorry you think I care about that.'

He rolled off the bed and undressed, stepping out of his jeans. 'I know how to do this right. Back home I'd play music, open a bottle of wine, light a candle ...'

'I'm sure you're really smooth.' She held out her open arms and beckoned him. 'Come.'

He grinned wickedly. 'Why do I get the feeling you're using me for my body?'

'Because I am.' Samantha got on her knees at the edge of the bed and drew him to her by the waistband of his boxers. 'Hope that doesn't offend you.'

'I'll patch my bruised ego in the morning.'

Samantha wasn't worried. His ego was cast in iron and could withstand a few blows.

He traced the bodice of her bikini top with a finger. 'This doesn't look very comfortable. Let me help you out of it.'

He'd had the good sense to change before they'd escaped the beach. She still had her damp swimsuit on under her clothes and could use the help. He pushed the stretchy fabric over her head. His hands roamed over the newly exposed skin. Then his mouth travelled from the dip at the base of her neck down to her navel. She arched forward, her arms falling to her side. He pinned her to him with a hand on the small of her back. She whispered his name, but he had found her breasts and nothing would distract him from them. And thank God, too. Every lick, every playful bite, ignited a small fire inside her.

They toppled onto the bed again. Samantha couldn't get enough of him. She wanted to feel, taste, and clutch every part of him. She gathered his T-shirt, pulled it over his head and dropped it onto the floor. Roman was just as eager. Samantha closed her eyes and focused on the feel of his breath fanning her hot skin, the ripple of his muscles under her hands, and every faint moan rising from his throat. The few words she uttered made no sense. She was begging him for more or less – or something just beyond reach.

Roman entwined his fingers with hers and pinned her hands over her head. With the tip of his nose, he nudged a wayward curl of hair out of the way before whispering against her lips. 'What do you want?'

Samantha raised her chin, defiant even when caught in a trap of her own making. 'You already know.'

He kissed her deeply, but when he broke away there was the teasing grin she loved to hate. 'That's not how it works. I can't read your mind.'

That wasn't true. From the moment they'd met, she felt he could see right through her. There wasn't much she could hide from him. Right now, he knew exactly what her body was asking for. That didn't mean she couldn't guide him along.

She took his hand and brought it to the bikini bottom. 'Take this off.'

His laugh was gritty. 'So demanding.'

'Thought you loved that about me.'

'You know I do.' He sat back and helped her wiggle out of the last bit of clothing that kept him from her. Then he yanked open the top drawer of the bedside table, producing two strips of condoms. 'Ribbed or bare skin?'

'Any sparkly ones?'

'Ribbed it is.'

'Really?' Samantha propped herself up onto her elbows and gave him an appreciative look. The man was sculpted to perfection. Broad shoulders, tight abs, toned thighs – there was no part of him that needed enhancement. 'What exactly are you compensating for?'

He ripped off a square packet from a strip. 'You kill my self-confidence.'

Samantha laughed into the soft darkness. 'As much as I'd like to believe that, I do *not* have that power.'

Roman reached down and stroked her ankle. It felt like the most intimate touch. 'You have that power over me.'

Why then did she feel so powerless when he stripped off his boxers and joined her on the bed? She closed her eyes. The part of her who wanted only to return home to England with her heart intact did not want this to be as good as she'd imagined.

Roman kissed her eyelids. 'Are you nervous?'

'Yes and no.' She was excited and anxious. She was everything all at once.

'Look at me.'

His gaze was steady. Samantha could not tear herself away. It wasn't supposed to be like this. She thought they'd have a fun, sexy time. This was more, much more. She hadn't expected to feel so safe with him. Roman was watching her, waiting. Damn it, she was just going to say it. 'This feels special.'

'Because it is.'

Unlike with her, there was no hesitation, no fear lurking in his words. 'That doesn't scare you?'

'No.' He ran the pad of his thumb along the length of her brow. 'If you want to stop, we can.'

He moved away from her, but Samantha did not let him get far. She wrapped her legs around his waist to keep him close. 'I don't want that.'

Roman took her hand and pressed a kiss at the exact spot where her pulse skimmed beneath the tender skin of her wrist. 'Want to know what I want?'

Too fascinated to speak, she watched him drag his lips to the groove of her elbow, connecting hidden dots. 'I want you to remember every second we spend together. I want you to want me even when you're hundreds of miles away. I want you to miss this.'

He didn't have to work so hard. It was a done deal. 'I don't think I could ever forget.'

'Good.' He moved to kiss her shoulder before returning to her throat. 'Now show me what you want.'

CHAPTER NINETEEN

That feeling she'd described in her blog posts, of standing at the edge, weightless, breathless, dizzy out-of-your-mind? Roman knew it all too well.

At first, he thought this thing between them could be fun, but he had his eye on the meter and they were way past 'just fun'. Samantha Roberts had him hooked with the first glare. With each smile, she'd reeled him in. In no time, he was addicted to her laugh. And now she was naked under him, her messy hair sprawled over his messy sheets. Her sunbaked skin, crisscrossed with tan lines, left trails of goosebumps everywhere he touched. She slung her leg around his hips and drew him to her. He pulled away. Roman wanted to taste her first.

He licked and sucked. She swore and scratched his back. Roman only relented when she covered her face with her hands, giggling as she cried, 'I *hate* you!'

Laughing, he withdrew. 'Not what I was going for!'

'That's what you get,' she fired back.

'You don't have to love me, but still …' Roman looked around for the condom and found it under one of the pillows. He sat at the edge of the bed and put it on.

She hugged him from behind. 'I love hating you.'

'That's more like it.'

Roman flipped her onto her back and put an end to the taunting and teasing. He eased inside her. Her sigh swirled around him and his mind went blank. He heard his own voice, distant, raspy and thick. 'If I fall for you, I'm taking you down with me. I won't play fair.'

'Get a clue,' she whispered back. 'I'm way ahead of you.'

He kissed her hard and kept her lower lip between his teeth. They moved together, round and round, faster, tighter, until she pressed her face to his chest. Her cry sliced through him. He shuddered and collapsed. She gathered him in her arms and held him as if he were precious. Roman closed his eyes. This woman, knowingly or not, had pushed him from darkness into light.

Official Wedding Weekend

Friday 15 August:

~~3 p.m. Rehearsal~~

~~5 p.m. Cocktails and Barbecue at the resort (beach cocktail attire)~~

CHAPTER TWENTY

Sometime past midnight, the rain Naomi had predicted finally came crashing down. Roman slipped out of bed to shut windows and lock doors, leaving Samantha alone, half awake, half asleep, listening to the tap of rain on the corrugated tin roof. She picked up the sounds of Roman moving about the house. It had felt like the most natural thing in the world. They slept intertwined and woke up around seven. He made her coffee and drove her back to the resort. She hadn't wanted to leave so early, but had promised Naomi to help set up for the rehearsal and prepare mentally for the arrival of her future in-laws.

Roman walked her to her door. 'I'll see you later, then?'

Samantha wasn't ready to set him free yet. She lured him inside with an offer of tea or coffee or whatever. A moment later, he had her pinned against the closed door, a hand slipped under her cotton T-shirt. A furious knock on the door jolted them apart. It was Naomi, looking frazzled.

All week Naomi had sailed about unruffled, graceful as a swan. Now she stood on the veranda with her arms rod stiff at her side, hands balled into fists, the way she used to as a child.

Samantha held open the door to invite her in. She shook her head. 'I need you to come with me to Amelia's.'

'Is something wrong?'

'There's been some … developments.'

Samantha looked around for the sandals she'd kicked off earlier. 'I'll just tell Roman—'

'Roman's here? So early?'

Roman had backed into the sitting room, discreet and out of sight.

'He stopped by this morning and—' Naomi's pointed look stopped her short. Samantha sighed and started over. 'Yes, Roman's here.'

He came in from the sitting room, crowding the narrow foyer. 'Hey, Naomi!'

Naomi eyed him. 'Glad someone is in a good mood this morning.'

'I just got a text from Anthony,' he said. 'Says he needs to talk. Is something up?'

'You may want to check in on him.' Naomi cuffed Samantha's wrist. 'I'm taking this one with me.'

Samantha barely had a chance to wave goodbye. Naomi marched her down the stone path leading to Amelia and Gregory's bungalow. At some point, Samantha worried she was under arrest. She urged Naomi to stop. 'Tell me what's going on.'

Naomi finally let it out. 'Anthony's family can't make it.'

'They can't make it to their son's wedding?'

'Well, no. Just the rehearsal dinner.'

'When will they get here, exactly?'

Naomi took a breath and launched into an explanation. The Connecticut contingent had missed their connecting flight in Miami. They were now booked on a 5 a.m. flight the following morning. Which meant they'd arrive on the wedding day with only hours to spare. The carefully drawn schedule was worthless. Now they were headed to Amelia's for an emergency meeting.

'So long as they make it in time for the wedding,' Samantha said.

'I know, I know.' Naomi huffed. 'But first Ted *bails* and now this.'

The absentee best man … His abrupt departure was a mystery to this day. 'What really happened with him?'

'Please, Sam, I don't want to get into it.'

Samantha raised her hands to show that she meant no harm. Naomi was in such a state that the slightest provocation could split her in two.

'Let's go. Amelia is waiting.'

★★★

It was such a lovely day. After the night's rain, the Caribbean sky was spotless and bright. But it didn't look like they were going to get a chance to enjoy it.

Amelia's bungalow was way larger than Samantha's and located in the secluded side of the resort. Amelia came to the door in a floral print housedress and matching turban, a cup of tea in her hand. She invited them into the sitting room. Once they were settled, she got to the point. Amelia had called for the emergency meeting to announce that she'd cancelled the rehearsal. 'You all know what's expected of you. A mock ceremony before the ceremony is superfluous.'

Naomi sank into the cushions of the rattan chair. 'I had a dress and a photographer booked to take photos.'

'Do you want to get married, or do you want to play dress-up?'

Samantha winced. Amelia could be cutting at times.

'Don't do that,' Naomi said.

'Do what?'

'Take every opportunity to treat me like a petulant child.'

Amelia shrugged. 'Well …'

'Well, nothing! I have every right to be upset. Everything is falling apart.'

'*Nothing* is falling apart!' Amelia shot back. 'Try thinking of others for a change. Your future in-laws are stuck at Miami International Airport, which we can all agree is a portal to hell.'

'They've booked a hotel room,' Naomi muttered. 'They'll be fine.'

Amelia looked to Samantha for help. But she walked over to Naomi, sat on her chair's armrest and rubbed her back. 'We can still rehearse, if that's what you want to do. Everyone who matters is already here. Hugo and Jasmine can fill in for anyone who hasn't made it yet.'

Naomi thanked her. 'No … She's right. It's just … I don't know …'

Amelia changed her approach. 'Darling, they missed a flight. These things happen.'

'What if it's by choice?' Naomi asked. 'What if they've changed their minds?'

'Don't be ridiculous.'

Samantha looked from Naomi to Amelia, certain she was missing something crucial. Why would Anthony's parents change their minds about attending their only son's wedding? No doubt for the same reasons Ted had bailed? Samantha was dying for answers but Naomi's harried expression told her now wasn't the time to ask the tough questions. Besides, mother and daughter were locked in a staring match.

A moment later, a faint knock on the door gave Samantha the opportunity to slip away. 'I'll get it.'

Naomi had recruited her for emotional support, but she was not strong enough to come between Amelia and her daughter.

Anthony was at the door, unshaven and dishevelled, with Roman standing behind him.

'What did I miss?' Anthony asked in a hushed voice.

'The rehearsal is cancelled. Naomi is not OK with it.'

'Well, I am. I didn't see the point in it, anyway.'

'Don't tell her that.'

'OK.'

Samantha stepped aside to let Anthony in. Roman didn't move and gestured for her to come out. She silently shut the door behind her.

'Anthony is freaking out,' he said. 'I know it doesn't look like it, but he is.'

'It definitely looks like it,' Samantha said. 'Something is going on.'

If Anthony's parents didn't arrive by daybreak, she would charter a plane and pick them up herself. She could not live in a world where Naomi's destination wedding extravaganza was derailed. They would never know a day's peace until the end of time. It didn't matter that only days ago Samantha had plotted to derail the wedding herself. That was then, this was now. Naomi, Goddess of Thunder, would wreak havoc on this little island if her dreams of marrying her one true love tomorrow at sunset did not come to pass.

Anthony and Naomi joined them on the porch. Naomi appeared

calmer, settled. 'No use sitting around here,' Anthony said. 'We never got the chance to go to Englishman's Bay. Wanna go?'

Samantha gave up on her dream of getting any sleep. 'Absolutely.'

Roman was on board. 'Give me time to head home and pick up some stuff.'

'You got it,' Anthony said. 'We'll meet at the usual spot in an hour.'

Naomi pulled Samantha into a one-arm hug. 'Could you let the others know?'

'No problem.'

'Tonight's barbecue is cancelled, too. It was a terrible idea to begin with. I should get to bed early.'

'How about a picnic at the beach?' Anthony proposed. 'It was just meant to be us at the barbecue.'

'There's a shack at the cove that sells really good food,' Roman said.

'It's settled,' Naomi said. 'We'll have a picnic. Tell the others.'

Samantha whipped out her phone. 'I'll take care of it.'

The couple strode off, hand in hand. Samantha watched them go, a lump in her throat. Roman curled a finger around the belt loop of her shorts and pulled her close to him. 'Come here,' he said. 'Let me take care of you first.'

Samantha leaned against him, her body still tender from last night.

'Are you OK?' he asked.

She nodded as she typed. 'Looks like we're heading back to the beach.'

'No complaints here,' he said. 'I needed an excuse to spend the day with you and now I have it.'

Samantha rose onto the tip of her toes and rubbed her smooth cheek to his rugged one. 'I love the beach, but there's one place we haven't been.'

'Where's that?'

'Guess.'

'Give me a hint.'

'All right,' she said. 'There's a four-poster bed.'

'I wouldn't worry about that. We'll make it there.'

'When?'

'Tomorrow night.'

'After the wedding?'

'The perfect time. I'll be wearing a tie. It'll come in handy.'

Friday 15 August, 8.45 a.m.
Sam's phone to Hugo, Jasmine, Jen

Samantha: Please be advised that the rehearsal and subsequent rehearsal barbecue at No Man's Land are cancelled.

Hugo: WHAT NOW?

Jasmine: What's going on?

Samantha: The Connecticut contingent sent word they missed their flight. They won't make it until tomorrow.

Hugo: Forget blogging. You should go into PR.

Jen: Damn it … Is Naomi losing it?

Samantha: Yes.

Jasmine: The wedding is still on for tomorrow?

Samantha: Yes. Yes. Yes.

Jen: So what's the plan for today?

Samantha: An excursion to Englishman's Cove. Get ready.

Hugo: Adrian and I were heading out to breakfast.

Samantha: Skip it. A picnic lunch will be served on the beach.

Jen: I'm in! I've been dying to go to the Cove.

Samantha: Please inform your significant others and/or friends. Any more questions?

Jasmine: Yep. When we get a chance, can we talk in private?

Travel Blog

Title TBD : ~~The Group Chat~~ [Maybe not]

DRAFT ENTRY #8: WHERE THE RIVER MEETS THE SEA

Meet me at the spot where saltwater and freshwater mingle.
Make me believe that someday we can make our way to each
other, too.

CHAPTER TWENTY-ONE

Englishman's Cove was paradise. A curved shoreline, hugged by a dense tropical forest, slanting into the turquoise sea. Tucked away on the quiet side of the island, far from the touristy hustle and bustle, it was the calm backdrop they needed on this day.

After a swim, Naomi set up the picnic using the fancy plates and cups she'd ordered for the evening's cancelled barbecue. Anthony and Roman went off to order lunch at a nearby seafood shack. The rest of them were hanging out.

'Who wants to check out the river with me?' Jasmine asked. 'It's a short walk in that direction.'

This was the cue.

Jen scrambled to her feet and wiped sand off her bum. 'I'll go.'

Hugo slipped on his sunglasses. He gave Adrian a peck on his bare shoulder. 'I'll be right back, babe.'

Samantha grabbed her camera. 'I'll shoot video for the blog.'

Jason, Adrian and Chris knew what was up. They politely declined. Naomi was too absorbed with her task to notice their theatre production. She waved goodbye.

They set off, Samantha and Hugo trailing behind Jasmine and Jen, and soon arrived at what looked to Samantha like a shallow stream running perpendicular to the sea. Every so often, a strong sea wave crashed through it.

'Here's where the sea runs into the river,' Jasmine said. 'Freshwater and saltwater don't usually mix. When they do, it changes everything. They make something new.'

'Lovely,' Hugo said. 'Get to the point.'

'I didn't want to spread gossip,' Jasmine said. 'That's why I kept this to myself. Jason knows, but otherwise—'

Jen shielded her light eyes from the sun with her hand. 'You can tell us.'

'I may have some insight on the best man drama.'

Samantha edged closer. Now they were getting somewhere.

'Our first night here, after dinner, Jason and I went for a walk. It was such a gorgeous night. We walked past Anthony's bungalow.'

'Honey, sweetie,' Hugo said. 'Get to the *point*.'

'Don't rush her!' Jen said.

'We heard shouting. Anthony and Ted were arguing.'

'What about?' Samantha asked.

'I didn't hear much,' Jasmine said. 'Ted was definitely trying to reason with Anthony. *What's the rush?* he kept saying. *Why can't you date a while like normal people? Give it six months. Give it a year.* It got heated and we didn't want to get caught eavesdropping, so we took off. The next day, Ted was gone.'

Guilt churned in Samantha's gut. Hadn't she come to Tobago with the intention of saying all those things?

'They fell in love!' Jen exclaimed. 'What's so strange about that? Some people, honestly!'

Hugo, Jasmine and Samantha swivelled to face her. Jen buckled under the strength of their combined glare. 'I'll admit when they announced their engagement I thought they were pranking me. We met for drinks and I nearly spit out my apple martini. They'd only been dating a few weeks.'

'I feel terrible,' Samantha said. 'I might've said all those things to Naomi given the chance.'

'That may be true,' Hugo said. 'But you wouldn't have bailed on her.'

'None of us would have,' Jasmine said. 'At the end of the day, we're here, doing the right thing, supporting our friend in sickness and in health.'

'Not to mention we had the *decency* to make our flights,' Jen added, furious. 'Think about it. Why did they cut it so close? We've been here all week.'

Samantha nodded, eager to flush out the guilt clogging her conscience.

'What do we do now?' Jasmine asked.

'I don't think there's much we can do,' Jen said. 'She obviously doesn't want us to know about Ted.'

'I knew what was up,' Hugo said. 'His vibe was off.'

They exchanged worried glances. The truth was there, swirling around them, yet no one dared put it into words. Maybe Anthony's parents flat out disapproved of this rushed wedding, or perhaps they objected to Naomi as a future daughter-in-law. They might have hoped their son would bring home an easygoing girl, someone from New Haven or New Hampshire or New England or even New Jersey, not this bossy British girl with Caribbean roots.

The sound of heavy footsteps caught their attention. It was Roman, approaching at an even pace. Samantha had never been happier to see anyone in her entire life.

'Is this where the Illuminati gathers?' he asked.

'Too late,' Hugo said. 'Meeting adjourned.'

'That's good timing. Naomi wants you back at the camp.'

'That must mean lunch is ready,' Jen said. 'I'm starved.'

Samantha stood by Roman. 'You go ahead. I want to show him the freshwater–saltwater situation.'

'Pretty sure he's seen it,' Hugo said. 'Considering he's from the island and all.'

Jasmine and Jen grabbed Hugo by the arms and marched him away.

'I've seen it,' Roman assured. 'Many, many times.'

'Not with me, you haven't.'

'Everything is better with you.'

For a while the only sound was the hushed murmur of the stream. But Samantha's thoughts were roaring in her head.

'Hey, you,' she said, nervous. 'Remember that deal we struck? Our pledge of allegiance.'

He looked confused. 'To the flag of the United States?'

'To each other, you fool!' she said. 'As the only two singles, we pledged to share information.'

'Ah … the Rum Punch Agreement.'

Samantha laughed. 'I like the sound of that.'

'I remember everything about that first night.'

'Good,' Samantha said. 'Because I'm invoking it now.'

Roman narrowed his eyes and took a step forward. 'What's going on? What do you know?'

She took a step back. 'Promise you won't say anything to Anthony.'

'Not if he's in some kind of trouble—'

'It's nothing like that,' she assured him. 'It's delicate, and I don't want him to know we talked behind his back.'

'I won't say anything. You have my word.'

If Roman's word was as solid as just about everything else about him, she was in good hands. 'All right,' she said. 'Here's what I know.'

Samantha relayed everything Jasmine had shared. Roman listened intently, nodding every once in a while, his jaw tight. When she was done, he let out a sharp breath. 'First of all, Ted is the worst. You should know that. I met him a few times in the past and I never liked him.'

'I got that vibe.'

'Second, don't worry.' He stroked her bare arm with the back of his hand. 'I knew all this.'

'You *knew*?'

'Who do you think broke up that fight?' he said. 'I went over to speak with Anthony after I left you that night. I must've just missed Jasmine.'

'You knew and you didn't tell me?'

Samantha was outraged. Obviously, the Rum Punch Agreement wasn't as strong as the cocktail it was named after.

'Anthony asked me to keep it quiet,' he said. 'If it makes you feel better, I went to see him that night to ask about you.'

'Yeah? Like what?'

He smirked. 'The usual. Your sign ... Your favourite colour ...'

'Oh, shut up!' It was hard to stay mad when he was so cute.

'I've got Anthony's back. I'm willing to put on a tux and step in as best man if it comes to it.'

She pictured Roman in a well-cut tuxedo. 'Could you wear the tux, anyway?'

'For you? I'll consider it.'

They were way off track. 'You broke our agreement the same night we made it. To my mind, you owe me some information.'

'What do you want to know?' he asked.

'Is there some other reason Ted objected to the wedding, apart from the lightning-fast courtship?'

'I think that was it,' Roman said. 'Fun fact about Anthony: he's never been in love before.'

That was odd. 'Never?'

'Never,' Roman said. 'Naturally, people think he's gone and lost his mind.'

The follow-up question just leaped out. 'Have you ever been in love?'

'Yes,' he said, as matter of fact as ever.

Roman in love with someone, anyone, head over heels in love, drowning in love – well, she couldn't picture it. Or maybe she just didn't want to. The thought made her sick. It was best to move on. 'Do Anthony's parents approve of Naomi?'

He cocked his head. 'Approve?'

'I think you understand.'

'Naomi is smart and successful and gorgeous. Any man would be lucky—'

'You and I know that, but Ted wasn't sold.'

'Again, Ted has proven to be the worst kind of—'

'I got it the first time,' Samantha said. 'I'm trying to see if there's a trend here. Have you met them?'

'Anthony's folks? Briefly.'

'What sort of people are they?'

'Normal. Simple. One's a teacher. No … a school principal. The other … I don't remember. Anthony is their only kid.' After a pause, he said, 'They love me.'

'Well, you're not marrying their only child.'

'True.'

Roman hunched low and picked up a cracked seashell on the riverbank. After brushing it off, he planted it in her open palm. Samantha closed her fingers around it, hoping it gave her the courage needed for one last difficult question.

'Are Anthony's parents the sort to stop a wedding?'

'Babe, I can't vouch for them,' he replied. 'But who knows what they're thinking? Even if they were pulling a stunt, it wouldn't matter. There's nothing they can do. It's a done deal.'

Nothing rattled this man. He was certain everything would work out. She could use some of that certainty. After all, it was possible that Ted's abrupt and early departure had nothing to do with Anthony's parents' late arrival. Maybe they were all too thrilled for their only son, relieved that he'd found the love of his life at long last. Possible, but unlikely ... Unfortunately, the only two people who could shine a light on this were stuck at an airport hotel in Florida.

'If they don't show up tomorrow, it's safe to assume they don't want to be here,' Samantha said. 'And I don't want Naomi to be embarrassed, not on her wedding day. She's so proud, it would kill her. Besides, she and Anthony aren't doing anything wrong. Even if it turns out to be a huge mistake, so what? They'll deal with it. We'll deal with it. It'll be fine.'

A fresh wave of frustration washed over her. She looked around for a pebble to kick. Finding none, she aimed at a decent-sized rock – and stubbed her toe. *'Dammit!'*

Roman pulled her to him. He rocked her and kissed the top of her head. 'Calm down, baby. It's like you said. If tomorrow is a disaster, we'll deal with it.'

Samantha pressed her cheek to the flat of his chest. Roman had called her 'baby'. Rainbows formed inside her chest. Had she stumbled upon some neglected back door into heaven?

'As far as I know, Anthony's parents are good, decent people,' he continued. 'But I promise you this: if they pull any stunts, I'll straighten them out.'

Samantha clamped her mouth shut. If she uttered one word it would be 'love', as in 'I love you'. Clearly, Tobago had warped her brain. She blamed it on the enchanted waters of the Nylon Pool.

'Feel better?' he asked.

She nodded, and stepped away. 'No more secrets. OK?'

'I promise.'

As they slowly took the path back to the beach, Samantha lit up with an idea. 'Hey! Would it be rude to ask Chris to charter a plane for Anthony's parents?'

'More weird than rude,' he said.

'Come on! He must have access to a fleet of planes. He's filthy rich, you know?'

'Oh, I know,' Roman said.

'Did you, really? I had no idea.'

'Once we got talking, I figured it out.'

Roman and Chris *had* been talking a lot. Every now and then she'd caught them with their heads together. 'What have you been talking about?'

'Finance, investments, how things get done in the West Coast.'

She eyed him with suspicion. Roman's blank expression gave nothing away, not one hint. Would Roman ditch Wall Street for the West Coast? Next thing, he'd join Naomi and

Jen on long hikes and send her photos of the sun setting over the Hollywood hills.

'Anyway, Chris doesn't fly private,' Roman said. 'He's mindful of his carbon footprint.'

Bloody hell. That was pretty much on-brand for Chris.

'And there's no need to charter a plane,' Roman continued. 'Anthony's family will get here in the morning. There'll be a wedding in the afternoon.'

Samantha forced a smile. 'We're going to dance the night away and get drunk on champagne.'

He stopped walking to face her. 'You've got a deal.'

'I can't wait.' She tipped backwards just to look up at him.

'I love that you care so much,' he said quietly. 'Your friends are lucky to have you.'

'Maybe you should tell them,' she said. 'I don't think they know.'

'I'll book a plane with a banner if you like.'

'I'd like that,' she said. 'Could it fly over the wedding venue just when Naomi and Anthony are about to exchange their vows?'

'I don't see why not.'

Samantha raked her fingers through his short, cropped hair. 'You get me.'

'I think I do.'

She recalled the day they first met on the hidden path. She couldn't stand him then. She couldn't stay away from him now. Like the sea reaching out to the river, they'd made an unlikely connection. That had to mean something.

'Come on.' He draped an arm around her waist. 'If I don't eat, I'll kill somebody.'

After lunch, they stretched out on beach towels, basking in the sun. Samantha's head rested on Roman's lap. He was in a heated debate about American football stats with Anthony, Chris and Jason, but his fingers gently stroked her hair. Naomi had calmed down and was having a sleep. Jasmine and Jen were off searching for conch shells. Hugo and Adrian were talking quietly to the side. At some point, their discussion grew heated.

Samantha watched them out of the corner of her eye. Hugo, her most relaxed, most easygoing friend, was becoming increasingly animated. 'I'm through compromising!' he snapped.

Naomi, who could always feel a storm brewing, roused from her slumber and slipped off her sunglasses. Samantha had no idea what was going on between Hugo and Adrian, but Naomi knew how to fix it. She grabbed a red plastic cup and raised it high. 'Everyone! Sam has a few words to say.'

Samantha snapped to attention. 'I do?'

'You do,' Naomi whispered, brows furrowed. 'I asked you to say a few words at our rehearsal dinner.'

'Right!'

Roman likely felt her panicking. He kissed her. 'You got this.'

That was nice of him to say, but she didn't have this. In her backpack was a rough draft of a speech that she'd hoped to revise sometime today. That speech was no longer appropriate. It was chock full of platitudes about love and marriage, with some quotes pulled off the Internet. It could apply to just about anyone.

While Naomi got everyone to gather round and filled any empty cups, Samantha's mind raced. Next minute, she was standing with her friends, old and new, surrounding her. They waited expectantly. Roman stood back, giving her space. Samantha took a breath.

'I'd worked on a speech for today, but it's rubbish,' she admitted. 'So now I'm just going to talk from the heart and tell you how I feel about this trip, about all of you, and this wedding we're here to celebrate.'

'Hear! Hear!' Jason exclaimed, but it was premature and Jasmine shushed him.

'It's no secret I was a mess when I got here.'

'Don't be so hard on yourself,' Jen said, but Jasmine shushed her, too.

'I really was,' Samantha continued. She suddenly had a lot to say. This might not be the right time or forum for it, but she was going to say all the things swirling inside of her. 'I was bitter, angry and a little cynical. Naomi and Anthony kept talking about their great love, but I couldn't see it.'

Naomi stepped forward, ready to interrupt. Roman stopped her. 'You asked her to speak. Let her speak.'

Naomi backed down, still looking rather nervous.

'Here's what I want to say,' Samantha said. 'We weren't ready for your love. None of us were. We didn't understand. The emotions and experiences you were describing did not make sense to us. We thought you were living a fantasy. And then we came here, to this island paradise, and we saw it, lived it, and we can no longer deny your love is true. You showed us what real love looks like. Not only that, you showed us what it takes to fight for it. It's beautiful and inspiring and I believe we've all been changed. I have, for sure. Like I said, I was bitter and brokenhearted when I arrived here. I'd been dumped and was depressed about it. I didn't have much hope of ever finding my person and I didn't want to believe all the tales you were spinning. But you and Anthony inspired me to let new people in. Jasmine and Jason made me believe in magic. Chris and Jen taught me that love exists in quiet friendships. It doesn't have to be bold and boastful to be beautiful. Hugo and Adrian, you've always been role models for me. Having spent this time with you, I know the goal is to put a relationship first and work at it every day. There's no such thing as perfect.'

Samantha paused for a breath and turned to Roman. 'I came here thinking I would be the odd one out. I joked this wedding was a couples' retreat and that's not far from the truth. Roman, I'm glad to be in a couple with you, even for this short time. I believe we found magic. We've been at each other's throat and we've had each other's back. I'm the river and you're the sea. Normally we'd never have met. But I'm so glad we did meet … here, of all places.'

Roman stared at her, his big brown eyes cloudy with emotion. He moved to kiss her when Naomi interrupted.

'Now you really are stealing my thunder,' Naomi said, wiping away tears. 'This is supposed to be about Anthony and me.'

Roman kissed her anyway and whispered against her lips, 'We'll take this up later.'

Samantha was smiling broadly when she raised her cup. 'To Anthony! Good luck because you're going to need it!'

Laughter erupted. But there were also tears and hugs and loud congratulatory slaps on the back. All that came to a sharp end when Chris raised his voice. 'I don't want a quiet friendship!'

A hushed silence quickly spread. Chris had been standing to the side alone. His hand gripped a beer bottle, his knuckles white on the amber glass. 'I don't want it,' he repeated. 'Jen, I love you. And I want to be bold about it.'

Jen had her arms around Anthony for a congratulatory hug. Chris's outburst froze her in place, arms extended and jaw slack. All eyes shifted to her. Samantha sent good vibes her way. It was time for Jen to take *her* shot.

Chris handed his bottle to Adrian and stepped forward. 'I don't know if you still want me after all I put you through. If you give me a chance, I won't let you down. I will show up for you as you have always, *always* showed up for me.'

That did it. She snapped out of her stupor. She brought her hands to her chest as if her heart might leap free. 'Of course I still want you! I love you, Chris. I've always loved you. I didn't value it before because it was so free and so easy, but I was stupid. I'm not that girl anymore. All I want is you.'

Jen and Chris ran to each other. Feeling the love, everyone cried, 'Awwww!' and rushed to surround them. Everyone but Samantha, who stood rooted in the sand. Jen and Chris had done the impossible. They'd leaped over a void of confusion and doubt and made it safely to the other side. She was happy for them, deliriously happy. More than that, she was hopeful for herself.

When she tore her gaze away from the happy couple, her eyes met Roman's. He stood apart from the group, his expression soft, eyes fixed on her.

Every cliché held a grain of truth. It was possible to look across a crowd, lock eyes with the person who had a claim on your heart, and know without a doubt that you loved them.

CHAPTER TWENTY-TWO

That night, Amelia hosted a dinner for everyone who had managed to arrive in Tobago ahead of schedule and with a positive attitude. The bride and groom retired shortly after. Amelia insisted the couple catch up on their beauty sleep. The rest of them went out dancing at a nightspot recommended by Maya. She'd been there the night before with friends and was over it, which made it perfect for the 'older' crowd. Located in a gingerbread-style building in the centre of town, Harry's Hideaway featured a restaurant on the ground floor and a dance-hall on the second.

They filed up the narrow stairs and barrelled onto the dance floor. Samantha shook off the day's heavy emotional shadow. She'd straightened her hair, slipped on a sparkly halter top and jeans, and slathered on lip gloss. She was ready for a party.

The DJ played the summer's hits. The crowded dance floor walled them in. Roman gripped her by the waist and they moved together. The first and only time they'd danced, they'd been cautious, aware of the spark between them and afraid to fan it. This time, they fused together. He cupped her face and they shared a rum-laced kiss. She ran her hands down his back, moulding him to her. He whispered in her ear. 'Let's go.'

'But we just got here!'

She was only teasing. They could turn around and leave right now. This day had been one long test of her patience. From one group event to another, she was desperate to escape with Roman. She wanted to go back to his place, close the shutters on the world and have him all to herself. How much better would it be this time around now that they knew each other better? They'd figured each other out, all preferences known and noted. This was the good part, new and exciting yet familiar. They had two nights to experience it and she did not want to waste time. She didn't want to play into his hands, either. She wanted him to want her.

'How much longer until I get you alone?' he asked.

'Not long. I promise.'

A few songs later, Jason and Jasmine, the seasoned couple, were sipping rum and Coke at the bar. Jen and Chris, the newly minted couple, were making out in a corner. Adrian hadn't joined them, opting at the last minute to stay in, which meant Hugo was wild and free, dancing with a group of women from Trinidad on a girls' trip. She and Roman made their way to the edge of the dance floor.

'I'm going to the bar,' he said. 'Want anything?'

'Ice water.' She didn't plan on getting much beauty sleep tonight. However, if she reported for bridesmaid duty with a hangover, the bride would toss her into the pool to sober her up.

'I'll be right back.'

She pointed to the double doors behind her. 'I'll be out there.'

Samantha made her way through the crowd and stepped out onto a narrow terrace overlooking a quiet side street. The night air made her shiver. Hugo was in a corner, slumped on a wooden stool, nursing a beer. He called out to her, 'Hey, Sam!'

She went to him and ruffled his hair. 'What are you doing out here all alone? Where's your new girl gang?'

'I couldn't keep up.'

'I don't believe it.'

'Are you having a good time?' he asked.

Samantha leaned against the wooden rail. She felt light, bubbly. 'I'm going to have exceptional sex tonight. I mean premium, top-shelf sex. Possibly the best of my life.'

'*Maravilha!*' Hugo exclaimed. He raised his bottle high.

Samantha saw through the cheerful demeanour. She noticed the creases at the corners of his mouth. 'What's up with you?'

Hugo ran his hands through his curls. 'Nothing much.'

'Come on. You can talk to me.'

'What's there to say? Everyone else came here to find love or fall deeper in love. Meanwhile, it looks like Adrian and I are splitting up.'

Samantha's heart tanked. 'Don't say that!'

'It's true.'

This was a crisis. Apart from her parents, Hugo and Adrian were the most stable couple she knew. Even when she'd caught them arguing on the beach earlier, she hadn't worried for them. She'd assumed they'd work it out by sundown.

Samantha looked around for a free stool, dragged it over and sat next to him. 'Tell me everything.'

He shook his head. 'I'm not going to ruin your night.'

'Don't worry about that, just talk to me,' she said. 'This is my area of expertise.'

'One break-up makes you an expert?'

'I'm a quick study.'

Hugo slumped lower. 'I don't even know where to start.'

'Is it the move to the suburbs?' she asked. 'Is Weston truly horrendous?'

'It's fine for the rich moms, but it's not for me.'

'Damn.'

'But that's not it,' he said. 'It's *everything*.'

Samantha nodded. That made perfect sense to her. 'What else is going on?'

Hugo stared out ahead of him, his square jaw tight. 'He's got the money, which means he's got the leverage.'

'Oh my God, are you broke?' The question just flew out of her. Samantha clamped a hand over her mouth, mortified. 'Sorry! You don't have to answer that.'

Hugo didn't mind. 'I'm not *broke* broke. Business is good. But I'm a freelance graphic artist and he's a surgeon. At the end of the day, it's not apples and oranges. It's melons and grapes. Marrying rich is overrated. Don't do it.'

Samantha didn't make much money, either. That didn't mean she was going to let a well-off partner call the shots. 'You listen to me. You're not just any grape. You're Cabernet Sauvignon.'

'Calm down,' he said. 'I'm Chardonnay at best.'

'My favourite,' she said. 'If Adrian wants to live out his posh suburban dreams in a gated community, let him go. You rent a flat near a beach and start over. Life is too short to compromise.'

Hugo took a swig from his bottle, considering her words. 'You're off script,' he said. 'You're supposed to say, *love will find a way.*'

She didn't believe in that rubbish, not anymore. There was no rhyme or reason to love. People made of it what they liked. If

Hugo wasn't being heard or his contributions to his relationship were undervalued, love alone couldn't fix it.

'I want you to be happy. You deserve it.'

Samantha meant every word. Hugo brought so much light to their lives. It would be a tragedy if he, of all people, ended up miserable to please a man.

'I want you to be happy, too,' he said. 'Do you know what you're doing with Roman?'

'Not really.'

He nodded. 'That sounds about right.'

★★★

Roman found his way to her, and not long after they dipped out of Harry's Hideaway, hand in hand. However, her talk with Hugo had stung. The love bubble was leaking air fast. While they drove along the dark and quiet streets, she watched him, studied his sharp profile. He kept his eyes on the road and one hand on the wheel. There was so much about him she didn't know. She tried to convince herself it didn't matter. She was leaving soon. Their time in Tobago wasn't the start of anything. It wouldn't lead anywhere. This was the entire adventure, beginning, middle and end.

When they arrived at his place, he pulled into the carport and cut the engine. 'Now tell me what you're thinking.'

Typical. He could read her; with him, she was illiterate.

'The fun ends on Sunday.'

He reached out and stroked her cheek with the back of his hand, his knuckles grazing her jawline. The gesture was familiar. She filed it away for future reference.

She saw a shadow of an expression. He knew exactly what she was talking about. Until she'd met him, she firmly believed relationships had to last to have meaning, if not forever then at least more than a couple of dates. But this man had wrecked her in a few days. What they'd shared was somehow deeper, richer than her most stable relationship had been even in the best of times.

He got out of the car, went around to open the passenger door and helped her step out in perilous heels. They entered the house through the side door and under the glassy gaze of the cat. He locked the door behind them. The kitchen was tidy except for the little table that served as his desk. He opened the refrigerator and pulled out two beers. She declined, but it looked as if he needed one for courage. He twisted the cap open.

'Go on,' he said. 'Tell me what's really bothering you.'

Samantha hopped onto the tiled countertop. Her mind was blank. Naturally, she'd forgotten all the little things that had been plaguing her these last days. Her eyes fell on the desk again. It was a good place to start. On the surface, leaving your job and relocating to the Caribbean seemed like a boss move. What was the story behind it? Even if he were dissatisfied at work, surely there were less drastic ways to make a career change. Helping his grandfather with his business was generous. However, Naomi's words had stuck with her. Tobago was a place to heal. If Roman had come home with wounds and battle scars, she wanted to see them.

'Why are you really here?'

'In T and T, you mean?'

'Yes.'

'I think I told you.'

Samantha swung her legs. She knew how this was going to go. He was going to dance around her questions. In the end, he'd give her just enough to pacify her. She did not want to do this dance. *Screw it. Let's get back to having fun.* She wasn't going to interrogate him. Not tonight, anyway.

She slipped off the counter and went to him. She took the bottle out of his hands and took a swig. The beer felt cool going down her throat. Roman stood with his back to the refrigerator door, arms folded, eyes bright. It was time to get this night back on track. 'What else do you have in that refrigerator?'

His expression softened with relief. 'Let's see.'

There was a container of chicken empanadas, leftovers from Candy's Shop. 'Are you hungry now?' he asked. 'Or do you want to work up an appetite?'

She smirked and reached for the container.

They ate it cold and washed it down with beer. 'So good,' she murmured, her mouth full.

Roman had finished his empanada in just two bites. He wiped his fingers on a napkin and looked at her as if he were still hungry. He was leaning against the closed refrigerator door again. It was as if time had looped back to when they'd first arrived, before she'd pestered him with questions, giving them a chance to start again. She took a step toward him and rested her palms on the cool surface of the refrigerator, trapping him in place.

His eyes glimmered with amusement, but also pure, unadulterated desire. 'You make a move like that, you better be ready to back it up.'

'I'm ready.' She moved to kiss him.

Roman moved fast to regain the upper hand. He cupped her

chin and brought his mouth to hers. Her lips parted, welcoming the hard kiss. She lost herself in the thrill, allowed her hunger for him to consume her. He broke the kiss far too soon, leaving her gasping. Before she knew what was going on, he lifted her back onto the counter. Dizzy, she threaded her arms around his neck to hold steady. He pushed away the straps of her halter top and swept his lips down her throat, along her collar bone. Her breath came out sharp as he traced a trail with the tip of his nose down between her breasts, then up again to that spot at the base of her neck. He knew how to make her tremble.

'It wasn't just fun,' he said. 'You had the best of me.'

These gentle words, spoken in a rough baritone, ravaged her. He'd pinpointed the fear that she'd been too much of a coward to admit. It wasn't that she wanted this 'experience' to matter or their 'time together' to count for something, she wanted him to demonstrate in word or deed that she mattered to him. Once she boarded her plane, Sunday at two, it was over. He may not see her ever again. She wanted him to remember her for more than just a good time because she was never, ever going to forget him.

Tonight she would show him.

Samantha slipped the sparkly halter top over her head and tossed it over her shoulder. She caught a glimpse of that wicked, dirty grin before he knocked a stack of pots and pans off the counter in his rush to get to her. Samantha gasped. Roman dismissed it. 'Never mind that. I don't cook.'

She wrapped her legs around him. He gripped her and lifted her off the counter. Together they stumbled backwards, crashing into the refrigerator and it rocked on impact. Roman lost patience and raised her by the hips back onto the countertop. 'Sorry. I can't be bothered right now.'

'It's OK,' she assured him. It was more than OK. She watched him peel off her jeans, excitement pulsing through her. She reached for his belt buckle when a bolt of common sense struck. 'It's *not* OK! The condoms are in the bedroom.'

Roman swore, swept her up again, and hauled her into the bedroom.

★★★

Later, when they lay wrapped up in each other, their damp skin touching, it occurred to her that she'd been going about it the wrong way. When she asked about his past, he clammed up. His answers were short and deliberately vague, leaving her craving more. It drove her a little crazy. But most people hated talking about their past. In the end, what did it matter? The past was irrelevant. She was a carpe diem type of girl herself. What mattered was the future, the one he was striving toward. What was in his heart? What did he dream about at night?

She twisted around to face him and smoothed his brows with her fingertips. 'What do you dream about?' she asked, her voice raspy and low.

He rested a hand on the curve of her hip. 'Besides you?'

A smile parted her lips. Such a flirt. 'Yes, besides me. What are your dreams for the future?'

That lazy hand slid down the length of her thigh. 'Samantha,' he whispered. 'I only dream of you.'

She squeezed her eyes shut. It wasn't the answer she was seeking, but it was the one she wanted.

CHAPTER TWENTY-THREE

Samantha opened her eyes to dazzling sunlight. The bedroom window framed a lush banana tree, its large, flat leaves swaying lazily. A green iguana raced up the trunk. The bed was warm. Roman's arm, slung across her torso, weighed heavy. She couldn't recall the last time she'd greeted a new day with such love and gratitude. That warm feeling quickly drained away as a flood of dread washed through her.

'Jesus!'

She'd overslept. What time was it? Her phone was nowhere in sight.

Roman was out cold. He slept on his belly with one arm curled around a pillow, the other flung over her body. He looked adorable. But now wasn't the time for mindless observations. She gripped his shoulder and shook him. He growled in his sleep like a Rottweiler.

'Wake up!' she cried. 'We're late!'

He opened one eye and peered at her. His voice was husky. 'What time is it?'

'I don't know!' she cried.

With a heavy sigh, he rolled over and reached for his smart watch off the nightstand. 'Relax. It's only eight o'clock.'

She could not relax. She'd never intended to sleep over.

The guys were off the hook until four in the afternoon. The bridesmaids had a brunch at ten and a visit from a hairdresser at twelve. The make-up artist arrived at two. Naomi would be barking orders all day. She had to get going if she didn't want to get murdered today.

'I have to get back in time for brunch. I can't show up in last night's clothes.'

Roman grumbled something and tossed back the sheets. 'I'm up.'

She swept her gaze down the length of his naked body. 'I'd say you are.'

'Look, don't touch,' he said, and rolled out of bed.

It pained her to oblige.

Roman pulled a fresh pair of sweat pants from the wardrobe. Samantha went on a treasure hunt for her clothes. The strapless bra was first; she found it at the foot of the bed. Her underwear was next. Her jeans and sparkly top were where she'd left them, on the kitchen floor. The copper pots they'd knocked over the night before were scattered on the terracotta tiles. She quickly picked them up and set them neatly on the counter. The next thing she knew, she was hunched over the counter under the watchful eye of the cat curled up in a corner, close to tears. She'd never be back here. Pain drilled through her chest. This was it.

'Hey, Samantha!' Roman called out from the bedroom. 'Mind if I hang out at your place? I've got to take Anthony to the barber in a bit. Might as well stay at the resort instead of driving back and forth.'

Samantha took a second to collect herself and find some way to feign a cheery tone. 'Sure! Just remember to pack an overnight bag, too.'

Roman tossed his duffle bag onto the wooden bench under her bedroom window. 'So this is the famous four-poster bed?'

'Yes, it is.' Samantha took the garment bag with his suit and hung it in the wardrobe next to her bridesmaid's gown. 'Very sturdy.'

He wrapped his fingers around one of the carved mahogany posts. 'Is that a challenge?'

'Can't a woman comment on the sturdiness of a piece of furniture without a man taking it as a personal challenge?'

Roman stretched out on the bed and joined his hands behind his head. 'What can I say? We're fragile creatures.'

They grinned at each other. They'd made it back to the hotel at breakneck speed. Samantha had a whole hour to get ready for brunch. Finally, she could relax. Just then, both their mobile phones and Roman's watch chimed with text messages as if to mock her. Samantha scrambled around, looking for her phone. Roman only had to tap on his watch. 'Cool,' he said. 'Anthony's parents just got here.'

Samantha let out a shout. 'Crisis averted!'

Well, hell … It was finally here. Today was Naomi and Anthony's wedding day. All the obstacles were cleared out. This was really happening. She looked at Roman, misty-eyed.

He sat up in one smooth movement and stood at the centre of the room.

'Did you want to marry that guy?'

That guy? He meant Timothy, of course. Why bring him up now? The answer was yes. She had wanted to marry him. However, what seemed like the logical next step only weeks ago now seemed utterly absurd.

'Sure,' she said, trying to sound casual. 'It's only normal. We were together a while.'

The topic of marriage made her nervous. She had deleted her various wedding mood boards and trashed her bridal magazines. She'd vowed that going forward, she would no longer obsess over weddings. If she met someone nice and he decided he wanted to make it official, she'd keep it simple: quick vows and a party at a rooftop bar under a sprinkle of fairy lights. Maybe she'd honeymoon in Tobago. No. Never. Absolutely not. Tobago was for Roman. She could never be happy here with anyone else.

'What if he'd proposed at Nylon or Argyle? Would you have said yes?'

Samantha weighed her answer carefully. 'I spent all my time in Tobago flirting with a cocky American boy. I wouldn't have had it any other way.'

That got him to smile. She smiled back.

'If I proposed, what would you say?'

Her smile faded. He had to be teasing. 'I'd start by asking if you'd slipped on the rocks and hit your head.'

'And then what would you say?' he asked.

'I'd probably say no.' His expression clouded so suddenly, she knew she'd made a huge mistake. Men *were* fragile creatures, in need of constant reassuring. 'Only because we've known each other for one short week. If we were dating a month or so, obviously I'd say yes.'

'Sammy, I'm not proposing,' he said. 'I'm wondering if I'm your type. From everything I've heard about your ex, we are very different.'

'Let's get a couple of things straight.' Samantha darted an index finger at him, noting that her nail polish was chipped on

Naomi's big special day. 'First, you're right. You're not my type. Before you, I dated nice guys and we did all the usual things.'

'Dinner and a movie?' he suggested.

'Not so much. We sat at a pub for hours, eating and drinking.'

He frowned, judging. 'Sounds like a good time.'

'Second of all, you should know you're every woman's type.'

His brows soared up to his hairline, as if this were big news to him. 'Is that right?'

'Give it a rest, Roman. You see how women look at you.'

'I don't see other women.' He yanked her close. 'I just see you.'

'Oh, no!' Samantha shook her head. 'I'm not falling for that line.'

'Are you falling for me, Sammy?'

'I don't like it when you call me Sammy.'

The childhood nickname was cute. She didn't want Roman to think of her as cute.

'Samantha is so formal,' he complained. 'What do I call you when we're alone like this, no one else around, just you and me?'

'I don't know.' He could call her anything, *propose* anything, if he looked at her like that. It moved something inside her, the stone sealing off the crypt where she safely stored all her warm and fuzzy feelings.

He whispered in her ear. 'I can be a nice guy.'

She held his face between her hands. He hadn't shaved yet. He'd packed a kit and would get to it at some point before the wedding. Samantha enjoyed the feel of the rough, scratchy stubble. 'Somehow I doubt it.'

Roman tightened his hold on her. 'I can't believe you're leaving tomorrow.'

She pulled back to better meet his eyes. 'I wouldn't mind staying in touch.'

That mild statement was way better than what she truly wanted to say. *Please, don't let this be the last night I fall asleep in your arms and wake up happy.*

'I'll take you to the airport and we'll talk,' he said. 'I know it's improbable, but I would like to see you again. Would you like to see me?'

She said yes, even though deep inside she worried that if they met up again, and it was just as crazy wonderful, they'd still only be stealing time before a final goodbye.

'Right now, let's just focus on getting through the day.'

And to that end, she was in need of a strong cup of black tea. Roman craved black coffee. She checked the time on his watch. She had ten minutes to spare and then she really had to get hustling. 'I'll be right back.'

'And I'll hop in the shower, if that's all right.'

'Enjoy it,' she said. 'It's like a spa in there.'

In the tiny kitchen, Samantha brewed a cup of tea for herself and coffee for Roman. He was still in the shower when she returned to the bedroom with the cups brimming with scorching hot caffeinated beverages. She set them carefully on the chest of drawers and knocked on the bathroom door. 'Coffee is ready!' she called to him. 'I don't drink the stuff, so it might be crap.'

'Get in here!' Roman called out.

She cracked open the bathroom door. He likely couldn't hear her over the running water. 'I *said,* your coffee is ready!'

He cracked open the shower door. Hot fragrant steam swirled out and fogged the bathroom mirror. 'I said, get in here.'

'No. Absolutely not.'

This was not the time for fun and games. She'd intended to use her travel steamer to smooth out her wrinkled dress while he was in the shower. She couldn't show up looking rumpled. The wedding photographer would be standing by to snap candid photos of the event. None of that mattered when Roman said 'please'.

He was wet from the shower. Water beaded on his strong shoulders and rolled down his arms. He stared at her through the veil of steam, his expression resolute. It did something to her. Freed her of free will. Samantha let out a sigh. She'd never do anything to intentionally bring on Naomi's wrath, certainly not on her wedding day, of all days. But a girl had to shower.

'Give me one second.'

She went to grab her dress from the wardrobe and hung it on a hook on the bathroom door. One way or the other, the wrinkles would come out.

Undressing, she said, 'This is not what nice guys do.'

He cracked open the door a little wider to welcome her in. 'You were right about me. I'm not a nice guy.'

★★★

An hour later, Samantha raced barefoot along the stone-paved walkway that snaked around the resort grounds, her sandals dangling from her hands. Her damp hair trickled streams of water down her back. She stopped twice for directions before landing on the event space almost by accident. Fifteen minutes late and severely out of breath, she burst through the French doors into the Palm Lounge. 'I'm here! I made it!'

The set-up was lovely, all pink and gold. A table was set for five and a buffet had enough food for fifty. Brunch-appropriate music poured in from hidden speakers. Jasmine was alone at the table, snacking on a bowl of cut fruit. Jen was at the bar, uncorking a bottle of prosecco. Naomi and Maya were noticeably missing.

'It's OK, sweetie,' Jen said. 'We're the only ones here.'

'Come have a seat.' Jasmine held out the chair next to hers. 'What happened? Did you oversleep?'

Samantha nodded. Yes, she'd overslept, but then she'd fooled around in a shower, too. She'd keep that to herself.

'Well, you look fantastic,' Jen said. 'Mimosa?'

'Yes, please.' Samantha hobbled over to the table, fell into the chair and slipped on her heels.

All three looked fantastic in the black midi-length dresses they'd been instructed to wear. Jasmine's dress was actually a smart jumpsuit. Jen wore a simple knit column with capped sleeves. Samantha had chosen a linen slip dress with thin straps that was still slightly wrinkled. The bride was expected to wear white.

'Where are the others?' Samantha asked.

'Anthony's parents arrived an hour ago, so maybe that's screwing up the timeline.'

So long as she wasn't the one screwing the timeline, Samantha had no objection.

Jen handed out champagne flutes. 'Cheers, ladies! It's been a trip of a lifetime and I'm honoured to have met you.'

Jasmine clinked glasses with her. 'The honour was all ours.'

'This trip has been incredible,' Jen said. 'I'm leaving Tobago in a much better place than when I arrived. I'll never forget it.'

Jasmine gazed down at her ring. 'Neither will I.'

Samantha wouldn't either, but for very different reasons. She was leaving something precious behind, something with real potential. She couldn't stomach the idea of not seeing Roman again. He'd said they'd try to figure something out. What would that even look like? She and Timothy couldn't make a long-distance relationship work and he only lived the next city over. She knew from experience how it would go. In the beginning, they'd talk and text all the time. They'd block out hours for video calls. They'd go so far as planning a visit. Then life would get in the way. Slowly, they'd lose momentum. A missed call here or there, texts gone unanswered, trips cancelled and rescheduled. With so much distance between them, their conversation would be strained. She'd miss their easy banter. Exchanges would be limited to lighthearted text messages, heavy with emojis. Before long, she'd forget his smile and the sound of his voice.

The photographer arrived and proceeded to set up. Samantha sipped her mimosa and snapped out of her funk. The goal was to get through the day. Besides, Roman wasn't Timothy. It wasn't fair to compare the two. She wouldn't appreciate being compared to anyone in his past.

'Naomi may not make it,' Jasmine said. She sank her fork into a cube of melon. 'They have to welcome Anthony's parents, show them around, get them settled. I wish they would let us know so we can eat. I'm starving.'

Samantha was starving, too. She and Roman had skipped breakfast. Her tea was too cold by the time she'd got to it. She went over to the buffet table and helped herself to fruit salad. The spread was typical hotel continental breakfast fare with the addition of coconut dumplings, Naomi's favourite dish.

'So, Jen,' Jasmine said. 'You and Chris look so happy together. Want to spill the tea?'

'I do!' Jen cried. 'I'm dying to.'

Samantha quickly filled a bowl with chunks of pineapple,

mango and melon and rushed back to the table. She didn't want to miss this. 'Go on,' she said. 'I need details. Tell me everything.'

'Is it as good as you'd hoped?' Jasmine added.

A week of fun in the tropics had bleached Jen's hair and darkened her freckles. When she spoke of Chris, she got red in the face. 'Better! He's so gentle and patient. I thought he'd be shy or I'd have to teach him things, but no …'

As eager as Samantha was to hear about Chris's hidden talents, she was distracted by her phone. A short text from Roman popped on the screen.

Heads up: Trouble brewing.

Samantha instantly broke into a cold sweat. She stared at her phone trying to decipher the true meaning of the message. What trouble? He could have provided some context. How were they going to make a go at a long-distance thing if he couldn't communicate properly?

WHAT ARE YOU TALKING ABOUT? I NEED DETAILS. TELL. ME. EVERYTHING.

The all-caps message was quite an accomplishment, considering her heart was in her throat and her fingers unusually stiff. In any case, the text was never sent. The French doors burst open and this time Maya came tumbling in. 'It's official! All hell has broken loose.'

Samantha's fight or flight reflex kicked in. She hopped to her feet. Her phone slid off her lap and onto the terrazzo tile floor. Jasmine's fork soon joined it.

Jen clutched her chest. 'My God! What is it? You nearly gave me a heart attack.'

Samantha now appreciated Roman's heads-up text, however vague it was.

'Is it Anthony's parents?' Jasmine asked. 'Did they lose their luggage?'

'If his mom needs to borrow a dress for the wedding, I packed a few,' Jen said. 'Some are loose and forgiving and will fit most people.'

'What size shoe does she wear?' Jasmine asked.

'Who cares?' Maya shouted. 'There's not going to be a wedding!'

'*What?*' Samantha, Jasmine and Jen cried out in unison.

Maya crossed the room. She wore a black skintight stretchy mini dress that restricted her movement. Her black hair was slicked back into a tiny bun at the nape of her neck. Her dark brown skin was naturally flawless and she wore very little make-up. She pulled up a chair and joined them at the table, clasping her hands under her chin. She was visibly shaking. Jen got up and poured her a glass of water. She took a few gulps, steadied her breath, and said, 'This morning Mum summoned me to her bungalow to meet Anthony's parents. I lost track of time and showed up late—'

Jasmine couldn't take it anymore. 'Maya, for God's sake, get to the part where they cancel the wedding.'

'All I know is when I finally got there, Naomi was crying, Mum and Mrs Scott were screaming at each other, and Anthony was huddled in a corner with his dad and uncles. Roman was there, too.'

Jen reached for her mimosa. 'I can't deal.'

The photographer cleared his throat to grab their attention. 'I'll just step aside.'

They waited for the door to close behind him before picking up where they'd left off.

'I'm confused,' Jasmine said. 'Do you think they flew all this way just to contest the wedding?'

'I have no clue!' Maya cried. 'I rushed out of there and ran straight over.'

Samantha scolded her. 'Go back! You have to find out more.'

'I'm not going back there. It was a mad house. Also, pour me a mimosa. I need one.'

'Are you old enough to drink?' Jen asked.

Maya rolled her eyes. 'Calm down, sweetie. I'm British.'

Head pounding, Samantha scooped her phone off the floor and worked on a new message for Roman.

Maya says the wedding is off. What exactly is going on??????????????

She considered whether to add a few exclamation points to better convey her state of mind. Maya dropped another bombshell, forcing her to abandon her edits.

'Sam, I came looking for you. Go and fix this.'

Jasmine shook her head. 'That's a big ask.'

'If anyone can, it's her. Naomi listens to Sam.'

'About random stuff, sure,' Samantha said. 'This is beyond me.'

Naomi had withheld so much. She'd kept quiet about the argument which had prompted the best man to abruptly pack up and leave. She'd put on a happy face and got on with the wedding planning as if nothing had happened.

'Maybe Jen should go,' she suggested.

'Me?' Jen shrieked. 'Why me?'

'She may be more comfortable talking to you,' Samantha said. 'So much has been going on and Naomi hasn't told me any of it.'

Jen set her straight. 'She's not exactly pouring her heart out to me, either.'

'Don't feel bad,' Maya said. 'She's been super tight-lipped about everything. She gets like that when she's stressed.'

'Maya, you're the only one with a right to be there,' Samantha said. 'I can't just show up. It would be inappropriate.'

'Sam, you don't need a formal invitation to put out a fire.'

'She has a point,' Jasmine said. 'We can't just sit here.'

Wasn't that exactly what the three of them intended to do, sit here sipping mimosas and wait on her to report back with news?

Her phone buzzed in her hand.

We have to talk.

This last text from Roman made her realize that she hadn't actually answered any of his previous ones. She deleted the draft riddled with question marks and typed: **Meet me by the pool.**

Too crowded. Let's meet at the rum punch convention spot.

She smiled despite herself. **Perfect.**

Samantha rose to her feet and squared her shoulders. 'I'm off to meet Roman.'

'How is that going to help?' Maya asked.

'Together we'll figure something out.'

CHAPTER TWENTY-FOUR

Roman wasn't alone, which explained the need for privacy. Anthony was slumped on the very same lounge bed where she and Roman had forged their alliance that first night. He held his head in his hands. Roman leaned against the iron rail, arms folded. He looked as if he were standing guard, as if Anthony might do harm to himself or others. Just the sight of him reassured her.

Samantha rushed to him. 'How bad is it?'

'Pretty bad,' he said. 'Don't worry. We can turn things around.'

She couldn't help but notice the worry lines creasing his brow. She reached up and smoothed them away. What a mistake it had been to cancel morning yoga. Everyone was on edge.

She turned to the one person who could provide answers. 'Anthony, what's going on? All I got from Maya is that all hell broke loose.'

Anthony's explanation was succinct. 'My mother has no filter; she's always been that way. This time, she put her foot in her mouth. Now Naomi's crying. I can't believe this is happening on our wedding day.'

Samantha looked from him to Roman. Fear curled around her heart. What could Mrs Scott have said to cause the Goddess of Thunder to break down and cry? Honestly, she didn't want to know. She'd have to take the older woman down. That would be a shame after all the work she'd done on her inner peace.

'I don't know what to do,' Anthony muttered.

'Well, I do,' Roman said. 'Get your mother to apologize to Naomi *and* her mother.'

Anthony scoffed. 'Naomi won't accept a lame ass apology.'

'I can attest to that,' Samantha said. 'She absolutely won't. It has to feel real.'

'She will if she wants to marry you by sunset,' Roman said.

'We're already married!' Anthony bellowed.

Samantha tore away from Roman's embrace. 'Wait! What?'

Anthony looked up at her and blinked. 'We did the city hall thing. I thought you knew.'

'I didn't.'

Maybe it wasn't as big a deal as she was making it out to be. Maybe it was a formality to comply with California law. She scrolled through every conversation she'd ever had with Naomi regarding the wedding, but it was Amelia's words that popped into mind. She'd said Naomi was only interested in playing dress-up. Amelia knew this wedding was mere window dressing, and likely not very pleased about it.

She took Roman aside. 'Why didn't you tell me?'

'Baby, I found out twenty minutes ago. I tried texting you. You didn't answer.'

'Sorry about that. So much was going on.'

She gazed out at the view. The terrace overlooked a veranda where the hotel staff were setting up for the ceremony. They arranged white chairs into neat rows and tied flowers to the backs of each one. All this couldn't go to waste.

He took her hand. 'Look at me.'

She met his eyes and was hooked by the intensity there.

'None of this is about us,' he said. 'Let's focus on getting these two married.'

'Remarried.'

'Details,' he said. 'Are you with me?'

Samantha's breath caught. Was now a good time to tell him how sexy he was when he took charge? Probably not.

'All right,' she said. 'What did Anthony's mother say that was so outrageous?'

Roman turned to Anthony. 'Want to tell Sam what your mother said?'

'Not really,' Anthony replied. 'I'd prefer she hear it from Naomi.'

Naomi was the one person she hadn't heard from all morning. And she hadn't necessarily been forthcoming lately. Chances were she'd give her a glossy smile and tell her everything was going great.

'I'm so lost. How do you expect me to fix this? I don't have enough information.'

'We know enough to get the ball rolling.' Roman laid out the plan. 'Here's what we'll do. I'll work on getting Lucy to apologize.'

'That's Anthony's mother, right?'

He nodded. 'Mrs Scott.'

She tried to focus. Hunger had its claws in her now. She thought fondly of the fruit bowl she'd left behind. Maya had probably eaten it.

'Work on getting Naomi to accept the apology,' Roman continued. 'We'll move forward from there.'

Samantha didn't know what Lucy had said, but it had to be vile to cause all this drama. 'Naomi is not one to forgive and forget very easily.'

'You're missing the point,' he said.

'Oh?' She raised her chin, defiant. 'What am I missing?'

His answer surprised her. 'I want to dance with you tonight. For that to happen there has to be a wedding. We're going to make it work.'

Samantha's salty mood dissolved instantly. 'And here I thought your intentions were pure.'

'Eye on the prize, babe.'

His cocky smile made his brown eyes dance. To think she'd dreaded this wedding. Now she couldn't wait.

He took one of her limp locks and curled it round his finger. 'By the way, your hair is still wet.'

She smacked his hand away. 'And whose fault is that? I didn't get a chance to dry it this morning. I have a whole routine and it takes forever.'

'Sure,' he said. 'Blame it all on me. If I remember right, there were two people in that shower.'

If she remembered right, those two people were doing very naughty things.

'I'm going to need another shower before this wedding,' he said.

'Don't even think about it.'

On the other end of the terrace, Anthony was bouncing off the nonexistent walls. 'Hate to interrupt!' he cried out. 'I'm in crisis here!'

Roman tossed him a look over his shoulder. 'Get a grip! We're figuring it out.'

'He's right,' Samantha said. 'We should get going. Do we synchronize our watches?'

'Cutie,' he whispered, and drew her close for a kiss. 'Just answer my texts.'

'I'll do my best.'

Samantha's phone rang. She had left it on the cocktail table tucked between the lounge chairs. All three of them turned to stare at it. Anthony peeked at the screen. 'It's Naomi!' he cried. 'Answer it!'

Roman squeezed her waist. 'Go on.'

Samantha rushed to answer before the third ring. Out of breath and coming across unnaturally chipper, she said, 'Hey there!'

'Sam.' Naomi's tone was wet. 'Where are you?'

'Well, I *was* at brunch when—'

'*Shit!* I totally forgot about brunch! Did the photographer show up? Was the food OK? I ordered dumplings.'

'Never mind that. Where are *you*?'

'I'm hiding out at your bungalow.'

Maya was right. Naomi sought her out when things got crazy. Growing up, Naomi hid in Samantha's bedroom when Amelia was on the warpath. Together they'd strategize how best to get her back in her mother's good graces before the weekend came around. They could always figure something out. Why would it be any different now? It came down to something Samantha had always known: Naomi only allowed herself to be vulnerable around a handful of people, and she had the privilege of being one of them. She wouldn't let her down, not today of all days.

'I'll be right there.'

'Come alone,' she said, her voice shaking. 'I need to talk to someone who isn't my mother … or Anthony's mother.'

'Sure thing.'

Samantha tucked her phone in the pocket of her dress. She tucked away any lingering insecurities, too. From the beginning, she'd considered this destination wedding extravaganza a test of her friendship with Naomi. It wasn't. Their friendship was fine. Now it was time to act.

Anthony crept forward. 'What did she say?'

'She wants to talk. I'm going to meet with her.'

'Good,' Roman said. 'We're on track.'

'Could you please tell her I love her?' Anthony asked.

The poor guy looked a wreck. 'I'm sure she knows.'

He repeated his request, desperate. 'Could you tell her anyway?'

Samantha had struggled to distinguish the man from the fitness guru. On this fine morning she saw him for who he was, a guy with a finely chiselled face and body, but just a guy nonetheless.

'Let Sam handle this,' Roman said. 'She knows Naomi better than anyone. She'll know what to say.'

CHAPTER TWENTY-FIVE

Samantha found Naomi waiting for her on the porch swing. With her legs tucked beneath her and her cheeks wet, there was something almost childlike about her demeanour. Gone was the Goddess of Thunder. Samantha climbed the steps to the porch and stood before her. 'It's a fine day for a wedding.'

Naomi made a face. 'It's a little hot, if you ask me.'

'It'll cool down by sundown.'

'Sam, there's not going to be a wedding.'

'I came all this way for a wedding. There'd better be one.'

'Sorry to disappoint.'

'You'll disappoint your fiancé. He's a wreck.'

'You saw Anthony? I thought you were at brunch?'

'Well, I was, but then—'

'How is he?'

'Honestly? Not great. He says he loves you.'

'I'm a wreck, too.' Naomi wiped her cheeks with the back of her hand.

'Come inside. Samantha unlocked the door to the bungalow and escorted Naomi into the sitting area. Naomi collapsed onto the sofa with a long sigh. 'How did things get so bloody awful?'

Samantha handed her a bottled water from the refrigerator.

'Here is what I've gathered so far. Your future mother-in-law said something awful, which set off a chain reaction.'

Naomi shrugged. 'Everyone has been pretty much awful. Lucy had the courage to say what everyone was thinking.'

'Not true!' Samantha pushed aside her laptop and her crystals and sat down on the coffee table. 'Your friends have your back. We've been supportive.'

'That's rubbish, too.'

'Naomi! I resent that.'

'Give it a rest. You've been against this wedding from the start. You haven't even tried to get to know Anthony.'

Samantha's outrage stalled. To this day, she knew nothing about Anthony except that he was shredded and had a nice smile. She racked her brain for more. He was easygoing, playful, loyal, a sentimental fool who believed in love at first sight, and an only child who wanted a big family.

Samantha shot to her feet and grabbed a banana from the complimentary fruit basket on the kitchen counter. She had to eat something before she passed out. As she chewed on the overripe fruit, the gears of her brain started spinning. Anthony wanted a big family. Naomi wanted a mini van to join the neighbourhood carpool. By the time she sat back down on the coffee table, she'd connected all the dots. 'You're pregnant, aren't you?'

Naomi's gaze fell to the floor.

Samantha was hurt that her best friend would keep something this big from her. But they were no longer girls sharing secrets in a pillow fort. Anthony was Naomi's person now, not Jen, not anyone else. Samantha had to find her person, too. Someone to dream up a future with and share secrets deep in the night.

She knew for certain Timothy was not that person. She could not rule out Roman that easily, and that made her heart break just a little.

After a long stretch of silence, Naomi looked up and said, 'If we're going to dive into this, I'm going to need something strong to drink.'

Samantha was on it. 'Should I raid the mini bar? I haven't touched it because who can afford—'

'Tea, Sam,' Naomi said. 'I'd like a strong cup of tea, please.'

'Right.'

Naomi was pregnant. She wanted tea, not whisky. Why was she having trouble keeping up? She rummaged through a tin replenished daily by the housekeeping staff and came up with nothing stronger than an English breakfast. She held up the packet for Naomi's approval. 'This OK?'

'It's fine.'

A moment later, with her strong cup of tea in hand, Naomi was finally settled enough to begin. 'I didn't lie to you,' she said.

Samantha sat in a wicker armchair and propped her feet on the coffee table. 'About what, specifically?'

They were dealing with too many half-truths. She needed clarification.

Naomi rested a hand on her belly, which was as flat as an ironing board. 'When I told you Anthony proposed, you asked if I was pregnant. It was the first thing you asked. You didn't ask about the ring or any details about the proposal itself, which was lovely by the way. You only wanted to know why he'd bothered to do it. I was very upset.'

And she was clearly resentful, too. 'I'm sure I congratulated you first, Naomi. I have some manners.'

Naomi stared at her from over the rim of the paper cup. 'You get my point.'

'I was *stunned*, OK?' she said. 'First, you win a man at auction. Next, you're marrying him.'

'Don't say it like that! Anthony isn't a mail-order groom.'

'I know that now. But when you called with the news, I literally fell out of my office chair.'

Naomi resumed sipping her not-so-strong tea.

'I'm sorry,' Samantha said. 'How was I to know you were living a fairy tale?'

'I'm not,' Naomi said soberly. 'We're taking a chance. How were we to know it would throw everyone in a tailspin?'

'I'm not spinning,' Samantha said. 'Not anymore, anyway.'

'Anthony doesn't play it safe. He takes risks. I love that about him. When he started to train local celebrities, he realized he was onto something. Within a month, he sold everything except his car and moved to Los Angeles. It was a risk. His family wasn't supportive. They never are. They're too busy protecting him to ever *listen* to him. Part of the reason he moved was to get away from them, but that's another story.' Naomi paused for a breath. 'Anyway, look how well it turned out! He's one of the most popular fitness trainers in Hollywood.'

Samantha nodded, impressed. That was the sort of energy she needed to turn her life around. 'Roman says Anthony can make a person feel like they can do anything.'

Naomi laughed. 'That's true. He says we can make all our dreams come true, and I believe him.' She took a long sip from the cup and set it down. 'I'm not like you, Sam. We lived next door to each other, but we led very different lives.'

She needn't say more. Naomi had always envied Samantha's

219

boring, stable parents. Her parents' divorce wasn't as neat and tidy as they sometimes made it seem. It was a miserable, drawn-out affair. For as long as she could remember, they quarrelled. The slightest incident could provoke a row. It had to do with her father's gambling and her mother's reluctance to just leave him already.

One night she packed up Naomi and spent the night at a nearby motel. Naomi was about eight or so and hated the entire experience. To Samantha, it had sounded like the beginnings of a great adventure. When Naomi returned the next day, she told Samantha the room had smelled of cigarette smoke and pine air freshener. Still, it had been worth the sacrifice if it meant her mother was finally ready to walk away. Naomi loved her dad, but blamed him for the chaos in her life. Plenty of their friends had divorced parents and they were happy. A week later, Amelia discovered she was pregnant with Maya. There was no talk of divorce after that, not for a long time.

Eventually, Naomi's parents split up for good. Her father was the one to leave this time. By then, Naomi was thirteen and seemed to have bounced back from her early years. She brought home high grades, starred in every school play, and had loads of friends. It was quite an aggressive comeback, come to think of it. The energy she put in to rise like a phoenix could fuel a jet. Was it all to cover up a deeper longing? Was that the dream that she and Anthony shared? To have a stable home, filled with kids, love and support?

Samantha's eyes prickled with tears. All this talk of love at first sight had thrown everyone off. This wasn't a story about two people who'd locked eyes across a crowded room. This story involved two deeply wounded people who had found refuge in each other. What right did anyone have to question that?

'So when he proposed, I said yes,' Naomi continued. 'I wasn't drunk. I wasn't pregnant. I was in no way impaired. I said yes because I want a life with him.'

'But you're pregnant now?'

Naomi nodded. 'Eventually, we got drunk and celebrated. A month later, we were pregnant.'

'Thus fulfilling the prophecy.' So much made sense now. When Samantha arrived in Tobago, she'd had trouble connecting with this new, calm and mature version of Naomi and had no explanation for it. It also explained why she'd turned down a hen do, ate like crazy and only drank water, carried around water biscuits for queasiness, and retired early almost every night.

'Once we were sure, we went ahead and got a licence and took a trip to city hall. We wanted to be a family.'

'Congratulations. I'm happy for you two.'

'Thank you, Sam.' Naomi was smiling through tears now. 'I'm nervous. But Anthony is so excited. He's going to be the best dad.'

'And I get to be the cool aunt who brings sweets from the motherland.' Samantha was eager to establish a role for herself in this new world order. She was not going to be left behind.

'We didn't tell anyone because, well …' Naomi shrugged, defeated, 'we knew what you'd say.'

This got Samantha back to the reason Naomi was holed up in her bungalow, like some wartime bunker, drinking mediocre tea, hiding from everyone.

'What exactly did Anthony's sweet mum have to say?'

Naomi let out a small groan. 'It's stupid really. I might have overreacted.'

'If it's so stupid, could we get back to brunching?' Samantha asked.

Naomi looked down at her hands folded on her lap. Samantha couldn't help but notice her nail polish was chipped, too. An irrational anger coursed through her. This was her big special day. They were meant to brunch, laugh and pose for silly photos. Later, they had a glam session scheduled. There wasn't time for any of this drama.

'Is there even going to be a wedding today?' Samantha asked.

'I don't see the point.' Naomi's voice was small. 'The secret is out and—'

'Oh, who the hell cares?' Samantha's voice filled the room. 'The Naomi I know wouldn't let what anyone thinks or says keep her from going after what she wants.'

Naomi gave her a weary look. How exhausting it must have been to battle everyone's perceptions all this time! Unfortunately, the battle wasn't over. Good thing Samantha had enough juice to continue the fight.

She rose and planted her hands on her hips. 'If you don't want to tell me what went down with Anthony's parents, that's fine. But could we please—'

Naomi waved away her protest. 'Settle down. We're just getting to the good part.'

This was quintessential Naomi. She was in pain, hurt and confused, and still enjoying it. As ever, she was the main character in a film in which everyone else had minor supporting roles.

Samantha sat back down. 'Go on, then.'

The Connecticut contingent arrived promptly at 8 a.m. Naomi, Anthony, Amelia and her stepdad, Gregory, were standing ready to greet them. Eager to impress, Amelia wore a linen pantsuit. Naomi wore the billowy white dress she had set aside for the morning's brunch. Anthony got his height and green eyes from his lanky Irish dad and his dark, good looks from his petite Cuban mother. They unfolded from the car and took in their surroundings with glee. They 'oohed' and 'ahhed' over the resort's charm and the striking beauty of the lush mountains in the distance. Naomi could feel the tension roll off her mother's body. They were off to a good start.

This was the first time the families were meeting in person. All the video chats in the world couldn't make up for good old-fashioned face-to-face interaction. Naomi had only to look into her future mother-in-law's eyes to know that they were not out of the rainforest yet.

Anthony's favourite uncle, Peter, and his wife and kids pulled up in a second car. Anthony threw himself into his family's arms. The hotel staff took care of the luggage. Very soon, they were off to Amelia's bungalow for coffee, tea, scones and breakfast pastries.

It had been decided, well into last night, that Naomi and Anthony would announce the pregnancy to their families over breakfast. It was the right time to do it. Their sincere hope was that the announcement of the arrival of a grandchild would unify the two families. Excitement would boil over and melt any lingering ice. When the time came, Anthony winked at her. She was nervous and did not share his confidence. Deep inside, she'd wanted to keep their secret a while longer, bury it deep in her heart. She'd come this close to changing her mind when Anthony rose and tapped a spoon to a teacup and said the dreaded words. 'Naomi and I have something wonderful to share.'

At which point Amelia froze, dropped a scone and blurted, 'Daughter, are you pregnant?'

'Wait …' Now Samantha leaned forward and planted her elbows on her knees. 'She called you … daughter?'

Naomi threw her hands up. 'This is why I love you! When has that woman ever called me *daughter*? She was putting on such a show.'

Too stressed to laugh, Samantha coughed. 'This is insane.'

'It gets even crazier,' Naomi said. 'Everyone stops what they're doing and stares at me. The room is as quiet as a church. It's painfully awkward. I am dying inside. Finally, Anthony says yes, we're expecting a baby in February. Amelia starts to cry. She's overwhelmed with emotion and wants everyone to know. Anthony's dad and uncle congratulate us. Good old Gregory breaks out his stash of Cuban cigars. For a second, I'm fool enough to believe our plan has worked and then—'

Samantha was at the edge of her seat, just as Naomi wanted. 'Hurry up! My heart's going to explode.'

'Lucy Scott pulls me aside,' Naomi said. 'She wants to talk "woman to woman". We step out onto the porch. I figure she wants to welcome me into her family or share some thoughts on motherhood or whatever. Instead, she says she can tell that I'm overwhelmed from the look on my face.'

'Which you were, and understandably so.'

'There's more,' Naomi said. 'She offers to help in any way. Whatever I decide, she has my back. If I want to cancel the wedding, she'll talk to Anthony and get him to understand.'

Samantha's anger burst before her eyes like fireworks. 'You're joking!'

'I'm not.' Naomi's lips had flattened into one grim line, betraying how hurt she was.

'And you're not exaggerating or embellishing in any way?' Samantha asked.

Naomi shook her head. 'Not at all.'

'And what did you say to her? Please tell me you gave her a piece of your mind.'

Naomi shook her head. 'I didn't know what to say. Blame it on the baby hormones. All I could do was cry.'

Naomi started to cry again. Samantha leaped over the coffee table and joined her on the sofa. 'Please don't,' she whispered, pulling her in for a hug. But Naomi's tears doubled. Samantha held her close and let her cry for as long as she needed. 'It's OK,' she murmured. 'It's going to be OK.'

Her thoughts ran to Roman. He had to get Lucy Scott to apologize. The woman was brazen. Samantha did not envy him his task.

Naomi reached for her tea. After a few sips, she was composed enough to continue. 'Lucy carries on. She's sure Anthony is rushing me into marriage. In her opinion, he's always been impulsive, quick to rush into things. She would welcome her grandchild with love, but in this day and age, a pregnancy is no reason to marry.'

Samantha was feeling sick. 'Oh, God …'

'Predictably, Amelia opens a bottle of champagne and calls us in for one of her famous toasts. She takes one look at me and turns into the helicopter mum she never was. I mean … she went at it *hard*. I thought she was going to throw champagne in the poor woman's face.'

'It must have been spectacular.' Samantha could just picture it: Amelia finally finding an appropriate outlet for weeks and weeks of pent-up frustration and letting Lucy Scott have it.

Naomi sat up and crossed her legs. 'It was fabulous.'

Laughter ripped through Samantha. It must have been contagious because Naomi started to laugh, as well. Torrents of uncontrollable laughter poured from them. They slipped off the sofa onto the rough sisal rug, cackling with laughter.

'You should have seen Lucy's face!' Naomi managed to say between fits of laughter. 'She kept apologizing and apologizing. She said sorry so many times and … ugh! By then it was too late. Everything had gone off the rails. Amelia whisked me away and asked her to leave.'

They climbed back onto the sofa, gasping for air, still twitching with laughter. Naomi dabbed at the happy tears at the corners of her eyes. Samantha sobered up first. 'Roman is going to get Mrs Scott to apologize.'

Naomi dismissed her with a wave of a hand. 'She's done plenty of that.'

'Hmm.'

About an hour ago she, Roman and Anthony were convinced that a well-crafted apology could clean up this mess. Roman was actively negotiating the terms of the peace agreement now. It was a total and complete waste of time. Mrs Scott had said what she'd said, and probably meant it. Her opinion didn't matter, nor did anybody else's.

Samantha hopped to her feet. 'Come on! Get up! Time to get going!'

Naomi shot her a quizzical look. 'I'm not going anywhere.'

'Oh yes you are!' Naomi had had a good cry – and a good

laugh – and the time for rolling in the deep was over. 'Today is your wedding day and we're well behind schedule. It's time to clean up this mess and get back on track.'

'Have you lost your mind?' Naomi asked. 'I'm not giving that woman the satisfaction—'

'Respectfully, Naomi, this isn't about you and it isn't about *that woman*, either.'

Naomi brought her hand to her flat belly. 'It's about the baby.'

'Not even,' Samantha said. 'It's about the family you want to belong to, the one you want to start.'

There was a chance to set the tone for the future. They had to get it right. 'You and Anthony have convinced me that love is real and worth fighting for. Now you have to convince Lucy. Wedding or no wedding, she's going to be in your life forever. She's your child's grandmother. You can't just walk away.'

Naomi didn't need an apology – or approval. But she and Lucy had to reach some sort of understanding.

Naomi leaned forward and held her head in her hands. 'Christ! I'm starving!'

All Samantha had on hand was the bloody fruit basket and a tin of tea. 'Want a banana?'

'Yes, please.'

She grabbed the basket off the counter. 'If the baby turns out to be anything like Anthony, you're in trouble. He'll eat you out of house and home.'

'May we call him Timmy?' Naomi asked sweetly.

Samantha threatened her with the business end of a banana. 'Don't you dare!'

Naomi grabbed the banana, peeled it and stuffed her mouth. 'We should have gone to brunch,' she said between bites.

No truer words were ever spoken. Samantha was rinsing an apple for herself when she received another text message from Roman.

We're ready. How about you?

She quickly dried her hands and typed her answer. Not sure. How do we proceed?

We lock them in a room and leave them to it.

Could we lock ourselves in a room while they're at it? For safety reasons.

I don't see why not.

'Why are you giggling?' Samantha looked up from her phone to find Naomi glaring at her. 'I'm in a crisis and you're flirting with your new boyfriend.'

'You only have yourself to blame!' Samantha snapped. 'You practically threw me at him.'

'Now I need you back!' she insisted.

'Listen, my "boyfriend" was nice enough to arrange a peace summit for you and your mother-in-law-to-be. She wants to speak with you. Name your time and place.'

'Ha! You admit he's your boyfriend.'

'I admit nothing,' Samantha growled. 'Name your time and place.'

Naomi settled comfortably in the sofa. 'I'm not leaving this spot.'

'I'll have him bring her here.'

'Fine.'

She sent a reply to Roman. Now all there was left to do was wait.

CHAPTER TWENTY-SIX

Samantha was in her happy place, locked in a bedroom with Roman. Except they had their ears pressed to the wall, trying to hear what was being said in the next room. Naomi and Lucy now occupied her sitting area. Anthony was with them, but he'd been advised to keep his mouth shut. This clash of the titans required no male interference or arbitration.

At first, Naomi and Lucy's voices were loud enough for anyone to hear. Lucy opened with a suitable apology. She was heartsick for making a bride cry on her wedding day. Her intention wasn't to split up a happy couple. Naomi replied hotly that she found Lucy's statements hard to believe.

'My sister married when she was pregnant with Ted,' Lucy explained. 'A miserable marriage, which she regretted until the day she died, but that was a different time.'

'Not so different,' Naomi said. 'Children still need parents.'

'Parents don't need to be trapped in a loveless marriage.'

Anthony interfered at this point. 'Enough!' he bellowed. 'Naomi is not Aunt Paulina and our kid is not going to turn out like Ted.'

A static-filled silence spread throughout the bungalow. When the conversation resumed, it was in muted tones. Samantha gave up. She flopped onto her bed, taking Roman with her.

'How much is this due to plain old bad luck?' she asked. 'Everybody knows the groom is not supposed to see the bride on the wedding day.'

Roman propped himself up on an elbow. 'Can't your crystals clear the air?'

She considered this. 'I should have lit sage.'

'Whatever works,' he said.

She listened for their voices. 'At least they're not shouting anymore.'

'I need them to work this out,' Roman said. 'I'll be damned if I have to spend my last night with you talking Anthony off a ledge.'

Samantha grinned. 'We're salt of the earth people, aren't we?'

'Hey,' he said. 'We turned this whole shit show around.'

'True.'

'And we make one hell of a team.'

She slid a hand under his T-shirt and stroked his warm skin. 'We do work well together.'

He nuzzled her neck. 'Could we monetize this, d'you think?'

She drew him closer and breathed him in. 'You Wall Street boys … Is money always on your mind?'

Roman caught the lobe of her ear between his teeth and tugged. In her rush this morning, she'd forgotten to wear earrings. She would have forgotten underwear if he hadn't reminded her. The entire morning had been one great panicky mess. She couldn't wait until things slowed down later.

'I'll need a wedding date next year for Jasmine and Jason's wedding,' she said. 'Who knows what drama might unfold there? They might need our services. Maybe we could work out a fee schedule.'

Roman pulled away and ran a slow hand through her hair. 'Are you asking me to be your date?'

'In a roundabout sort of way.' They might make it if they had something to look forward to. 'Would you come?'

'Sam,' he whispered. 'When will you understand? I'll go anywhere for you.'

Unable to contain her joy, she pushed him onto his back and pinned him down with a kiss. A sloppy one, but sincere. She could never put it into words; her heart and mind were too much of a mess. He made her feel seen and understood, cared for and desired. Nothing made her giddier than the flash of his smile. She would go anywhere in the world if he were waiting.

The bedroom door suddenly flew open, startling Samantha. She gasped and pulled herself upright, her palms planted on Roman's chest and her thighs straddling his waist. Anthony filled the doorway, a smirk twisting his handsome features.

'What the hell, man?' Roman protested. 'Ever heard of knocking?'

Samantha's heart was slamming in her chest. She tried to move off Roman, but he held her in place with a hand on her bottom – which only made the optics worse.

'Sorry,' Anthony said. 'My bad, but we gotta get going. The wedding is on. We need to get haircuts and this lovely girl,' he gestured to Samantha straddling Roman, 'needs to do whatever is left on the day's schedule.'

This was tremendous news, the best possible outcome, but the timing! Lord! First Anthony and Naomi were conspiring to put them together, now they were conspiring to pull them apart. She touched Roman on the cheek. 'To be continued?'

He brought her hand to his mouth and kissed the palm. 'Bet on it.'

With a resigned little sigh, Samantha eased off Roman and climbed off the bed. She smoothed her wrinkled dress. 'All right. Let's go.'

Naomi and Lucy were still crying when Samantha walked in on them. Only this time, the tears were joyous. They were hugging and laughing, too. Samantha snapped a quick photo, certain this was the day's high point.

'OK, everybody! I'm getting married at five. Let's get moving!' Anthony said in the fitness coach voice that had made him famous.

'Actually, we're getting married at six,' Naomi corrected.

'Any time is Trinidad time!' he exclaimed, then grabbed Roman and his mother, blew a kiss to his bride, and took off.

Once they'd cleared out, Naomi turned to Samantha, beaming. 'Do you think there's still time for brunch?'

Samantha linked her arm through Naomi's. 'There's always time for brunch.'

***

Having given up on any semblance of normalcy, the remaining bridesmaids invited their friends and significant others to share the meal. When Naomi walked through the French doors, her heart set on coconut dumplings, she was greeted like a queen with cheers and 'Long live the bride!'

'What's going on?' Naomi cried.

Jasmine offered an explanation. 'Uh … We didn't want the food to go to waste.'

Maya told her the truth. 'We figured if there wasn't going to be a wedding, there might as well be a party.'

Prosecco flowed. Dance music boomed from the speakers. The dining table was pushed aside to make a dance floor. The new guests ignored the strict black dress code and showed up in their brightest, busiest beachwear.

'There's going to be a wedding!' she snapped. 'Nothing has changed.'

'Don't get cross with me,' Maya said. 'I'm entertaining *your* guests. Everyone was freaking out.'

Naomi looked slightly alarmed. 'Everyone knows?'

'They know there's drama,' Maya said. 'But even I don't know the details.'

'Don't worry. Mum will clue you in.'

Naomi ventured into the party, climbed onto a chair – which Samantha wasn't sure a woman in her condition ought to do – and waved a pink cloth napkin in the air. 'Your attention, please!'

She waited until a hushed silence settled in the room. Someone tactfully lowered the music. Naomi in her white cotton sundress, hair smoothed back in a simple bun, was beaming with joy. No one would ever guess she'd been crying moments earlier.

'Thank you all for coming,' she said, as if the impromptu party had been in the schedule all along. 'As you may have heard, there was some drama this morning, just a bit. All of that is sorted and we're back on track.'

'What's a wedding without some drama?' Jason called out. Samantha noticed that he was a little pink in the face.

'Exactly!' Naomi said. 'Now let's have some fun.'

More cheers, music, and the party kicked off in earnest. A gentleman, Adrian rushed forward to help Naomi down from the chair. Hugo made a beeline for Samantha. He was thoughtful enough to bring refreshments. 'Here, *gata*,' he said, pouring her a glass of fizzy wine. 'You deserve this.'

'I do, don't I?' Samantha took the offered champagne flute.

'You badass,' Hugo said. 'You singlehandedly kept the love boat from sinking.'

'I had help. Roman came through.'

He raised his glass for a toast. 'Teamwork makes the dream work.'

'How about you?' Samantha looked around and spotted Adrian clear across the room chatting with Chris and Jen. Still, she lowered her voice. 'How are things going with Adrian?'

'Downhill.'

'Oh, no!' Samantha lost her fizzy wine buzz.

'We've decided to shelve any talk of moving until we get home. From here on out, it's day drinking and dancing. If there's any drama, it won't come from me.'

'Day drinking and dancing sounds great, but I hate that you're upset.'

'I'm not. I'm frustrated. Drinking and dancing will take care of it.' He did a little dance, shaking his hips. 'Let's go!'

Frowning, Samantha set her glass down and followed him to the dance floor.

From the day she'd met two of her best friends, Samantha was drawn to Jasmine's ease and grace and Hugo's *joie de vivre*, the authentic kind, not this fake stuff he was serving up now. He was tense beneath the tan and his devilish little grin didn't quite reach his eyes. Even his dance moves were rote, uninspired. She sensed there was more drama to come.

How was it that they were all leading double lives? They hid so much from each other. Naomi's secret pregnancy, Jasmine's feud with her mother, Hugo's imperfect perfect marriage ... all this time they'd chatted nonstop about the shows they watched, the shoes they splurged on, the celebrity couples they obsessed over. They exchanged memes like crazy. No social media scandal went unexamined. Meanwhile their everyday burdens stayed buried.

Who was she to complain, really? Hadn't she kept her break-up a secret, not revealing it until the last minute? And even then, she'd withheld as many details as she possibly could. Advanced torture techniques couldn't get her to admit she'd been dumped. This was wrong. It had taken a once-in-a-lifetime reunion on a Caribbean island to get all this stuff out. Going forward, they had to do better.

Jen danced toward her. 'Get out of your head! Loosen up!'

That was easy for her to say. She got to stay here and unwind while Samantha went through an emotional spin cycle.

The doors flew open and a freshly shaved groom strutted in. 'I hear there's a party!'

'You can't be here!' Jen cried, no longer feeling loose. 'It's bad luck to see the bride on the wedding day!'

That outburst was a waste of breath. The bride threw herself in her groom's arms. He picked her up and spun her around to the delight of everyone. Samantha was just as taken by the happy couple as anyone, but she kept her eyes on the door, watching for Roman. After two seconds, she lost patience and asked Anthony outright.

'He's not far,' Anthony replied. 'One of the caterers stopped him to ask about his grandmother. It was sweet.'

It *was* sweet. It was also a stark reminder that she hadn't met

Roman's grandmother and likely never would. Their time was running out. Now that the happy couple's future was secure, Samantha had to focus on her own happiness.

She slunk out of the party unnoticed. As she hurried down the path, she heard Roman call out her name. She stopped and swivelled around. There he was, heading toward her from the opposite direction, cutting through the grass, clean shaven and fresh as the day. She was slightly resentful that fifteen minutes in a barber's chair was all it took to complete a man's glow-up.

'Where are you sneaking off to?'

'I was looking for you.'

He had reached her with a few strides. Now he was towering over her as usual. She did that thing where she let her head fall back to gaze up at him. He did that thing where he bent forward and touched the tip of his nose to hers.

'Don't you want to stay and party with your friends?' he asked.

'If I know Amelia, and I do, she will shut down this party in a few short minutes. When she does, we won't want to be there.'

'You're right. Let's get out of here.' He tucked her arm under his and their steps fell in line. 'I hear there'll be something of a rehearsal at three and then you'll be in lockdown until sundown.'

Samantha slapped a palm to her forehead. 'I can't deal with all these changes!'

'But it's early still,' he said. 'That gives us a few hours. What would you like to do?'

She ran down the mental list of all the things they hadn't had a chance to do. Top of the list was a midnight swim. Would a midday swim make up for it? 'The pool is likely deserted. We could go there.'

'I came around that way. Anthony's nephews have taken it over. But I know somewhere we could go.'

'You do?'

'You didn't think there was just one pool in this entire resort, did you?'

'Actually, yes.'

'Well, you're wrong. Come with me.'

***

The heated whirlpool was located in a remote corner of the property. Samantha slipped into the warm, churning waters, and sighed with delight. 'I can't believe this oasis was here all this time. How do you know about it?'

'The guys hung out here the night before you arrived, drinking beer and talking trash. A low-key bachelor party.'

'Not fair! Naomi didn't get a hen do.'

They should have insisted on a girls' night out. Sheet masks and Chardonnay didn't count.

'It wasn't planned. Her doctor didn't approve of her simmering in a tub of hot water in her condition.'

'You knew about the pregnancy.'

'I was sworn to secrecy about that, too.'

Roman came closer. Water swirled between their bodies. His hand found the curve of her hip and rested there. 'What's the matter? You look upset.'

'I'm not … it's just …' He waited expectantly while she grappled with what to say. 'It took this trip for me to realize that my friends and I are not as close as I thought. We keep so much from each other.'

'I don't believe that,' he said. 'There's so much love there. I'm envious.'

'All you have to do is say the word and they'll count you in. They love you, too.'

'That love is conditional,' he said. 'They'd kill me if I ever hurt you. I can see it in their eyes.'

Samantha took his newly smooth-shaven face between her wet hands. 'Don't hurt me, then.'

'I don't plan to.' He studied her quietly. 'Did they hurt your feelings?'

'They wouldn't. Not intentionally, anyway. So many secrets have come out these last few days, it's made me wonder. I had no idea they were dealing with so much. I thought their lives were perfect.'

Roman was pensive. 'Is that the measure of a friendship? The number of secrets you share?'

'Not a measure … an indicator. If not, what do you have? Just gossip and small talk to fill the time.'

'Not everything is worth sharing.' He kissed her neck, sending a shiver down her body. 'Some things are better left dead.'

He *would* say that. 'How many bodies are you hiding, Roman Carver?'

He grinned. 'A whole lot. I won't lie.'

'Are you secretly married?'

'No.'

'Secretly divorced.'

'No.'

'Are you in the CIA?'

'I'd like that, but no.'

'What is it, then?'

He kissed her shoulder. 'Right now, you like me. I don't want to mess with that.'

'That bad, huh?'

'It's not good.'

'Are you a fugitive?'

'Stop.'

He kissed the freckles between her breasts, making her ache inside. Before her thoughts unravelled, she had to make this last point. 'I'll like you no matter what.'

'You say that now. Wait until my probation officer shows up.'

'Are you kidding?'

'I'm kidding.' He pulled away from her. 'How about this? Tomorrow, we skip whatever is on the schedule, sleep in, order breakfast and talk.'

So tomorrow they would talk about their future *and* his past. That was a lot of ground to cover. How convenient for him that all this revelatory conversation was scheduled for the day of her departure.

'Why delay it?' She'd much rather have the difficult conversations now.

'Because look at where we are, Samantha. Think of all the things we could be doing.'

He was right. They were in paradise and all she could do was obsess about the past. Had she crossed the line of healthy curiosity?

'How about some rapid-fire questions?' she proposed. 'You can't overthink your answers. Just say what comes to mind.'

He looked uncomfortable. 'OK. What are the topics?'

'All of them. We'll start with dentistry. Were your teeth always that straight or did you get work done.'

'Braces at sixteen.'

She splashed him with water. 'See? Easy!'

Roman went quiet, as he tended to do when deep in thought. 'I'll answer the question you haven't asked, but first tell me why it matters. What will my answer change between us?'

'I want to know you,' she said. 'My ex and I never talked, not about anything important. I don't want to fall into that habit again.'

'Well, I'm not your ex.'

She reached out for him, entangling her legs with his under the water. 'I know that, but give me something.'

'Once I was in love. I messed it up. Does that make you want to run?'

'I think I'm past that point,' she admitted.

'Same here,' he said. 'You're stuck with me.'

'Were you hurt?' she asked. In most cases, a nasty break-up was a two-car crash.

'Pretty bad, but I'm over it.'

Samantha had so many questions. Who was this person? How long ago was this? And just how bad was 'bad'?

Roman had a single question that negated all others. 'May I kiss you now?'

It was suddenly very hot in the hot tub. 'Please.'

CHAPTER TWENTY-SEVEN

After a quickie rehearsal, the wedding party retreated to their respective bungalows for much-needed rest. She and Roman had curled up on her bed for a long nap. Later, they locked up and left together. She was on her way to Amelia's for an intensive glam session: hair, make-up, the works. Roman was off to join Anthony after discovering a stream of messages demanding to know where he'd gone and what he was up to and why he wasn't replying to any of his texts.

'I won't see you until sunset,' he said.

He was walking away backwards, as he'd done that first night. Her heart swelled with nostalgia. She wanted to do it all again. 'That sounds romantic.'

'Except it's not our happy ending, is it?'

Samantha wasn't so sure. She'd dreaded this day. Now it was shaping up to be the best day of her life. 'That's fine! I don't believe in fairy tales.'

'What?'

He was too far along for them to carry on like this. 'Never mind!'

'What?'

'Careful! Look out for the tree!'

Before she could finish her sentence, he'd veered off the path and slammed into a skinny palm. He bounced back with his usual grace, but that didn't stop Samantha from laughing. 'Ha!'

He grinned, waved goodbye, and disappeared around a bend. Samantha fought the urge to chase after him for one more hug, one last kiss. It wasn't like her to be so needy. If she couldn't collect herself now, how was she going to handle tomorrow? Would she cling to him at the airport gate?

She forced the gloomy feelings out of her mind and headed down the path leading to Amelia's domain, lugging her make-up kit and bridesmaid's dress in its garment bag. She wondered whether a glam session was even necessary. She felt gorgeous. She wouldn't brag about it, but that was how she truly felt deep inside. Roman made her feel beautiful with every look, every touch. He couldn't keep his hands off her wild hair, said outrageous things just to catch her smile. She could wear a potato sack to the wedding and still feel like the most beautiful woman there, although it was best not to test that theory.

Maya greeted her at the door, took custody of the garment bag with her bridesmaid's dress, and invited her in. Once she got a glimpse of what was in store for them, Samantha got into the spirit of things. The vast living area had been transformed into a day spa. Rattan peacock chairs were arranged in a semi-circle, uniformed aestheticians set up mani-pedi stations. They sprinkled pink and red hibiscus petals and drops of essential oil into foot baths. Flickering candles and soothing music added to the vibe. She wondered why she'd ever questioned this. Of course, this was necessary.

Amelia handed her a cup of cocoa tea. 'It does all the good things that coffee does and none of the bad.'

'Thank you.'

As she accepted the cup, Samantha asked herself if this was the same woman who'd come close to emptying a bottle of champagne on another woman's head mere hours earlier. She couldn't get over Amelia's calm demeanour. It was as if the morning's unpleasantness had happened to someone else. In a lavender silk housecoat with 'Mother of the Bride' embroidered on the lapel, she was ever the sophisticated host. Samantha understood at that moment that the wedding had never been in peril. Amelia would have never allowed it, not after all the trouble and expense she'd gone through.

Amelia nudged her along. 'Go join the others.'

The others were scattered about. Naomi was already soaking her feet, headphones on, eyes closed, taking deep rhythmic breaths. Jen was gabbing to anyone who'd listen about the virtues of guided meditation. Jasmine was in a corner, tapping on her phone. Samantha assumed she was texting Jason, but when she put away her phone and reached for her own cup of cocoa tea, she announced that Hugo would be joining them.

Maya squealed with joy. 'Yay! He's my favourite.'

Samantha took her tea to her appointed chair, to the right of the bride. 'Good to know, Maya.'

'I'll always love you, Sam!' Maya fired back.

At Maya's directive, a chair was added to the circle and a pedicure bowl placed at its feet.

Jen took the seat to Naomi's left. 'I hate to bring this up now 'cause we're all so cosy, but I don't think Hugo and Adrian are clicking.'

Jasmine responded with a sad little smile. 'That's why I told him to join us here. He needs a break.'

Samantha thought back to the evening when Adrian and Jason arrived to great fanfare. How happy they'd seemed to be reunited with their partners. Now Hugo and Adrian couldn't stand to be together. How easily happiness unravelled. It was heartbreaking.

Jen had a plan. 'Let's lock them in a bedroom until they reconcile their differences.'

Naomi slipped off her headphones. She'd been listening all along. 'If anyone locked me in a room with a soon-to-be ex, I promise you only one of us would come out alive. And it wouldn't be him … or her.'

If there was a woman among Naomi's exes, this was the first Samantha had heard of it.

Naomi offered her an indulgent smile. 'Don't look so shocked, Sammy. I don't tell you everything.'

'Correction: you don't tell me *anything.*'

Naomi's smile grew even more indulgent. 'Not true. I tell you everything that matters.'

'Anyway,' Jasmine continued. 'Hugo wanted to work on his marriage on this trip. You recall him saying that, right, Sam?'

'In passing … but I thought nothing of it.' He'd tossed out the comment as if it were a punchline to a private joke. She hadn't thought to ask why his marriage needed work in the first place.

'Neither did I,' Jasmine said. 'And I probably shouldn't be telling you this.'

'You absolutely should,' Naomi interjected. 'Anthony and I have been speculating on this all week. We need a resolution.'

'All week? Really?' Samantha teased. 'Didn't you two have a wedding to plan, a life to envision?'

'It's not just them,' Jen said. 'Chris and I are invested in this, too.'

'Is that all couples do?' Samantha wondered.

'You tell us,' Naomi said. 'You were in a couple just last week.'

'She's in a couple now,' Jen said. 'Don't forget.'

'Believe it or not, Roman and I don't spend our time gossiping about other couples.'

'We get it,' Jen interrupted. 'Don't rub it in.'

'Give it a few months,' Jasmine said. 'Jason has been hanging out with Adrian and he's learned a thing or two. I'm only telling you guys because this is a circle of trust.'

'It's a semicircle,' Maya said. 'But go on.'

Samantha had learned a thing or two straight from Hugo. She wouldn't betray his confidence, but she wasn't opposed to hearing what Jasmine had to say.

'Jason told Adrian that he and I haven't nailed down where we want to live after the wedding: Montreal, Toronto or even England if Jason is asked to relocate.'

'I'd love that!' Samantha cried.

'I know!' Jasmine cried.

'And then what?' Maya asked.

'It seems Adrian came prepared to deliver an ultimatum about the move to Weston. We assume he's followed through on that and Hugo isn't taking it well.'

'An ultimatum?' Jen cackled. 'Like that ever works.'

'Their condo is in his name,' Jasmine explained. 'And it looks like he's prepared to sell.'

Jen sipped her tea. 'I'd follow Chris anywhere.'

Naomi looked sharply at her. 'It's not just a change of address.

It's a complete change of lifestyle. They have to be on the same page.'

Something occurred to Samantha. 'Adrian probably wants kids. Why else move to the suburbs?'

Naomi's hand went to her lower belly, a gesture only Samantha caught.

'The American Dream,' Jen mused. 'Two kids and a two-car garage. What's the British version of that?'

'Who knows?' Naomi said. 'A gin and tonic at the end of the day? We're not fussy.'

'I'm on Hugo's side,' Jasmine said. 'Adrian can't bully his way into starting a family.'

Samantha wished it wouldn't come to picking sides.

Just then, Hugo arrived.

Amelia greeted him at the door. 'Come in. The girls are inside. We're just getting started.'

'Thanks for including me,' he replied sheepishly.

Amelia served him tea. 'You're always welcome, dear. Take a seat next to Sam.'

She welcomed him with open arms. 'Come to us!'

Hugo slipped off his flip-flops and dipped his feet in the warm water bath. 'I hope I'm not messing with your feminine mystique.'

'Don't be stupid,' Naomi said. 'We were about to summon Venus, but we can wait on that.'

'I'm not exactly from Mars,' Hugo quipped. 'She might make an exception for me.'

'She may,' Naomi replied. 'As long as you're ready to paint your nails and talk trash about boys, there shouldn't be a problem.'

'Count me in.'

'Hold on!' Jasmine said. 'Before we dive into trash-talking, there's something I've meant to ask Sam. How's the blog going?'

She blinked, caught off guard. 'It's going, I suppose.'

'Just checking in,' Jasmine said. 'I mean … you packed all that equipment. Consider me your accountability coach.'

Naomi yawned. 'Don't let us stifle your creativity, Sam. I know we can be a bit much.'

Jen offered her photography services. 'If you need to stage a photo shoot at dawn, I'm your girl.'

Samantha sipped her tea. 'Thanks.'

Hugo sighed. 'I had a blog once. It didn't last long.'

'It's a lot of work,' Naomi said. 'Have you decided on your niche?'

'Travel is good.'

'Travel is broad.'

'Narrow the scope or go the clickbait route,' Jen suggested. 'Ten places to visit before you die, before you turn thirty …'

'Before you marry your sugar daddy,' Hugo chimed.

Jen laughed. 'Good one!'

'Before you marry for money, consider visiting Monaco or Marrakesh,' Naomi droned with the inflectionless tone of a television broadcaster.

Jasmine pushed past the noise. 'Narrowing your scope isn't a bad idea. I have my go-to eco-tourism blogs. I check with them before each trip to make sure I don't miss anything.'

Jen's eyes went dreamy. 'I live for a hotel room tour. Show me the bed. Show me the view. Show me the clawfoot tub.'

'Double down on photography and video,' Hugo suggested. 'From now on I want to see a camera in your hand. It doesn't matter if you piss people off. You're making content.'

'It wouldn't kill you to hop on some dance trends,' Maya said, reminding them all of her presence.

Suddenly her friends were social media mavens. Samantha mimed taking notes. 'Hotel rooms. Dance trends. What else?' She caught Jasmine's eye and realized that she was doing the very thing she'd accused everyone else of doing, glazing over the hard truth with humour. It had to stop.

There was a brief pause in the relentless onslaught of encouragement during which they chose their nail polish colours. The bridesmaids agreed on classic red, the bride went with traditional pink, and Hugo chose a striking electric blue.

'I'm no longer sure about a travel blog,' Samantha blurted.

'But you've been dreaming of travelling since we were kids,' Naomi said.

'I've dreamed of spontaneous trips with friends. We book a cheap hotel, drink cheap wine, sleep in, get out at some point to see the sites.'

Jen nodded her approval. 'All of that sounds amazing, except for the cheap hotel part. Not really my style.'

'My point is: I don't want to document the experience. I want to live it.'

Naomi urged her to do both. 'It's called multitasking. You're too good a writer to give up.'

'I'm not giving up on anything.' Samantha looked from one to the other, trying to decide whether this was the right time to float her idea. After careful consideration, she decided to hell with it. 'I'd like to write about us.'

Jasmine studied her cuticles. 'You can't mean *us*?'

'That's exactly what I mean,' Samantha said. 'Roman read some of my draft posts and he thinks—'

Naomi's big-sister instinct kicked in. 'I don't care what Roman thinks. What do *you* think?'

Heat spread across Samantha's face. 'I think I can do more than a generic travel blog.'

Jasmine took her self-appointed coaching duties seriously. 'We're listening.'

'I want to write about my travels, but I want to write about my life, too. That includes all of you. We've all been through a lot this past year alone. I'm interested in writing how we've processed and dealt with our issues.'

'We still have issues,' Hugo said. 'It's an ongoing thing.'

'I agree, yet sometimes it's hard to tell.' Samantha shot a look at Naomi. 'We don't always talk about the things that matter.'

'Who started that trend?' Naomi asked hotly. 'Does the great late break-up announcement via group chat ring any bells? I came close to having a stroke.'

'You're as tight-lipped as she is,' Hugo said. 'I figured it had something to do with your uptight British upbringing.'

'You're one to talk,' Naomi snapped. 'All you do is send out silly memes.'

'Memes are my love language.'

'I'm willing to admit I don't share as much as I should,' Jasmine said, contrite. 'Going forward, we'll all do better.'

Naomi reached over and squeezed Samantha's hand. 'I say this with love. Nobody gives a damn about us.'

'Not true,' Samantha said. 'They don't have to know us or love us to relate to what we're going through. Take our relationships with our parents. I'm sure people would like to know how to handle conservative parents, or divorced parents, or—'

'Absentee parents?' Jen offered.

Hugo chimed in. 'Or parents who wanted you to be a doctor, so you marry one?'

'Or perfectly wonderful parents like yours,' Naomi said. 'What could you reproach Patrick and Diane about? They're lovely. I'm still disappointed they chose not to attend the wedding.'

Patrick and Diane would never cross the pond and then catch another plane to cross the Caribbean just to attend a wedding. 'My parents are cautious people who never venture far from home. I love them, but I don't want to turn out like them.'

Hugo was the first to get on board. 'Write about me all you like. My life is an open book.'

Naomi was still on the fence. 'Would you change names to protect the innocent?'

'I wouldn't name names. Like you said, no one cares about us. I'd use our issues as starting points. If it sounds vague, it's because I'm making this up as I go.'

Jen's approval was rooted in her digital marketing experience. 'Personal stories work in any field. It's the best way to connect with an audience.'

'I say: go for it,' Jasmine said. 'I trust you, whatever you do.'

'Why not?' Naomi said. 'Our hot takes and hot messes should benefit *someone*.'

'Regardless, I'm still your accountability coach,' Jasmine added. 'I'd like a glimpse of those early drafts you showed Roman, if you don't mind.'

'But will you cuddle up in bed and tell her she's pretty?' Hugo quipped. 'That's a huge part of the deal.'

'You guys are the best and the worst,' Samantha said. 'I love you all.'

Everyone broke out in a collective 'Awwwww!' Except for Maya, who stared at them, stone-faced. 'You guys are a trip.'

Travel Blog

Title TBD: ?? [Note to Self: Really? Is this the best you can do?]

DRAFT ENTRY #9: Bridesmaid Duties

A bridesmaid is as close to a lady in waiting as you get these days. She's made to wear a frilly, unflattering dress, attend to the bride, assist her in every way, spread rose petals at her feet, and dispose of her bouquet at the end of the night. Say nothing of the weeks and weeks of preparation leading up to the big special day.

Parties. Luncheons. Gifts. More gifts. It's an expensive, thankless task. A basket of bath products or speciality cheese is not fair compensation for the time and effort spent. Lifelong friendships will be tested. Tempers will flare; it's unavoidable. If you walk away, you're labelled a bad friend never to be reinstated in the circle again. If you take your job too seriously, ridiculed. Repeat performances lead to social suicide. Always a bridesmaid and all that …

Groomsmen aren't subject to any of this. In their tailored suits, they are admired, desired and hunted like prize game. Their duties are limited. They get their mate to the venue on time and tackle him to the ground should he panic and attempt to run.

Chances are if you're invited to serve, you're either a close friend of the bride or a distant cousin. Either way, you're privy to a lot of information the average wedding guest is not. You've witnessed mother-daughter battles, lovers' quarrels, and vicious rows over the guest list, seating chart, floral arrangements and money. You know how long and tortured the road to 'I do' truly is.

When the big day finally arrives, you're exhausted and eager to get it over with – that's a given. But you're rooting for this couple and revel in their joy. If the officiant asks whether anyone knows of any reason they should not be joined in matrimony, you keep your reservations to yourself. Let the loving pair say their 'I dos' and be done with it.

Cheer up! You've made it through this ordeal with your dignity intact and your friendships in good working order. Well done, you! The reception is your time to shine. Tear off the tiara and chuck aside the flimsy bouquet. Take full advantage of the open bar. Flirt shamelessly. As soon as the first dance wraps up, grab a groomsman and hit the floor. Dance like no one's watching even though you know bloody well everyone is watching and wondering when it will be your turn to make the trip down the aisle.

CHAPTER TWENTY-EIGHT

The setting sun gifted Naomi and Anthony a gold-and-violet backdrop to perfect their island paradise wedding aesthetic. Was the bride lovely? Achingly so. Did she drift down the aisle with the grace of a swan to an acoustic rendition of 'Here Comes the Sun'? Absolutely. Did the handsome groom beam with joy? If he were any brighter, he'd set himself on fire. It was no exaggeration. The ceremony was perfect in every way. The couple said their vows with quiet confidence, exchanged rings and kissed to cheers and applause. Anthony's mother bawled her eyes out. Amelia dabbed the corners of her eyes with a lace handkerchief. Maya made little hiccup sounds as she sobbed. Samantha exercised supreme self-control to keep from dissolving in an ugly cry right there in front of everyone.

That was all she remembered of the ceremony. She couldn't describe it in finer detail and would have to rely on the wedding video to fill in the gaps. While Naomi and Anthony promised to love, honour, cherish and all of that, she'd had an honest to goodness out-of-body experience.

It started when the wedding planner lined them up on the red carpet leading to the altar at the veranda's edge. Samantha scanned the guests looking for Roman. Amelia had invited the who's who of Trinidad and Tobago, so it was hard to find him at first. Then she spotted him in an aisle seat, second row to the last. It took a while for her brain to sync the man in the dark tailored suit with the man in the rumpled T-shirts she'd got to know these last few days. He was looking straight at her, just waiting for her to connect all those dots in her mind. They locked eyes and from that moment on, Samantha walked among the clouds.

That dizzy feeling, that lightheadedness, never left her. It was like falling from the sky and not giving a damn where you landed. She hadn't come to Tobago to find love or anything like it, yet she'd found Roman and there was no denying he had a hand on her heart.

★★★

'Ladies and gentlemen, I present to you Mr and Mrs Anthony Scott!'

Husband and wife danced their way down the aisle. Samantha took her place in the procession and would have gladly exited when she reached Roman if she could. Better or worse, she was committed to bridesmaids' duties. A photographer was waiting to make up for the photo opportunities missed due to all those last-minute cancellations.

The hour-long photo shoot in the resort's garden kicked off with the bride and groom and their parents. Jen, Jasmine, Maya and Samantha, in deep blue chiffon dresses with saffron-coloured flowers in their hair, collapsed onto lounge chairs and wiggled their aching toes in the grass. They were starving. Meanwhile the guests were enjoying crab dumplings. Before long, they were summoned to pose for photos with the bride, the groom, and of course Amelia.

A while later, they stood in a queue outside the banquet hall, waiting to be announced. Before the ceremony, Samantha had silenced her phone and tucked it in the pocket of her dress. It buzzed now and the vibration tickled her thigh. She didn't have a death wish, so she checked to determine if the coast was clear before checking her phone. Amelia was fussing with the train of Naomi's dress; this gave her all of two seconds. The message was from Roman:

I'm over this. How much longer until I can be with you again?

Samantha turned away from the others, concealed her phone in her bouquet of yellow roses and typed an answer.

I'll ask them to speed things along. I'm sure they'll take your feelings into consideration.

Roman: I'm not the only one who feels this way. We may start a riot.

Samantha: Do what you have to do. So long as you set aside a few dumplings for me.

Roman: What do you think of my tie?

It was a gorgeous shade of blue, matching her dress. Even so, she wasn't going to gush. It's nice, I guess. Pretty colour.

Roman: We're not going to do nice things with it.

She strained to control her smile. Hmm ... Is it silk? I've got standards.

Roman: Only the best for you, pretty lady.

A funnel of emotions spun inside her. With a few playful texts, he'd made her tingle from head to toe. She'd never felt this rush of excitement, never wanted anyone as much. She was screwed, wasn't she? Was Roman Carver the gold standard of men? Was she doomed to spending the rest of her life comparing every man she met to him? It certainly seemed that way.

The wedding planner swung open the doors to the ballroom-cum-banquet hall with her usual flourish. Samantha tucked away her phone and snapped to attention. Their instructions were clear: enter before the bride and groom and take a seat at the head table, where they were mandated to remain through dinner and the inevitable toasts and speeches.

Samantha stretched onto her tiptoes to glance into the room over Jen's shoulders. She admired the ivory linens and floral centrepieces that Naomi had selected. All the guests were seated and chatting amiably except for Hugo, Jason, Roman and Chris, who had a table to themselves. They were laughing hysterically.

By the looks of it, Hugo was telling one of his famous stories. Jason and Chris were doubled over with laughter. Roman kept his head low and bit back his laugh, but Samantha could tell he was having fun. He fit so seamlessly into her world. Timothy had never made an effort to fit in with her 'crazy' friends.

She started to imagine future holidays, beach getaways where they gathered under one roof. Naomi and Anthony would pull up to the rented cottage in a mini van loaded with kids. She and Roman would—

Without warning, the wedding planner slammed the doors shut in their faces. Thank goodness, too. Her imagination was spinning out of control.

'The DJ is experiencing some difficulties. He's asked for ten minutes to sort it out.'

'What difficulties?' Amelia cried.

'Of the technical sort, madam.'

'Calm down, Mum,' Naomi said. 'It'll be fine.'

Maya proposed they plug her phone into the sound system. 'My playlists are unparalleled.'

Samantha took advantage of the commotion to break away. Ten minutes was enough for a quick dash to the ladies' room. She handed her bouquet to Jen. 'Hold on to this. Heading to the restroom. I'll be right back.'

'Ah yes,' Jen said. 'You're going to *pop to the loo*.'

'You don't get to say that, Jen!'

As she dashed toward the restrooms, she passed a man slumped on a bench outside the men's room. Adrian! 'Hey, there!' she called out cheerily, without stopping. She used the facilities, washed her hands, arranged and rearranged the yellow flowers in her hair, and came out to find Adrian in the exact same position. He was staring at his phone as if willing it to ring. Samantha had no choice but to stop and check in on him.

'Are you feeling all right?'

The only socially acceptable answer to that question was: *Yes, I'm fine. Go on and enjoy your night.* For some reason, Adrian made another choice. 'No, I'm not.'

Samantha stammered. 'Are you ill? Should I get you a bottle of water?'

'No thanks. I'm not dehydrated. Only deeply disappointed in you all.'

Now she was really confused. 'What are you talking about?'

Adrian arched an eyebrow. He had the most symmetrical face she'd ever seen. The effect of the single arched brow was devastating. 'You know exactly what I'm talking about. You've ignored me. It's like you're pretending I'm not here.'

She couldn't speak for the others, but she hadn't gone out

of her way to snub him. It was true his rift with Hugo had gone a long way to isolating him. He'd mostly kept to himself. Nonetheless, she couldn't recall a single conversation with Adrian since their arrival. And she'd had deep, meaningful conversations with just about everyone, including Chris. That was saying something. Except now wasn't the time to get into it. She had to march in step with the other bridesmaids shortly.

'I'm sorry we didn't get a chance to chat this trip. We can catch up later, maybe?'

'Hey, missy!' Jen flagged her down from the end of the hall with both their bouquets clasped in one hand. She looked ethereal, a bridesmaid fairy, with her long blonde hair worn in a French braid strewn with flowers. 'It's showtime!'

Samantha turned to Adrian, feeling a pinch of regret. She had to leave him with something. 'I know you and Hugo are going through tough times, but I'm rooting for both of you. You're my favourite couple in the world.'

He smiled wanly. 'Doesn't that honour go to the newly-weds?'

'It goes to whomever I'm speaking with at the time.'

'Fair enough.' Adrian stood and tugged at his cuffs. He was a striking man, smart, stylish and serious. His stern demeanour complemented Hugo's playful, freewheeling ways. They were proof positive that opposites attract. What a shame their differences were now driving them apart.

'Come, my friend.' She offered him her arm. 'I've got to make a grand entrance and you've got to clap and cheer.'

Adrian sighed. 'We each have our roles.'

She tightened her fingers around his arm. He sounded so defeated; it broke her heart. 'Adrian, you and Hugo love each other. It's palpable. We can all feel it. And we're all rooting for you.'

He smiled wanly. 'You're sweet. You know that?'

'Yes,' she said. 'Now let's go.'

***

The honour of delivering the first speech of the night fell upon the best man. Anthony's uncle read from a piece of hotel stationery. His speech was designed to gloss over his family's role in the couple's chaotic journey to the altar. Next Gregory Thomas spoke up, extending a warm T&T welcome to everyone. Naomi's Aunt Donna offered the newlyweds life advice. Anthony's mother was invited to say a few words. She had the good sense to keep it short and sweet, but then was followed by a long-winded local politician. It was basically open mic.

Samantha managed to applaud at all the right times and keep a pleasant smile pasted on her face while stealing glances at Roman, who could no longer hide his impatience. At one point, he lowered his head and pinched the bridge of his nose. Finally, Anthony rose to say a few words, signalling the end was near.

'People … Can I just say … This is the happiest day of my life. My heart is so full. You all look beautiful. Thank you for being here to help us celebrate. We may not know each other very well, but trust me that'll change before the end of the night. We're going to be best friends.'

Anthony rambled for a good while. Naomi, a gifted public speaker, was awash with admiration for her incoherent husband, a true testament of love if ever there was one.

'My family is here,' Anthony continued. 'We're a small, mighty bunch. We party hard. We get loud. Get used to it.'

'Woop! Woop!' his uncle called out, provoking a bout of nervous laughter in the room.

Samantha slipped out her phone and typed from under the table. It's quite possible the groom is drunk.

Roman: Think so?

Samantha: He's waffling.

Roman: We had a couple of tequila shots earlier to take the edge off. The man's a lightweight. He hasn't had anything stronger than vegan beer these past five years.

Samantha: What if he never stops talking?

Roman: I'll tackle him.

'Amelia and Gregory, you're stuck with me now. Maya, have fun tonight, but come tomorrow I expect you to start counting your steps. The family that trains together sticks together. Am I right? Seriously, though, I love you guys.'

Samantha: Would you, please?

Roman: Anything for you. And the public good. This can't go on.

Samantha: Isn't it customary for guests to give speeches in Tobago?

Roman: And it's customary for me to grab a bottle and duck out with friends.

Samantha: That sounds like fun.

Roman: Say the word. I'll grab a bottle and meet you at the door.

'Now, to our friends who spent the week with us, what can I say? You guys are the best.'

Samantha: Oops! We can't go now.

'It was amazing to get to know you all better. All those memories we made ... I swear, it was magic. I love you to death.'

'Love you, too, man!' Hugo called out, much to Anthony's delight.

'Ride or die!' Anthony cried out in response, at which point Naomi's eyebrows crept upwards, betraying her rising concern.

Roman: You really want to stay for this?

Samantha: It's sweet.

Roman: It's stupid.

'Before I wrap this up, I have one more person to thank ... Roman Carver. Dude, I love you like a brother.'

Samantha: You gave him the tequila. You brought this on yourself.

'You've held me together this week and for that I'm truly grateful. There's nothing I won't do for you. Count on me for anything.'

Roman gave Anthony a look that said, *Love you. Wrap it up. This isn't going over as great as you think.* Anthony ignored it and went on with his verbal soup.

'Finally, to this beauty I get to call my wife.'

Roman: The man is 200 pounds of muscle. He ought to handle it.

Samantha: Just wait until Naomi finds out you got her groom drunk.

Roman: You'd snitch on me, babe?

Samantha flushed. He might as well have stroked her back. She glanced around to make sure no one was onto her before risking a glance at Roman. He was focused on his phone, typing.

Roman: What happened to ride or die?

Samantha: I'm more of a safe and sound type of girl.

Roman: **You're safe with me.**

That was a lie. He had her careening over an emotional cliff. Even as she sat texting him from under the table like a schoolgirl, she felt the pulse of danger. Nothing about this high-wire act felt safe, least of all their uncertain future.

Anthony was now professing eternal love to Naomi, who didn't seem to mind this more expressive side of him. Roman might be in the clear.

'There's never been a dull moment since you've come into my life,' Anthony said. 'It's been one crazy thing after another, hasn't it, my love? You're so strong. You're my rock. You take everything in your stride. I'm in awe of you. Truly, I am. You make me so happy. I've never met anyone like you and I'm more than proud to call you my wife.'

As sappy as Anthony's words were, the emotion behind them was serious. He loved Naomi. It was that simple. Maybe he wasn't drunk, after all. Maybe this was what love looked like, a swirling pool of emotion. Samantha wanted someone to look at her that way and say all those things, preferably not within weeks of their first meeting, but sometime down the road.

Samantha: **Do you think you could love intensely like that?**

She braced herself for a dry, sarcastic reply. He was probably too jaded. She could never imagine him pouring his heart out like Anthony, but could he crack open the shell just a bit?

Roman started to type, then stopped. Samantha gripped her phone even tighter, eagerly watching the bubble with the dots pop and disappear from the screen. Finally, he responded:

Would you want that kind of love from me?

Samantha's fingers hovered over the virtual keyboard. All she had to do was type 'YES' in all caps and punctuate with a heart emoji. She wanted to stand up and shout across the room, *I want you to love me, damn it!* She wanted to skip all the nonsense and get to the part where he loved her. This was not a conversation they should have via text. It felt too big to put it into tiny words. A heart emoji wasn't going to cut it. Perhaps now was the time to grab that bottle and sneak out.

To Samantha's relief, Anthony raised his glass for a final toast. She dropped her phone onto her lap and reached for her champagne flute. She would join Roman at his table soon enough. They could talk in private then.

Anthony filled his lungs, ready to end strong. Samantha raised her glass higher, should he need some encouragement.

'Friends, family, join me in raising your glasses to …'

Anthony lapsed into silence, leaving everyone with their glasses raised and no one to toast. Samantha's smile grew wobbly, her outstretched arm hurt. All he had to do to end their collective misery was say his wife's name. Had he forgotten it? Not possible. He wasn't *that* drunk. Finally he cleared his throat, hesitated a moment, and said, 'Tara, is that you?'

CHAPTER TWENTY-NINE

'Sorry about the mix-up, folks!' Anthony spoke over the rising murmurs of confusion. 'I was caught off guard. Everyone, my college buddy Tara Evans is here. We weren't expecting her. What a surprise!'

He pushed out a dry, choppy laugh that didn't help the situation. Everyone, including the catering staff, swivelled around to stare at the woman hovering awkwardly outside the ballroom doors. Anthony's 'college buddy' was a beauty. Short and curvy, she had a creamy almond complexion and long glossy black hair. Smiling broadly, she stepped forward, brought her hands to prayer and bowed slightly. 'I come in peace, and bear gifts from the airport duty-free shop.'

Anthony threw his hands up. 'Who could ask for more?'

The quirky exchange worked to release only some tension in the room. All eyes were on Naomi now, gauging her reaction.

Most people left behind the friendships forged at uni after a couple of years or so, but not Anthony. His mates trailed him everywhere. Which was a testament to him, really. Still, Samantha had never heard of Tara Evans. Naomi had never mentioned her. Where did she come from? What fresh batch of drama was this?

Naomi remained calm and composed even under intense

scrutiny. Anthony didn't call her his rock for nothing. In an award-winning show of solidarity, she broke into a smile and extended a warm T&T welcome to this last-minute guest. 'Tara, don't just stand there! Come in! We're thrilled you made it! Someone find her a seat.'

The wedding planner took over, ushering the newcomer to the one table with available seats. Tara made a beeline to the seat that Samantha had mentally reserved for herself, the one next to Roman.

He rose to greet her. She gave him a warm embrace. Evidently Anthony's college buddy was Roman's, too.

A distant conversation with Roman bobbed to the surface of her mind.

I had a date.

Where is she?

Thought we weren't talking about our exes.

'More champagne, miss?'

The server appointed to their table had done a great job keeping their glasses full and generally being helpful. Only now he was in the way, blocking her view of Roman's table. It was a blessing in disguise. Samantha was in free fall and didn't want anyone to see when she hit the ground.

★★★

Once the dinner plates were cleared away, Naomi rose from her overstuffed seat and addressed them. 'Ladies, one last photo before the party gets going.'

Maya chucked aside her napkin. 'For the love of God, set us free!'

'It won't take long,' Naomi promised. 'I have to get back in time for the first dance.'

'You heard the bride.' Jen pushed back her chair. 'Let's do this.'

Samantha could think of a thousand things she'd prefer to do than be photographed. But Jasmine was tugging at her arm. What would she even say? *Sorry, can't stand still and smile right now, I have the sudden urge to rip a man's head off?*

Roman had not looked her way once since Tara Evans had made her grand entrance. She commanded his attention; not in a good way, she could see that. The tension between them was thick. But what difference did it make? She could have stood to give a speech of her own and he wouldn't have noticed. She wasn't jealous. She just wished that stabbing sensation in her gut would stop so she could breathe.

Naomi led them to a small adjoining balcony. The photographer trailed after them, but didn't get far. Jen shut the glass door in his face and stood guard. Jasmine eased Samantha onto a wrought-iron banquette and the others gathered around. This was how she became the subject of an intervention for the second time in one month.

'Sam,' Naomi began. 'There's something you should know.'

She closed her eyes. There was nothing Naomi could tell her that she didn't already know. It was all painfully obvious.

Naomi snapped her fingers to get her attention. 'Are you listening?'

'Save your breath. I've figured it out. Tara was Roman's date, right?'

Naomi gave her a pitying look. 'Oh, Sammy. It's *way* more complicated than that.'

She stiffened. 'How so?'

'Well, it's a long story.'

'For heaven's sake!' Maya cried. 'Give it to her straight. She can handle it. It's not like she's in love with the man. She's only known him a week. Isn't that right, Sammy?'

'Absolutely. Whatever you have to say, I can handle it.'

Her voice was too thin to convince anyone, let alone herself.

'If you say so,' Naomi said. 'I would have preferred you hear this from him, but I can't leave you in the dark.'

Samantha nodded encouragingly, but she was one heartbeat away from grabbing Naomi by the throat.

'Roman and Tara were engaged.'

'What?'

'They were together for the longest time and got engaged soon after Anthony and I started dating. It didn't last long. One month tops.'

Samantha wasn't sure if the tingling sensation spreading through her limbs was a sign of shock or something more serious and life threatening.

'After they split up, he quit his job and came down here to lay low a while, sort things out.'

'That's over the top,' Jasmine said. 'Why did he have to quit his job?'

'He hated it,' Samantha said flatly.

'Apparently so,' Naomi said. 'It's a shame, too. You should have seen his flat. The views were insane.'

'Found her!' Maya brandished her phone. 'Tara Evans has a profile on a networking site.'

Jen moved away from her post at the door. 'Let's hear it.'

'Tara J. Evans was born and raised in Philadelphia. She earned a BA at Stony Brook and an MBA at Carnegie Mellon. She's currently employed at a venture capitalist firm. An avid reader and a runner. Knits, too. I love that about her.'

Naomi held up a hand. 'Thanks, Maya.'

'He never mentioned an ex-girlfriend or any other kind of ex?' Jasmine asked.

Samantha raised her chin, hoping the slight gesture would make her feel less of a fool. 'He said he'd had his heart broken once, but he was over it. He's moving forward.'

Maya tucked away her phone. 'Well, if he's over it, we're over it. Onward!'

'Something tells me Tara isn't over it,' Jasmine said.

'No one expects him to declassify his ex files,' Jen said thoughtfully. 'But an engagement is heavy stuff. You might want to drop it into the conversation.'

'I can't believe he didn't mention it,' Naomi uttered under her breath.

'Why didn't you mention it?' Samantha snapped. 'While trying to fix us up, it would have been useful to point out his baggage.'

Naomi waved away her concerns. 'At our age we're bound to have a significant ex or two. I figured it would come up organically.'

'It certainly has,' Maya said.

Samantha turned to Jen. 'Did you know?'

'Depends what you mean by that,' Jen said. 'I … might've heard something.'

Naomi snapped her fingers again. 'You're focused on the wrong things! Who cares who knew what, when?'

'What is she even doing here?' Jasmine asked. 'That's what *I* want to know.'

'I'm as shocked as anyone,' Naomi said. 'Tara is such a cool girl, but she didn't bother to RSVP. She showed up unannounced. Anthony didn't have a chance to wrap up the toast. And now Samantha's upset.'

The most egregious offence was failing to RSVP, obviously. Interrupting Anthony's speech was a close second.

'How upset are you, honey?' Jen asked. 'You can be real with us.'

Samantha looked from her newest to her oldest friend and laughed. She felt *really* stupid. How about that? Roman had a life he'd never hinted at. It included a flat with killer views and a fiancée who knitted for fun. She thought about his last text, the one she hadn't answered and her laughter died in her throat.

'None of this matters,' Jasmine said. 'Roman left his old life behind to start over here. He met Samantha and vibed with her. The past *is* past. Over. Done.'

'Except the past is very present at my wedding reception,' Naomi said.

If Samantha were keeping score, she'd have to award Naomi with a point. Tara wasn't some shadowy figure in Roman's past. She was sitting at her seat and seducing her date. And she'd had no choice but to sit from her perch of honour and watch. It was a miracle she wasn't sick.

With the door left unattended, there was no one to stop Hugo and Adrian storming in. Hugo assessed the scene and took charge. 'Hate to break this up, but they're waiting on the bride.'

'Right.' Naomi smoothed the skirt of the dress. 'Do I look OK?'

Adrian gave his professional assessment. 'A little shiny.'

'Hmm … We want a glow, not a shine.'

Jen came to her rescue with a face mist and absorbent tissues. Samantha couldn't help but feel embarrassed. It was her fault the bride was drenched in sweat. She should be indoors, in a temperature-controlled environment, chatting up her guests, working the room, and collecting envelopes stuffed with cash. This wasn't her big special day. The spotlight shouldn't be on her.

Within minutes Naomi was ready to return to her guests with a fresh and dewy complexion. She slid a worried look Samantha's way. 'Will you be all right, Sammy?'

'She'll be fine,' Hugo answered. 'Adrian and I will take over. Get out of here.'

Left behind with her new caretakers, Samantha felt ridiculous. 'I should go with them. I'll miss the first dance.'

'Just relax,' Adrian said. 'If you've seen one princess bride twirl around a ballroom, you've seen them all.'

She'd seen her fair share of twirling princesses, almost exclusively on TV.

'Besides,' Hugo said, 'don't you want to know what Roman and the mysterious Tara were up to at our table?'

'No, not really.'

'They weren't up to anything,' Adrian said. 'Don't give the girl a heart attack.'

Hugo sighed. 'You're naïve. It was so charged, Anthony asked them to clear the room in case they started a fire.'

'But not in a good way,' Adrian rushed to add.

The image of Roman and Tara out there somewhere, sipping from an open bottle, hashing out their problems and reaching a compromise, made her nauseous.

'This is what we know,' Adrian said. 'Tara is sorry for her behaviour – whatever that behaviour was, I couldn't say for sure. She flew down here on a whim. She's staying at the Blue Moon Beach Resort.'

That last bit of information was superfluous.

'Roman handled it like a boss,' Hugo said. 'He asked her point blank what she hoped to get out of this stunt. Want to know what she said?'

Samantha glared at him. Was he really going to make her ask?

Adrian implored Hugo to adopt a more straightforward approach. 'Darling, please, no more guessing games. You'll wear her out.'

'Come on! You're taking the fun out of this.'

'Fun?' Samantha cried. In what world was this fun?

'Point taken,' Hugo said. 'The bottom line is this: she wants him back. Dropping in like this was a *grand gesture* to melt his heart.'

Adrian confirmed this. 'Those were her exact words.'

Samantha covered her sadness with sarcasm. 'You two are thorough.'

'We had the scoop of the night,' Adrian said sheepishly.

'Don't worry,' Hugo said. 'Roman wasn't moved.'

'I'm not worried,' Samantha said. 'He can do what he wants.'

'Uh huh.'

Adrian and Hugo were seated on either side of her on the wobbly iron bench, holding her down as if she were a flight risk. They made a great team and were arguably one of the most handsome couples in the world. It would be a shame if they couldn't work things out. This was probably the most time they'd spent together in days. Focusing on someone else's relationship woes was likely therapeutic. In a way, she was glad to be of service.

'The *look* Roman gave her,' Hugo said. 'Did you catch it, babe?'

Adrian frowned. 'I felt bad for her. She's desperate to hold on to what she had. I can relate.'

Hugo could not relate. 'She was wrong to show up like this.'

'Right or wrong, does it matter?'

'It matters.'

'People act on impulse. They make mistakes.'

The conversation had taken a slight turn. It was probably a good idea to step away and let the couple talk privately. She wanted nothing more than to sneak back to her bungalow, fall asleep and wake up back home in England.

'Like the time you hired a real estate agent behind my back?' Hugo said. 'I don't think so. Not everything is a mistake, my love. Some actions are deliberate and intentional.'

Oh dear ... Samantha massaged her rigid neck. Things were about to get ugly.

'I'm sorry!' Adrian cried. 'How many times do I have to say I'm sorry?'

'What are you talking about? You never once apologized.'

'Well, I am now.'

Samantha let out a sigh. If she had to endure this, she might as well intervene. 'Adrian, your apology lacks substance. Hugo obviously feels betrayed. You have to address that.'

'Ha!' Hugo spat. 'Sam thinks you lack substance.'

'Not you, Adrian,' she corrected. 'Just your apology.'

'I'm sorry I went behind your back to list our home. I didn't realize how much you loved the place.'

'Yes, you did,' Hugo said. 'That's why you went behind my back. You knew how I'd react.'

'I thought you'd come around. I could make you fall in love with the house I had my eye on.'

Hugo wasn't swayed. 'You can't make me do anything.'

'I know that now.'

'Good.'

Samantha cried foul. 'Hold on! He apologized. Now it's your turn.'

'I've nothing to apologize for.'

'Think of something.'

Hugo drummed his foot on the terrazzo floor. 'Sorry I wouldn't tour houses with you. But I refuse to leave Miami so why would I waste my time?'

Adrian turned to Samantha. 'How substantial was that apology?'

It was rather thin, as was her patience. 'I can't go around in circles with you two. You have no idea how lucky you are to have each other. Sort this out.'

'I know how lucky I am,' Adrian said. 'And I know I screwed up.'

'Tell me what got into you,' Hugo pleaded. 'You've turned into someone I don't recognize.'

'It's Victor. He got to my head.'

'Victor? What does your brother have to do with this?'

'He bought the house in Orlando and hosted the family reunion last spring. I can't fit two people and their luggage in our guest bedroom.'

'We went through all this for some petty sibling rivalry bullshit?'

'I can't say that for sure, but it was definitely on my mind.'

'Do you even want to host a family reunion?'

'Not really. The hassle alone.'

'Exactly.'

Adrian buried his face in his hands. 'I don't know what I was thinking.'

'Babe, we are never going to be the heteronormative couple your mother can't stop dreaming of. We're not giving her grandkids and we're not hosting big fat reunions. That's not us.'

Samantha tapped him on the knee. 'I think he gets the point.'

'Do you?' Hugo asked anxiously.

Adrian reached out and smoothed the one lock of Hugo's hair that had managed to escape the hold of his preferred gel. 'I do.'

Hugo caught his husband's hand and pressed the knuckles to his lips. 'You're a piece of work, but I love you.'

They kissed and made up while Samantha squirmed out from between them. 'OK, guys, mind taking this somewhere else? I need a moment alone.'

This was her private balcony of heartache and sorrow. She needed a few minutes to wallow in peace.

Hugo wouldn't hear of it. '*Gata*, we can't leave you out here by yourself.'

'I fixed your marriage,' Samantha replied coolly. 'You can do me this one favour.'

'I owe you one,' Adrian said. 'Thanks for your help.'

'You're welcome. Now go. Get out of here. Be happy.'

CHAPTER THIRTY

Tara approached the table. 'Is this seat taken?'

Roman studied her, taking in the defiant glint in her eyes. 'It is, actually,' he replied.

She sat down anyway. A leaping flame of anger scorched Roman's insides. He flinched in pain.

'Could you tell whoever it is whose seat I've stolen that I've been through a lot?' Tara kept her tone light and playful. 'I woke up in a cold sweat at 2 a.m., booked a flight which turned out to be three connecting flights, just to get here in time for one of my best friends' wedding.'

'There was no need to do all that. You had plenty of notice.'

She side-eyed him. 'My date dumped me last minute.'

'That's not even remotely true.'

'It's kinda true!' She rested a hand on his thigh. 'Relax, OK? Accept this as the grand gesture that it is.'

Roman stared at her blankly. He tried to see the traces of the woman he once loved. For years they'd been so close. He knew her inside out. Now he had no idea what she was thinking.

'This may very well have been a bad idea,' she said. 'Nevertheless, I'm persisting. I've come too far to back down now.'

'You're incredible,' he said under his breath.

'In a good way or—'

Roman wasn't in the mood for playful banter. 'When did you get here? Where are you staying? Did you fly in to Crown Point?'

'Aw, sweetie! You're worried about me.'

He pushed aside his place setting in annoyance. 'I worry about you wandering alone in a place you've never been.'

'That's very patriarchal of you, but as you can see I'm fine. I flew in this afternoon and I'm staying at the Blue Moon Beach Resort not far from here.'

'You could've called. I would have met you at the airport.'

'Except you wouldn't have answered my call. You blocked me, remember?'

'I haven't blocked you or anyone. I'm off the grid.' As evidence, he pulled out the basic smart phone that he used while in Tobago, instead of the iPhone that served as a portal to his New York life. He hadn't charged that one in weeks. The phone in his hand was a refurbished piece of junk that tied him to Samantha. That's how he liked it.

'*Off the grid* is just a clever way of saying you've buried your head in the sand. Everyone is looking for you.'

'I doubt that.'

'I'll fill you in later.'

She was aware – as was Roman – of their dinner companions actively eavesdropping. The only difference was that he didn't care. He was more concerned with what Samantha might be thinking. He didn't dare look at her, but he could feel her laser-hot glare on him. His phone had stopped chiming with her messages; a bad sign.

Dinner was served. Roman managed to make it through the meal without choking. Afterwards, Naomi stood and exited the reception hall followed sagely by her bridesmaids. Roman watched as Samantha made her way out of the room, her head held high. Soon enough, Anthony got up and made his way toward their table. He grabbed one of the empty chairs and wedged it between Roman and Tara. He forced out a laugh. 'Hey! Look who made it!'

Tara planted a kiss on his cheek. 'It's the man of the hour! How are you, buddy? Holding up OK?'

'Great! Never better!'

'You look a little pink around the ears. Have you been drinking?'

Anthony clasped his big hands together. 'You only get married once. Am I right?'

'In your case it's twice, and with the same woman,' Tara said. 'But never mind that. Congratulations!'

'Come here!' Anthony drew her into a bear hug and ruffled her hair. 'I'm happy to see you, T! But you know how Naomi is about seating charts.'

'I don't want to hear it. There are plenty of empty seats here.'

'Pretty sure these seats are reserved.'

Roman looked from Anthony to Tara. There was nothing easy in their interaction. It was all forced, and a part of him ached. For ages, the three of them had been like family. Three amigos who'd met in college and stayed tight throughout the years. Those bonds were fraying, and it was mostly his fault.

Anthony's arms fell away from Tara. 'How about you two step outside to clear the air?'

'Good idea!' Tara said.

Roman glanced at the side door the bridal party had exited. Anthony reassured him. 'Don't worry about it. I'll tell Sam.'

'No, don't,' Roman said. 'It has to come from me.'

'Gotcha.'

★★★

Tara followed him out to the hotel lobby, trailing behind him by several steps. He couldn't shake the thought that everything could have been different. They could have flown down to Tobago together weeks in advance of the wedding to explore this island that he considered his true home. He could have introduced her to his relatives. They could have swum in the waterfall and toured the beaches. That's not how things had worked out. Instead, Roman had met Samantha, and had all those experiences with her. It was exactly as it should have been. He would trade nothing for it.

He pointed to a pair of rattan armchairs in a corner. 'How about here?'

Tara shook her head. 'No,' she said. 'I want to get out of here. Take me back to my hotel.'

'You just got here.'

'I've wished Anthony well and pissed off the bride,' Tara said. 'I'm good to go.'

Roman glanced at the ballroom doors. He could see straight through to the head table. Samantha still wasn't there.

'Come on,' Tara said. 'It's not far, and we'll talk along the way. You'll be back way before the groom tosses the garter.'

★★★

They did not talk along the way. He drove in stiff silence and she stared out the window. Roman pulled through the resort's gates and parked in the lot reserved for guests. He cut the engine.

Tara toyed with the gold strap of her purse. 'Any chance I can convince you to come up for a glass of wine? The view from my balcony is breathtaking.'

Roman curled his fingers around the steering wheel. 'Listen, Tara—'

'Did you meet someone?' she interrupted. 'Is that why you're acting this way?'

'How do you act when your ex shows up to ambush you?'

'I'm here to *reconnect* with you. There's a difference.'

Roman left the car and leaned against the closed door. He was feeling claustrophobic in the small black saloon.

Tara soon joined him. Her heels made click–clack sounds on the paved lot as she rounded the car bonnet. 'Believe it or not, I didn't come all this way to ruin your night.'

He turned to her. The animosity he'd felt all night was gone. Mostly, he felt tired. 'Why did you come? Tell me.'

'The firm wants you back. I've been authorized to make you an offer and it's generous. You get the VP title, which you've earned, *and* the corner office you deserve.'

'Isn't Doris head of HR?' Roman asked, confused. 'Or have things radically changed since I left?'

'No … Doris is still … Doris. When she couldn't reach you

by phone or email, she asked if I could relay a message. So I'm here to tell you they want you back.'

'You flew all this way, crashed Anthony's wedding, to get me back to work?'

'Or to get you back, plain and simple. Your old life is waiting.' She went to him and rested a hand on his arm. '*I'm* waiting.'

Roman covered her hand with his. For a long while they stood like this, connected but apart. 'That life is over,' he said.

'It doesn't have to be,' she said. 'So we made a mistake. We rushed things. It's not too late for us. We can have everything we wanted.'

'I want other things.'

Tara's hand slipped out from under his. She must have known this expedition was doomed. Why did she go through the trouble?

'Tara, we did everything we could,' he said. 'I want to move on. I want that for you, too.'

'Sleep on it. You may see things differently in the morning.'

'I won't.'

She swept her gaze over him, considering him with new eyes. Roman stayed silent. He'd said all that he was willing to say tonight. They were not going to rehash the past or plan a future. It was over between them. Done.

Tara retrieved her purse and shawl from the car, and slammed the passenger door. He did not stop her when she marched off toward the hotel. Halfway up the path, she swivelled around. Her voice cracked as she made one last point. 'I didn't crash the wedding. I was *invited*.'

Roman watched her go. *This wedding,* he thought. *This god-damn wedding.*

CHAPTER THIRTY-ONE

Five minutes alone on the balcony was all the time Samantha needed for a proper meltdown. There was a hive of angry bees trapped in her chest. Screaming into her cupped hands was the only way she knew to let them out. She couldn't go at it with her friends watching.

Samantha's head was reeling. Was Mercury in retrograde? Was that it? How else could she explain this strange twist of events? Against all conceivable odds, she'd met a guy she truly liked and he seemed to like her, too. Time was not on their side; she knew this and was OK with it. She was prepared to leave on Sunday a little sad, a little hopeful, but overall better off for having met him. No drama. No stress.

The funny thing, the thing that cracked her up, was that she'd hoped Roman would help dispel the drama of her last break-up. Now look what he'd done! To get dumped and then ditched, and in such a public way, was just tragic. She'd never shake off her well-meaning friends. It was going to be 'poor Sammy' until the end of days. They would *never* move on from this. In a quarter century's time, at Naomi and Anthony's silver anniversary gala, they'd gather around to tell the tale of Tara Evans.

Her five minutes were up, but her rage hadn't died down.

How could she go out there and face everyone, face him … and *her*? Maybe she could climb over the ledge and slip into the night. With the exception of Amelia, who was keeping tabs on every member of the bridal party, would anyone miss her?

The door to the balcony squealed open. Samantha had her answer. Naomi's head pushed through the crack, knocking her crystal tiara askew. 'There you are, Sammy.'

She was so moved she nearly burst into tears. Screw Roman and his fiancée. She had real friends and would always be missed.

'What are you still doing out here?' Naomi asked.

'Just needed some fresh air.'

'That's enough of that. Come inside.'

'Yes, ma'am.' Samantha took a step toward the door and froze. 'Are they …?'

'No, they're not,' Naomi replied. 'I haven't seen them around. Even if they were, what would it matter? You've done nothing wrong. Now let's get back out there before Amelia sends a drone to track us down. You can't hide all night. I won't have it.'

From stilted speeches to surprise guests, the reception finally got lively. The guests were up and mingling. Roman and Tara were nowhere in sight. Whether Naomi approved or not, hiding in plain sight was Samantha's plan for the evening. She stuck close to the flock of bridesmaids, hoping their matching dresses would work like camouflage. Her plan worked for a while. When the DJ turned up the volume, playing a Soca staple, she followed everyone onto the dance floor. When the tempo slowed, and everyone drifted off in pairs leaving her standing alone in the middle of the dance floor, she plotted her next move.

The head table was empty, abandoned by all except Anthony's uncle, who appeared to be dozing off. If she returned to her seat, she might as well stand under a spotlight. It was time for another trip to the restroom. A long queue snaked out of the ladies'. Since her goal was to avoid people as much as possible, Samantha changed route, cut through the lobby to the private restrooms. The plan backfired. She ran straight into Maya.

'Hey, Sam!' the girl cried. 'Come with me!'

'Where are you headed?'

Maya waved a keycard. 'The honeymoon suite. I'm going to decorate, if you know what I mean.'

'Is that necessary?' She was sure housekeeping had turned down the bed and sprinkled rose petals on the sheets.

'It's tradition. I'm going to write lurid messages on their bathroom mirror in lipstick and trace a path from the door to the bed with these.'

She fished around in her basket for a condom wrapped in gold foil. Samantha eyed it with scepticism. Wasn't it late in the game for those?

'Carry on without me,' Samantha said. 'And take pictures. I want to see your handiwork.'

'Just so you know, I'm gunning for you,' Maya said. 'You and Roman make a cute couple. And sure, Tara is a baddie, but so are you. Don't forget it.'

That was one pep talk Samantha could have done without. 'Thanks, Maya. Now go on! Have fun with it!'

Maya was already on the move. 'Just don't mope around.'

Samantha took that as an insult. 'When have you ever seen me mope?'

Maya was no longer within earshot. But the man who'd given her cause to mope was.

Roman entered the lobby through the main entrance and stopped abruptly at the sound of her voice. Her first instinct was to run and lock herself in a bathroom cubicle. Only he seemed so relieved to see her, her stupid heart squeezed out one last drop of hope.

'What are you doing out here?' he asked.

She pointed to the ballroom doors. The DJ had switched things up again and a pulsing bass bounced off the walls. 'I'm avoiding all the happy couples.'

Roman stepped closer. 'You're avoiding me.'

He never let her get away with anything. 'With good reason.'

'Samantha, it's not what it looks like.'

She couldn't help but notice how tired he looked, but she could stop herself from caring. 'Life isn't always a mystery. Sometimes things are *exactly* how they seem.'

His lips flattened to a straight line. 'What did they tell you?'

'The truth! Something you couldn't do.'

Roman looked away. Samantha went to the bar cart set up for guests. Dry-mouthed, she grabbed a complimentary bottle of water. Her hands trembled so much she had trouble twisting the cap.

Roman took the bottle from her, opened it effortlessly, and brushed his fingers over hers when he returned it. 'We were going to talk tomorrow. Remember?'

She didn't believe him. 'Tomorrow you would have found another excuse to get out of it.'

'That's not true.'

'I told you everything, all my secrets, all my messy stories. If your fiancée hadn't walked in—'

'She's not my fiancée. We're not together.'

'What went wrong? Didn't you find her "grand gesture" appealing?'

Roman cocked his head. 'They really told you everything.'

'I hate to repeat myself, but *you* should have told me!' she cried. Before he could tell her to calm down, she warned him: 'Don't you dare tell me to calm down!'

He threw his hands up. 'I would never.'

'Good.'

Feeling overheated, she took a swig from the water bottle. It did not cool her off. Roman yanked at the knot of his tie, the object of so many fantasies. This was not the way this night was supposed to end.

'Do we have to have this conversation here?' he asked.

'We don't have to have this conversation at all.'

He approached her gingerly, as if she were a wild animal. 'Samantha, please. I know I hurt you.'

'You didn't hurt me,' she snapped. 'I'm fine.' Roman was smart enough not to state the obvious fact: she didn't look fine. 'You've disappointed me. That's all.'

Hurt flashed in his eyes. Samantha was torn. She suppressed the urge to reach for his hand and reassure him.

'So where's your fiancée now?' she asked.

'Again, she's not my fiancée. And to answer your question, I drove her back to her hotel.'

'You have a big place. Why should she stay at a hotel?'

'Sammy.' His voice dipped to a whisper. For once she didn't mind her nickname. It sounded loving and tender, not childish. 'You're the only one who has ever been to my place.'

'Oh.'

286

'By the way, you're not doing a good job hiding your jealousy.'

'I'm not *jealous*!'

'Now I'm disappointed. Didn't I do anything right this week?'

'This is not a joke, Roman!'

'All I ask is a chance to speak for myself. We didn't need our friends to find each other and we don't need them to fill in the blanks for us now. Let's go somewhere and talk. I'll tell you everything. If you still want to tell me to get lost in the end, that's fine.'

'I'll definitely still want to tell you to get lost.'

'Your call,' he said. 'I'll have to live with it.'

She tapped her stiletto heel on the tile floor. 'Where should we go?'

It couldn't be far. She had to return in time to catch the bridal bouquet and put an end to her bad luck once and for all. Her bungalow was close by. It was nice and quiet and well suited for conversation, but there was no way they were ending up there tonight.

'Come with me,' he said. 'I know a place.'

CHAPTER THIRTY-TWO

The terrace overlooking the sea was the ideal spot. The bar was closed and the lounge beds were free to use. With the hotel staff busy with the wedding, there was no one to enforce the two-drink minimum. The sky wasn't as clear as the first night they'd come out here. Then again, nothing was.

They bypassed the lounge beds and stood at the rail. Roman said he was too restless to sit still. This was fine with Samantha. Her dress was too restrictive for lounging. Roman shrugged off his jacket and draped it over her shoulders. His scent quickly enveloped her, the same fresh scent that clung to his bed sheets. Could she smuggle his jacket out of the country and crawl beneath it on nights she missed him? As hurt as Samantha was, she would still miss him, no question.

They stood side by side, facing the night. Roman dropped his elbows onto the rail and pushed out a breath. His neck was stiff. His clenched jaw sharpened his profile. He resembled the man she'd first met, hard, unapproachable.

'This has been one long day.'

'True.' Samantha stifled a yawn. 'I think Naomi stopped time.'

'I wouldn't put it past her.'

288

His gaze flicked to her face. She shifted uncomfortably. The distance between them wasn't great, but it was significant. It showed how far apart they'd drifted. They didn't say much after that. The slow rolling surf softened the silence.

'Samantha,' he said, at last. 'How badly did I mess this up?'

'Pretty bad.'

He bit his lower lip and of course it made her want to kiss him. 'Before I say anything, I have to make this clear. I don't want to lose your friendship.'

The word *friendship* stung. Were they back to being just friends? Deep inside, she'd hoped he would make things right and put them back on track in the same efficient way he'd taken Tara to her hotel. That was a fantasy. They'd come here to settle things and end things all in one fell swoop, nice and neat.

She opened her arms, inviting him into a *friendly* hug. He'd helped her through a dark time and would always have her friendship.

Roman stared at her. 'What are you up to?'

'I'm not up to anything. I thought we could hug it out.'

'That's a pity hug.'

'Call it what you want, but that's all you're getting from me tonight.' She folded her arms across her chest, withdrawing the invitation. 'Maybe Tara is up for more.'

'This is a clean fight, Samantha,' he cautioned. 'No hitting below the belt. If your ex had showed up—'

She interrupted him. 'He didn't show up, did he? That was *your* ex.'

Whatever argument he was about to make was pointless. For one thing, her ex would *never* show up. Unlike Tara, Timothy wouldn't crash a wedding reception just to get her attention.

Grand gestures weren't his thing and he'd never attempt one of this scale. Most reasonable people wouldn't, Samantha among them. Grand gestures were stupid, risky, and embarrassing for everyone involved. To put herself out there like that, to put the other person on the spot, she couldn't do it. Even so, the thought of never being on the receiving end of one made her sad.

'Besides,' she drilled on. 'You *knew* about my ex and how I felt about him. If for some strange reason he showed up here tonight, you wouldn't need a personal briefing from a team of experts to get you up to speed, all the while looking and very much feeling like a fool.'

'I told you about my past.'

'You told me about some past break-up. I had no idea—'

'OK, OK.'

'Roman, we can't stay out here all night. Now would be a good time to start talking.'

They were shoulder-to-shoulder now, but still worlds apart.

'How much do you know already?' he asked.

'Never mind that.' She hadn't come here to compare notes. She wanted him to open up to her, to trust her with his secrets. Even the most basic friendship required trust.

'Here goes,' he said. 'Tara, Anthony and I met in business school.'

'College buddies,' she supplied.

Roman paused to study her. 'Welcome to my circle of friends. It's not as large as yours, but we were tight. We had each other's back.' As he talked, he balled his hands into fists. 'Anthony brought us together. I was his roommate and Tara was a girl he'd met at orientation. She was friendly and resourceful. Pretty soon we started hanging out, but Anthony didn't have a lot of free time. My folks saved all their lives to send my brother and me to college. Tara had scholarships. Anthony had to work to afford books and stuff. He started coaching at a local gym and that was it for him. He'd found his calling. He would've dropped out of school, but his mother would've killed him. You met her, so you understand. Tara and I did what we could to get him through. We wrote his papers and coached him through presentations. We made him our special project. We'd started together and were determined to end together.'

'A noble sentiment.'

'He was the only one who knew how to cook, so … there's that. He got us all eating healthy. It beat frozen burritos for dinner every night. But don't get me wrong, that guy owes us a lot.'

Samantha loved his generous spirit. 'I'm sure he does.'

'Most nights Anthony went to bed early to meet with clients at dawn. Tara and I would stay up late, cram for finals, order pizza, all the usual things.'

Samantha had no trouble imagining Roman and Tara spread out on a dorm room floor, books piled everywhere, sharing notes and eating pizza straight from the box. That tightening in her chest was jealousy, no doubt about it.

'One night we slept together. One day she moved into my room. And that's it. We were a couple.'

'Sounds like a whirlwind romance to me.'

'I keep things simple.'

Samantha's chest was so tight, she could hardly breathe. 'She's obviously in love with you.'

'Is it obvious? I don't see it.'

'Roman, she flew all this way—'

'I wouldn't read too much into that.'

'Well, when did you fall in love with her? You asked her to marry you.'

'I wouldn't read too much into that, either.' Roman dropped into deep thought. 'But I loved her. I won't deny it. There was no lightning-bolt moment. One morning it snowed so bad our classes were cancelled. We stayed in and it felt right.'

For the first time tonight, Samantha wanted to cry. She loved the way he loved, the way he eased into it on a snowy day.

'After graduation we went our separate ways. Anthony had a job waiting for him in LA. He sent his diploma to his parents and took off. I got picked for a training programme at my firm. Tara went home to Philadelphia to sort things out. She was already enrolled in graduate school. I thought it was over between us. We didn't see each other again until she showed up in New York eighteen months later to interview with my firm.'

'Is this something she does? Turn up out of the blue wherever you are?'

Roman cracked a smile. 'I gave her the lead on the job, so I can't blame her for following through.'

'You picked up where you left off.'

'Pretty much. She moved into my building. She kept her own place, but we were living together.'

'Wait,' Samantha said. 'You got her a job at your firm, had her move into your building. Admit you wanted her in your life.'

'Oh, I admit it. I'd missed her and wanted things back the way they were. For a while, it worked out. We were happy. Anthony took his business bicoastal, meeting with big-name clients in the city. We got together often and it was like old times except he didn't have to cook. We could afford nice restaurants. We looked forward to his visits. He always stayed with us. One weekend he announced that he was coming with someone special. He'd never done that before.'

'Naomi.'

Roman nodded.

'She loved your flat. She said the views were amazing.'

'I'm glad she liked it. Her visit changed everything.'

'How?'

'Anthony took us aside and said he intended to marry Naomi before she realized how dumb and boring he really was. There was more to it than that. He was clearly in love with her. She was so good to him.'

'Weren't you concerned? They couldn't have been together long.'

'I wasn't concerned,' he said. 'It was classic Anthony. His intuition is sharp. He knew he was wasting time in school. He knew his future was in the West Coast. And he knew Naomi was the woman for him.'

'Naomi is the same way,' Samantha said. 'She packed up and left for California with one week's notice. I freaked out. Amelia broke down. Naomi never lost her cool. She never doubted it was the right move for her.'

'They're perfect for each other.'

'I want to be perfect for someone.' The words slipped out of her. She wished she could recall them.

'You may be perfect for me, Sam.'

She didn't believe it. This was their last night together and they'd spent it talking about the enigmatic Tara. There was a chance Roman was still in love with her.

'You'll forgive me if I doubt it. Not too long ago, you were all set to marry another woman.'

'There were practical reasons for doing it,' he said. 'Around the time of Anthony's visit, Tara's lease on her studio was coming up for renewal. What made sense at the beginning no longer made sense. Life would be simpler if she just moved in with me. After Anthony's visit, living together wasn't enough. She wanted to make it official.'

'You loved her. You'd been together a long time. What was holding you back?'

'That's what Tara wanted to know. To this day I don't have an answer. It didn't feel right. That's all I can say. Seeing Anthony so sure and in love brought all our issues to light.'

For the first time ever, Samantha was grateful Timothy had ended their relationship before things got complicated. Here was an account of how complicated things could be. It made her simple break-up enviable.

'We were together so long. It was simple, easy, routine. It wasn't like ...'

'Like what?'

Roman caught her gaze and held it until the air they breathed turned thick. She wanted to break away, but couldn't. His hold on her was just that strong. All he had to do to break the spell was lower his eyes.

'In the end, I figured we'd been together too long to just pull the plug. You know? Her birthday was coming up. Tara was born on January first and we usually celebrate on New Year's Eve. All I had to do was buy a ring. We were dressed for a party and had champagne on ice.'

'It doesn't sound like you put too much effort into it.'

It was tough not to draw a side-by-side comparison with the proposal she'd witnessed just the other day. Jason had gone through so much trouble to make the occasion special for Jasmine. She remembered how nervous he was beforehand and how euphoric he'd been ever since she'd said yes. That was how it ought to be.

'Next time I'll hire a hot-air balloon. Would you like that?'

'If I'm ever on a hot-air balloon ride with you, I'll push you out,' Samantha cautioned. 'I sat through a three-course meal watching you reconnect with your long-lost fiancée—'

'You're hung up on that word,' he said. 'How many times do I have to tell you? We were never engaged.'

'What happened? You bought the ring and everything. Did you change your mind?'

He cocked his head. 'Love how you're so eager to blame me.'

Samantha brought her hands to her face. 'Oh my God, she turned you down.'

'Bingo. She said it felt forced and she'd started to question her own feelings. That ring never made it out of the box. We fought. We cried. She moved out that night.'

'Sorry. I don't know what to say.'

Roman fell silent again. This time the surf roared in her ears. He might be over Tara, but he wasn't over the break-up. 'You asked if my heart was ever broken. My answer is yes. That night was the worst of my life. She was the only woman I ever loved.'

'She's here now. Don't you think you can work it out?'

Roman didn't hesitate. 'I don't want to. It was hard to let go, but once I did I felt free.'

'I think she turned you down out of pride.'

'She wants what Anthony has, that kind of love. Here's the

thing: before Anthony ever got to that point, he left everything behind and struck out on his own. I didn't do that. I took the first job out of school and tried to make things work with the first girl I loved. When none of it made me happy, I couldn't figure out what went wrong. But now I know.'

Everything he described was so familiar. 'We're the same,' she said.

'What are you talking about?'

'I took the first job out of university. I stayed with the guy I met there and tried to make our relationship outlive its shelf life. I'm unhappy at my job. It's not bad as far as jobs go, but it's kept me stuck in one place. How is it that we're the same?'

Roman smiled. 'What made me think you wouldn't relate?'

'I relate, and it's depressing as hell.'

If he needed freedom to start his life over or rebuild from scratch, as she did, for that matter, where did that leave them?

Roman extended a hand to her, palm face up. 'What do the lines say about bad timing and even worse luck?'

She traced a finger along the lines she'd once studied, looking for insight into his heart. Tears blurred her vision. 'No idea.'

He curled his fingers around her hand. 'Sam, look at me.'

She couldn't. She was crumbling to pieces inside and could not let him see.

Because the universe was kind, her phone rang giving her the excuse to withdraw her hand. She had a text from Jasmine.

Time for Cake! Where are you?

'I should go. Important bridesmaid's duties.'

Roman took a step back and buried his hands in his pockets. 'I'll walk with you.'

With a heavy heart, she slipped off his jacket and returned it.

CHAPTER THIRTY-THREE

Jasmine caught the bouquet. Her chances were vastly improved by Samantha, Maya and Jen's complete lack of interest. Her only true competition was a woman in her late thirties who, though motivated, did not have the wherewithal to lunge in four-inch heels.

At long last, it was over. Bride and groom were sent off under a hailstorm of rice and corn for luck and prosperity. They got as far as the pool where they stripped down to bikini and swim shorts and jumped in. A last-minute post on the wedding website with instructions to wear swimwear beneath their formalwear was a tip.

Maya kicked off her shoes, kept her dress on, and dived in after them. The small gathering started chanting, 'JASMINE! JASON! JEN!' for no reason other than it was catchy. Hugo didn't need prompting. He stripped down to floral print trunks, grabbed Adrian's hand, and leaped in.

Samantha sat at the edge of the pool and dipped her feet in the water.

'Jump, Sammy! Dive in!' cried Maya from the deep end.

'Sorry, can't!'

She couldn't dive in. Her heart was so heavy she might

drown. Roman had disappeared at the end of the night. Had he gone after Tara? Were they sitting in the moonlight wondering where they'd gone wrong? Although she kept repeating, *It doesn't matter. I don't care*, she cared very much and hated that he could make her feel this way, so freaking insecure. This was not like her.

'Why not?' Maya demanded.

Samantha held up her phone. 'Taking photos!'

The excuse was enough to satisfy the younger girl. Maya took social media very seriously.

Samantha snapped a few photos to avoid further questions. Since none of her friends were camera-shy, they leaped and splashed about, competing for her attention. She laughed and played the role of art director. In twelve hours, she would board a flight home. No matter how she truly felt, she would cherish these last few hours with these incredible people.

All of that was shot to pieces when Anthony called out Roman's name. 'Hey man, you're back! Where were you? Where's T?'

Roman walked onto the pool deck, looking very much like an off-duty model in his dark suit, shirt undone, tie hanging loose around his neck. All the laughing, screeching and general carousing came to a halt. The answer to those questions was of interest to everyone, Samantha included.

Anthony had the presence of mind to climb out of the pool and take Roman aside. They continued the conversation in hushed tones. Naomi and Jasmine slid quick worried glances Samantha's way. Anthony ended the summit by pointing her out. Roman caught her eye and crossed the deck, making his way toward her.

'Hey, you,' he said. 'Why are you sitting here alone?'

Not a minute ago, her heart was trapped in the icy grip of anxiety. And now, just the sound of his voice flooded her chest with warmth. This was not good. Roman Carver could squeeze a woman's heart, leaving nothing but the pulp. She couldn't let him. She had not come all the way to Tobago just to let a man derail her life once again.

It was clear he wasn't ready for a new relationship, and neither was she. He was still trying to sort himself out, which was his right. Samantha was searching for a thrill that wasn't necessarily tied to romantic love, which left her no time to fool around.

'I'm OK here,' she answered.

'May I speak with you?' he asked.

She was done talking, but didn't want to be rude, not in front of everyone. She allowed him to pull her to her feet. She turned her back to the others for some added privacy, but that was as far as she'd go. 'What's up?'

'I wanted to give you this.' He handed her the keycard to her bungalow. 'I cleared my stuff out.'

Samantha stared blankly at him. This morning she'd slid the spare card in his pocket while he kissed her. They had such grand plans for the night and the morning. They were going to talk about the future, see how they could keep this good thing they'd found going. She fought the childish urge to snatch the card from him and stomp it with her foot. Yet the urge that followed was too strong to overcome. She took the card, thanked him, and sent him plunging backwards into the deep end of the pool. She'd warned him what would happen given the chance.

***

The loud splash of water, and the even louder cries it provoked, still roared in Samantha's head when she made it back to her bungalow. She switched on the lights and took in her little sanctuary. The original plan was to spend some much needed alone-time here, indulging in intense self-care. Why had she strayed from the plan?

She peered into the bedroom from the doorway. It was stripped of any sign a man had been there, and she felt the sting of loss. Samantha was suddenly exhausted. She curled onto the bed and rested her head on the stack of pillows, hoping to relieve the pounding at her temples. A stiff piece of paper stuck to her cheek. She yanked it off and examined it. The square envelope with the hotel's logo was smudged with her make-up. The handwritten note inside was pristine.

You're perfect for me – R

CHAPTER THIRTY-FOUR

Early the next morning, Naomi showed up at Samantha's door. Because she had refused to cry herself to sleep like any well-adjusted person would do, she hadn't slept the night before. She knew what she must look like, eyes red from staring at a whirling ceiling fan, face puffy with fatigue.

'What are you doing here? It's officially your honeymoon.'

'That doesn't start until tomorrow. We booked a resort in Trinidad and we're turning off our phones. Today we're sending you off to the airport and sticking around to help Amelia get sorted.'

She stepped aside to let Naomi in. 'Still doesn't explain why you're out and about at seven in the morning.'

'The brunch is cancelled. Everyone is exhausted and would rather sleep in.' She held up a basket covered in a blue-and-white-chequered cloth. 'We're dropping off breakfast baskets so you can relax and pack without any hassles. Anthony and I are aware that we pushed you guys to the limit. You must hate us.'

'Don't be stupid. We love you. Come sit down.'

The bungalow was a disaster with clothes and shoes strewn everywhere. Samantha was busy packing up her laptop and camera when she'd heard the light tap on her door. She tidied up a corner of the sofa for Naomi to sit. This morning she wore a white T and shorts and designer slides. She was seriously committed to the bridal theme.

'If anything, we're grateful to you,' Samantha said. 'This trip changed our lives.'

'The others', sure,' Naomi said, wiggling to get comfortable. 'Jasmine got engaged. Jen finally pinned Chris down. Hugo and Adrian worked things out. How about you? I'm afraid you came all this way just to get your heart broken again.'

Samantha took the basket into the kitchen and focused on unpacking one item at a time. 'Rice cakes! I love rice cakes.'

'Sam … nobody loves rice cakes that much. Answer me.'

Samantha clutched the cellophane-wrapped goodies in her hands. She loved them because they reminded her of Roman. Yet anything that reminded her of Roman also reminded her of the crater-sized hole he'd left in her heart. That was the vicious cycle she was caught in. She didn't want to think of him. Roman had used his ex as an exit ramp. It was over between them the moment Tara arrived.

'I have a message from Roman,' Naomi said. 'Do you want to hear it?'

She shoved the rice cakes back into the basket. 'No.'

'Too bad. This message woke me up at dawn. You're going to hear it.' Naomi slipped off her slides, propped her feet on the coffee table and read from her phone. *'Please tell her goodbye. Tell her I didn't want it to end this way. I didn't want it to end at all. Tell her I'll never forget her smile, her laugh, her fire, her temper. She changed me. I did not think that was possible. And I'll never forget her.'* Naomi dropped the phone onto her lap with the flourish of a stand-up comedian. 'Now tell me that doesn't melt the ice cap of your heart.'

So much so, she was wiping away tears. But it didn't change anything. It sounded to her like a beautiful goodbye.

'I understand the fiancée business threw you two for a loop, but it needn't be that way,' Naomi said. 'From what Anthony tells me, the relationship was stale and they dragged it on for too long. They'd been together since they were nineteen. You can't expect a relationship forged in hormones to withstand the test of time.'

'Some people make it work.'

'Roman and Tara are not those people,' Naomi said. 'Are you going to eat the banana in the basket? I need my potassium.'

She brought it to her. 'I'll fight you for the rice cake, but you can have the banana.'

'Thanks, Sammy. Now, back to serious matters. Roman is distraught. You should have seen his face after you tossed him in the pool and walked away. Boss babe move, by the way. I applaud you. It was deserved. Any chance we could move forward now?'

'No.'

'Oh, come on! You two were so good together, so easy, so cool. It was a joy to see.'

It was a joy to live, too. But a relationship slapped together on holiday would not stand the test of time. That was for sure. 'It's over. I'm focusing on me. I shouldn't be in a relationship anyway.'

'Why not? Because of Timothy?'

'Because of *me*. Forget *him*.'

'Gladly,' Naomi said dryly.

'Do you know what all of you have in common?'

'All of who?'

'You. Anthony. Jasmine. Jen. Hugo. Adrian.'

303

'Go on.' Naomi added a rolling hand gesture to her request. 'I get it.'

'You've all sorted yourselves out before finding love. You have fulfilling careers and things you're passionate about. All I could come up with was a stupid blog.'

'I had my doubts about the travel blog only because it requires some financing and freedom to move about. Unless you plan to do all your travelling on weekends, it would be hard to sustain. The other idea I loved. You're passionate about people. You want to know what makes them tick, what's going on in their heads, and all of that good stuff. You ask questions and follow-up questions. You actually care. I've always loved that about you. Why not tap into that?'

Samantha moved aside a pile of folded jeans and made room for herself on the sofa. She nestled close to Naomi. Who knew when she'd have the chance again? 'You don't think it's stupid?'

Naomi pulled her into a pity hug. 'I think you're stupid for belittling your ideas. You're so bright.'

Samantha raised her head and studied her brilliant friend. 'You never second-guessed yourself. How?'

'What's the worst that can really happen?' she said. 'We're the lucky ones. We've got family and friends who love us and support us emotionally, and even financially, if it came to that. We can afford to make some mistakes.'

She couldn't afford to quit her job and take off to Bali, like in the movies, to hone her craft. Tobago had given her the taste of adventure and opened her eyes to what her real interests were. The trick was to find a way to combine the two.

'OK, my love, I have to spend quality time with my other little sister, Maya. Help me up, please.'

'You're not *that* pregnant.'

'I've had to hide this pregnancy for too long. Now it's time to milk it.'

Samantha got up and tugged Naomi to her feet. Then she gave her one last hug and whispered 'thank you' over and over again.

Naomi was weepy when she pulled away. 'One last thing,' she said. 'We're planning on having everyone over when the baby is born. A West Coast reunion! Save your paid time off for that.'

★★★

The happy couples boarded the bus two by two. Samantha flopped onto the first empty bench. They were all too tired to talk and the ride to the airport stretched out in silence. To pass the time, Samantha scrolled through the dozens of photos she'd taken the night before. Naomi and Anthony kissing in the water. Jasmine laughing hysterically as Jason paraded her on his shoulders. Jen and Chris spooning on the pool's steps, sharing a private laugh. Maya and the twins staging a photo shoot worthy of an editorial. She could hear the laughter and the taunting and the cheers. Samantha swiped at a tear with such force she nearly scratched her eye. These were her people. These were the relationships that mattered and would last far longer than this other round of heartache.

It was a relief when they finally approached the airport. Samantha tucked her phone away and checked her passport and boarding passes. In reality, she was checking for Roman's note folded within the pages of her passport. She ran her fingertips over its slanted letters. Then she tucked it back in its hiding place.

After the luggage was sorted, they handed their driver all their free bills and loose change, over six hundred local dollars in total. They travelled together to the international airport of Port of Spain. This was where they said their final goodbyes. Jasmine and Jason were flying to Toronto. Jen and Chris were headed to Los Angeles. Samantha was sticking with Hugo and Adrian to Miami, where she would catch a connecting flight back home. They made a big production out of it with group hugs, one-on-one bear hugs, tearful promises to keep in touch, and one last group photo with the aid of Adrian's selfie stick.

At their gate, Hugo and Adrian swore up and down that they were fit enough to manage the emergency exit in exchange for seats with extra legroom. Samantha didn't bother. There was a good chance Timothy's seat would be empty and she'd have a row to herself.

It wasn't until she boarded the plane and shoved her carry-on case into the overhead compartment that she noticed the woman in the window seat.

Petite. Curvy. Glossy black hair. Smooth almond skin. Sassy leopard-print face mask. A spool of knitting yarn on her lap.

Tara.

Samantha brought a hand to her mouth. Her disposable surgical mask scratched her cheek. Oh, God, she thought. There was no way she would make it to Miami alive.

'Ma'am, please sit down.'

Flight attendants had no patience for passengers in the throes of nervous breakdowns.

Samantha looked around in search of a vacant seat. 'Is there—'

'No. The flight is full.'

Damn it.

Tara reached for a sweater draped over the armrest connecting their two seats and a magazine tossed on Samantha's side of the fence. 'This seat is free,' she said, attempting to clear up any misunderstanding. 'Here you go. All yours.'

She unleashed that same charming, self-deprecating humour which served her so well when she'd showed up at the reception the night before. By comparison, Samantha's response was wooden and charmless. She lowered herself onto the seat before the flight attendant resorted to violence. Her bag slipped off her lap and her phone, lip balm and a pack of chewing gum scattered to the ground. Guess she wasn't a baddie, after all.

Samantha caught her phone before it went tumbling down the centre aisle.

'Are you nervous?' Tara asked. 'I get nervous when I fly, which explains the yarn … and why I'm so chatty. I'll shut up after take-off.' She scooped up the lip balm. 'Here you go. Love that brand, by the way. So moisturizing.'

'Thanks.'

'No problem.'

Tara was more than charm and a winning smile. She was a winner. Her eyes sparkled with intelligence. One day she'd lead the free world or the World Bank, whichever recruited her first. If Roman couldn't love her …?

'We ask that you please fasten your seatbelts at this time and secure all baggage underneath your seat or in the overhead compartments.'

Tara stuffed the ball of pink yarn in a duffle bag underneath her seat. 'Goodness, *look*, your passport!'

Samantha's passport was under Tara's foot, stuck to the sole of her smart loafers. For God's sake! Why couldn't she hold it together? She and Tara reached for the passport at the same time,

but Tara was quicker. It was stuck to her foot after all. 'British …
nice. Do you have family in Trinidad? Or were you on vacation?'

Samantha wondered how to play this. Tell the whole truth
or a slimmed-down version of it? Her brain was buffering. Why
couldn't she think? She had to come up with a plan. Was it too
late to text Hugo for advice? The short answer was yes. It was
too late to phone a friend or come up with any sort of plan.
Tara had found yet another one of her belongings, a short note
inked on hotel stationery.

'Flight attendants, prepare for take-off.'

CHAPTER THIRTY-FIVE

Tara studied the note, flushed beet red, and handed it over. Samantha stuck it back into her passport, which she secured in the zippered pocket of the tote bag she stuffed beneath her seat. She prayed that would be the end of it.

Tara was silent as they raced down the runway. She clutched the armrest when the aircraft rattled as the wheels pulled in. They hadn't reached cruising altitude when she loosened her grip.

'I was at that hotel just last night, at a close friend's wedding.'

'What a coincidence.'

'And I recognize that handwriting.'

Obviously.

'What's your name?' Tara asked.

Samantha exhaled. If Tara could play it straight, so could she. 'I'm Samantha Roberts. I was a bridesmaid at the wedding. Your close friend married my best friend.'

'You're *that* Sam?'

'Depends what you mean by that.'

Tara turned away and stared out the window, her eyes searching the clouds. 'I think we know.'

Samantha wasn't proud of it, but her heart swelled upon hearing those words. There was a part of her that revelled in finding Tara on her flight. It meant that she hadn't stayed behind with Roman, not that she cared.

Tara repeated the note from memory. '*You're perfect for me.*'

'I wouldn't read too much into that.'

'Did you know him long?' Tara asked.

'Barely a week. We were the only single people at the wedding and just started hanging out. I was perfect for him … under those limited circumstances.'

Samantha wondered what she was aiming to achieve, going on like this. Who was she trying to convince? Tara or herself?

'Roman only says what he means,' Tara said. 'If he said you're perfect for him, you are. Lucky you.'

The refreshment service marked the end of the first round. Samantha requested a green tea, no sugar. Tara went for a ginger ale, no ice. They attended to their beverages without saying a word. The tea was terrible, and Samantha's throat was too tight to drink anyway. She checked the time. Two and a half hours to go. What were her options other than locking herself in the tiny, smelly lavatory?

Tara reached blindly under her seat and pulled two small packets of chocolate-covered pretzels from her bag. She offered one to Samantha.

'No thanks.'

'They're far better than airline snacks. I stock up whenever I travel.'

'I'm sure, but …' Samantha paused. On second thought, it would be rude to turn her down. 'Thank you.'

Samantha ripped open the pack and made a point of munching on a few pretzels. They were delicious, the right sweet-to-salty ratio. 'Tasty.'

'Right?' Tara did a little shoulder shimmy. 'I love turning people on to gourmet snacks. You'll never settle for the cheap stuff again.'

'*The hell is going on here?*'

That was Hugo, and his little outburst earned him a reprimand from a young mother in the next aisle. He rushed to Samantha's side. 'My sixth sense told me to check on you. How did this happen?'

Samantha shrugged, helpless. There was no explanation. The universe had her in a spin cycle.

'I know you!' Tara exclaimed. 'You were at my table last night.'

Hugo showed his confusion with a slight tilt of the head. 'It was the other way around. You were at *my* table.'

'I guess so.' Tara made a face. 'I must have caused drama. Does everybody hate me? Do they think I'm a drama queen?'

Samantha popped a pretzel in her mouth and mumbled, 'I wouldn't go *that* far.'

Tara looked from Samantha to Hugo. 'OK. Scale of 1 to 10.'

Hugo gave it some thought. 'You're hovering around 7 to 7.5.'

'That's not good.' Tara frowned. 'I love Anthony to pieces. How can I fix it?'

'Send the couple an expensive gift,' Hugo suggested. 'That's what I'd do.'

'Good idea.' She tapped Samantha's shoulder. 'You're the bride's best friend. What does she like?'

'Shiny, sparkly things that come in pretty boxes.'

Tara decided on the spot. 'Crystal candlestick holders.'

Hugo approved. 'That'll do it.'

'Thanks, you two,' she said. 'I didn't intend to cause trouble.'

'What was your intention?' Hugo asked. 'I'm curious.'

'That's between Roman and me.'

Samantha choked on a pretzel and coughed up any good will she'd had for Tara. Hugo handed her the cup of green tea that sat cooling on the fold-down tray. 'Are you all right?' he asked.

She nodded, took a sip. 'It's nothing. I'm fine.'

A bout of turbulence prompted the captain to turn on the 'fasten seatbelt' sign and request all passengers return to their seats. No one other than Hugo was wandering about, so the request seemed directed at him.

'I should go,' he said. 'Are you going to be OK here? Want to switch seats?'

Tara laughed. 'She'll be fine. We have premium snacks.'

Samantha rewarded him with a chocolate-covered pretzel. 'Go back to Adrian. Tell him I said hi.'

'Holler if you need me.' A pointed glance at Tara, sharp enough to pin her in place, and Hugo returned to his seat.

'He has to be the fun friend,' Tara whispered.

Hugo was the most fun and the most nurturing. 'The best. I love him.'

Tara returned her attention to the window. Timothy had the aisle seat on this and all the flights they'd booked. He hated feeling boxed in. The window that Tara was gazing out of was hers. She'd boarded the plane early and just took the seat she wanted. Samantha decided that this was the last time she'd let Tara spoil anything else for her.

'I can't say for sure Roman meant what he wrote in that note,' Samantha said. 'All I know is that what we had was meaningful. It changed me, for sure. I have no regrets.'

It wasn't the right time for either of them to start something new. They had a lot to sort out on their own. In another world, maybe, they'd be perfect for each other. Saying goodbye now was the right thing, the mature thing.

Tara kept her eyes on the ever-changing sky. Another bout of turbulence had her clutching the armrest. She didn't speak up until the captain announced the weather in Miami. 'Sorry if I messed things up for you. Sounds like you had a momentum going and I crash-landed into it … Oops, poor choice of words.'

'No need to apologize,' Samantha said.

'I never got a love note from him, not once in six years. I guess that proves my point. We loved each other, but weren't *madly in love* with each other. We were nothing like Anthony and Naomi – those two take the cake.'

It wasn't so much a love note as a farewell note, but Samantha didn't point out the difference.

'It kills me to think I might've ruined his life.'

Samantha was confused. 'Why would you think that?'

'Maybe not his life,' Tara mused. 'Certainly his career.'

'I don't understand.'

'Our break-up was pretty dramatic,' Tara explained. 'He proposed, and I said no. I couldn't go through with it, even though I'd pushed for it. Blame it on Anthony and Naomi. All that talk about love at first sight …'

None of this answered Samantha's original question. What made her think she'd destroyed his career?

'Want to hear something stupid?' Tara said. 'Roman was my instant love. The first time I laid eyes on him, I was lost in the woods. I just had the good sense to shut up about it. I'd unsubscribe to anyone who tried pushing that nonsense on me.'

'It's not stupid,' Samantha said quietly.

She wasn't about to judge Tara when she'd had an eerily similar experience, except she was literally lost in a woodsy area at the time. She could see it clear as day. He came running past and the rest was history.

'Anyway, I went after him and I got him,' Tara said breezily. 'I'm very proactive, and I don't believe in luck or chance. You have to go out there and make things happen, for better or worse. The night he proposed, I knew I'd gone too far. I'd pressured him into it, and it wasn't right.'

Roman had proposed thinking it was the right thing to do, but it was a pity proposal, and nobody wanted that.

'It wasn't pretty.' Tara stared blankly ahead as if reliving the horror of that night. 'We had the mother of all fights *on my birthday*. I cried. He cried. We let it all out. It was necessary, therapeutic. When the dust settled, I thought we were in a good place. I thought we could start over and take things slow. Then he went and blew up his whole life. He quit his job and moved out to the middle of nowhere.'

'Tobago is a magical place,' Samantha said. 'We should be so lucky to get to live there.'

'We're *not* the lucky ones,' Tara fired back. 'I don't know how it is in jolly old England, but Roman and I are working-class kids. We can't afford to do that shit. Do you know how hard we had to work to get our foot in the door on Wall Street? Roman joined a mentorship programme and worked for free. I had to assist a guy way younger than me with way less credentials. I had to bring him coffee! That's the world we live in!'

'I understand the struggle is real,' Samantha said. 'But have some faith in Roman. He has a plan. He's pivoting to small businesses that cater to the tourist sector.'

'That's adorable, but how does that pay rent?' Tara said. 'Anyway, our firm wants him back. That's what I flew in to tell him. They'll give him the promotion he wanted and the office he was eyeing.'

'He hates that job.'

Practical-minded Tara rejected this wholesale. 'No one loves their job. Unless your nana left you a trust fund, you've got to work. I honestly couldn't believe he quit. We were finally living our dream.'

'Your dream, maybe.'

Tara sighed with impatience. 'You really are perfect for him.'

Samantha ignored the comment. She was too focused on something else Tara had said. *I'm very proactive.* 'May I ask you something?'

'Why not? I've been talking for so long my mouth is dry.'

'Did you somehow encourage management to rehire Roman and put that package together?'

Tara laughed. 'Girl, I'm not that powerful. They *want* him back. He's good at what he does. He's *great*. I had them add the office with a view to sweeten the deal.'

There it was. Tara had gone too far. Again. 'Let's forget Roman for a minute, if that's all right.'

'OK.'

'Why take it so far?'

'I still care about him. He shouldn't ruin his life because of me.'

'That's not what he's doing. And he has a right to quit his job.'

'I get that you don't want him to return to New York.'

'You're wrong. I'm on my way home to *jolly old England*. I may never see him again. It makes no difference to me.' To

Samantha's horror, her voice broke on that last phrase. She rushed to make her point before she came unhinged. 'You may not want to hear this, but it's not your place to negotiate with Roman's employer or otherwise use your influence to make him return to a life that he's rejected.'

'Are you a relationship expert?'

'I've yet to have a successful relationship,' Samantha admitted without shame. 'But I have loving, caring friendships. You'd like to be his friend, right? You're going about it all wrong.'

'You're a smart girl, Samantha,' Tara said. 'I want way more than to be his friend. You must've figured that.'

'My point is the same. You're going about it all wrong.'

Tara blinked, searching for something to say. Finally, she popped a chocolate-covered pretzel in her mouth and resumed staring out the window.

The landing was bumpy, but they'd made it safely to Miami.

★★★

Samantha gave Hugo and Adrian a final hug goodbye before they parted ways. They were heading to customs and she was off to catch her connecting flight. Hugo couldn't let go. He held her tight and swung her around while Adrian stood off to the side, scrolling his phone, giving them the space they needed.

'Bye, *gata*,' Hugo whispered. 'Take care of your heart.'

'You too,' she whispered back. 'And take care of him. He's all right.'

'Sure. I might kill him, though.'

'Don't!' She gently pulled away from him. 'I've got to run. *Try* to be good.'

'Never! Just wait until I break the news to the others about you know who.'

They would never ever shut up about it. 'Ugh! I hate you!'

'Love you! Bye!'

Samantha watched them go, chatting and wheeling their carry-on luggage behind them, then took a minute to check the information on her boarding pass. Just as she was ready to charge off, You Know Who walked right up to her and tapped her on the shoulder. 'Hello again!'

Tara had gathered her things as soon as the plane stopped moving and charged to the front of the line, past glares and goggle eyes. 'I hate waiting around' were her only parting words. However, it seemed she'd been waiting for Hugo and Adrian to leave to approach Samantha.

'I've got some time to kill before boarding my flight to New York,' she said. 'Want to hang out?'

'I can't. My flight boards in twenty minutes.'

Tara flashed that winning smile. 'Probably for the best, right?'

Samantha couldn't disagree. 'Probably.'

'Well, hey. I know this is awkward as hell, but I'm glad I met you. All in all, I feel better knowing Roman is in good hands.'

Samantha took a step back. 'He's not in my hands at all.'

'You're in denial. That's OK. Go home and get settled. You'll find out soon enough that it's not so easy to get over Roman Carver. It took me three tries to get it right.' Tara swung her duffle bag over her shoulder. 'Bye now! Safe travels!'

CHAPTER THIRTY-SIX

Gloomy skies welcomed Samantha back to England. It suited her mood perfectly. When she finally arrived home, a stale odour clung to the air inside the flat. Her monstera plant stood drooping in a corner. She put down her luggage and cracked open a window. Then she set her phone on the bedside charger. The group chat comprised texts, GIFs and endless strings of emojis. Hugo had kept his word and broken the news more faithfully than a BBC correspondent. Everyone on the chat, which now included Jen, had an opinion. Samantha didn't have to hear it.

She was exhausted. The last leg of her trip had gutted her. It was easy enough to keep up appearances with her friends around, and she would have leaped out of the plane before falling apart in front of Tara. Sitting alone in that transatlantic flight, without the perks of a first-class upgrade that got her through the last time around, she was a weepy mess. Tara's words haunted her. *It's not so easy to get over Roman Carver.*

After a shower, she pulled on her favourite jumper and yoga pants combo, tossed a half-empty container of takeaway into the rubbish, made a cup of mint tea, watered the monstera, lit a candle, and repeated her mantra until she fell asleep. *I can go it alone.*

In the dead of night, she startled awake. No tropical night sounds. She slipped out of bed, puttered into the hall and in the dim light, checked the zippered pockets of her travel bag until she found her passport, and in her passport, the note left on her pillow the night before.

Next thing, she dug out her laptop.

DRAFT POST #10: THE HIDDEN PATH

I was on the path to happiness and somehow lost my way ...

***

The following morning, Samantha dragged herself to work. The pandemic had significantly altered the office culture. Where she and her colleagues once crammed into one large office space divided into a cubicle farm, now only a handful of them were authorized to work from the office on any given day. The rest of the time, they worked from home. Samantha welcomed the change, but she was in the minority. Her colleagues missed their routines. They enjoyed setting their alarms the night before, waking up at dawn, commuting in the rain, scarfing down prepackaged lunches at their desks, arguing with co-workers over office supplies, office gossip, and bad coffee. Samantha didn't share their longing for the way things were.

The office was located in one of the modern buildings in the city centre. Riding the lift to the tenth floor, she worked out a strategy. If asked about her trip, she would hand over her phone and let her colleagues swipe through the carefully curated album she'd created for her mother. She would chalk up her lack of enthusiasm to jetlag. Satisfied with her plan, she marched to her workstation.

Of the nine writers in the web content division, Dawn Matthews alone was at her desk. A gift! Dawn wasn't one to chitchat. Channelling Naomi, Samantha did her best to sound as chipper as possible. 'Good morning, Dawn!'

Not me crying over some man I met last week. I've more sense than that.

'Look at you, all healthy and glowing.'

'A little holiday doesn't hurt.'

Dawn frowned. 'You're happy about the news, aren't you?'

'What news?'

Samantha dropped her bag on her desk. Her cubicle was smaller than the others, but it was closest to the window. That summed up corporate compromise.

'You haven't heard?' Dawn said.

'Heard what? I was on holiday.'

'Mary sent an email.'

'I was on ho-li-day.' Work-life balance was not a privilege of the few, but a right of the masses. 'Would you like to see the photos?'

Dawn's frown deepened. In her mid-fifties, she always looked polished and put-together in navy suits. 'Don't you know me by now?'

Samantha laughed, even though her insides felt like broken glass. 'Yes, Dawn, I do.' She took a breath and sat down. 'And I love you just the same.'

She fired up her desktop computer and froze when she spotted a note on her keyboard. Another damn note! This one was from Steven Shaw, her managing editor, a few words jotted down on a yellow square. *Come see me right away.* Samantha held it up over the cubicle partition. 'Dawn!' she cried. 'Do you know what this is about?'

'I do,' Dawn said dryly. 'And you would, too, if you checked your emails.'

***

The web content division was going remote. That was the news.

'As with everything, it's about money,' Steven explained. 'By going remote, we'll cancel the lease on this floor. We'll make an office available for any of you, should you need to come in, once or twice a month. Don't worry, you won't have to work in the break room.'

Samantha leaned forward. 'You're saying we'll be working from home 100 per cent of the time.'

'From home or a café in Paris, if you choose. The point is, we really don't care. So long as you have a secure connection, which we'll provide, turn in your assignments in a timely manner, and participate in our virtual weekly meetings.'

'Are you … serious?'

'Quite. We're cutting the umbilical cord.'

Steven's salt and pepper hair went every which way, but his glassy blue eyes were steady. That was his serious face. He *was* serious. 'It won't be all fun and games. If you can't keep up with our pace and consistently miss deadlines, we'll have to let you go.'

'I understand.'

'Not everyone is happy about this. How do you feel?'

'Free,' she whispered. 'I feel free.'

'Well, fly away, then,' he said, dismissing her with a flick of a fountain pen. 'And I want one thousand words on cryptocurrency by the end of the week as a companion piece for next week's cover story.'

Samantha left the meeting feeling weightless. She was free to fly away. She could pack up her laptop and head to the airport right now. Nothing was stopping her. A spark of excitement fizzled out quick. Where would she even go? Jetlag weighed her down.

***

That evening, she flipped open her journals in search of a list of travel destinations that she'd compiled way back when. Off the top of her head, she could rattle off a few: Rome, Athens, Barcelona … none of those places called to her now. Maybe somewhere quieter, less obvious. She could reach out to Jasmine for a recommendation. Last year, she'd visited Morocco and loved it. That was a possibility.

Samantha boxed up her journals and shoved them under her bed. Why wasn't she excited? The world was open to her now. All she wanted to do was lie down and nap. The answer was obvious. Now was not the time for dream-come-true scenarios. Her heart was broken. She did not want to fly. She wanted to curl up in her nest and sleep the days away.

***

On Friday evening, Samantha had to leave her flat. She rode the bus to her parents' house and showed up at their door with a bunch of balloons and a HAPPY RETIREMENT banner. Her mother greeted her with a hug and fitted a party hat on her head. She was wearing her official retirement uniform, the finest in athletic leisurewear and a pair of fuzzy slippers. At fifty-seven, her mother was a tall Black woman with a sweet disposition. She would have likely gone on working for two more decades if it weren't for her chronic migraines.

Her dad, on the other hand, was healthy as an ox and committed to his job.

Samantha had her mother's height and her dad's eyes and smile. Her curly hair and cinnamon brown skin were a combination of the two.

It was just the three of them at their dining table, as usual, but for some reason her mother felt the need to apologize. 'I know this is not as exciting as you would've liked but I wasn't in the mood to get dressed up.'

Samantha looked up from her plate of lasagne. 'Mum, this is great. I can't think of anything I'd enjoy more. Besides, this is *your* party.'

'I made chocolate cake.'

'Well, what more do we need?'

It hurt her that she'd made her mother feel like her life and experiences weren't grand enough or that she ought to crisscross the globe to find fulfilment. Some people were meant to wander and others were meant to keep the porch lights on. At this point, Samantha wasn't sure which she was cut out to be.

As a reward, her dad filled her wine glass. Samantha raised a toast. 'Happy retirement, Mum. I hope it's everything you're dreaming of.'

After dinner, Samantha took her glass of wine to her old bedroom. Only it didn't feel like hers anymore. There were no longer any posters on the walls, for one thing, and that was a big deal. For another, the books that lined the shelves no longer mattered to her and the clothes hanging in the wardrobe were hopelessly out of fashion.

She stood at the window that looked straight into Naomi's old room. The new owners had converted the bedroom into a home office. An exercise bike was crammed into a corner. Everyone had moved on. Surprisingly, Samantha was OK with it. Naomi was happy in her new world and happiness was within reach for Samantha as well. She just had to be patient … and proactive.

Come Sunday, she'd return with enough boxes and bags to clear out this room. That would be her gift to her mother. She wouldn't stop there. She'd splurge on a craft table and whatever else a person needed to do crafts. A top-of-the-line sewing machine or hot glue gun? Samantha made a mental note to look it up. And while she was online, she'd book a cheap flight; it didn't matter where. The trick was to get going, the rest would sort itself out. Tara had one thing right. You had to go out there and make things happen, for better or worse, come what may. You couldn't do that by clinging to the past, looking back, wondering what if, and wishing things were different. It was a waste of time.

Deep inside, she knew what the problem was. For all her dreams of travel, she had never expected to go it alone. She loved the shared experience. She'd first caught the bug in Vegas. The trip had changed her perspective entirely. Lounging poolside alone at a five-star resort wasn't terrible. Sprinkle in a few new friends, a fruity cocktail or two, and those dry hot desert nights were the coolest ever.

I can go it alone.

I can do the things that scare me.

Seriously, what was the point of mantras and affirmations if you didn't apply them to real-life situations? Maybe hers needed revision.

Each day I'll do one thing that scares me.

Today, I'll book a flight.

Tomorrow, I'll post my blog.

Sunday, I'll clear out my childhood bedroom to make space for growth.

Tuesday or Wednesday, I'll wake up in a new city.

Travel was the best way she knew to get out of a rut. Besides, she could always meet new people, make new friends. Until she'd met Jen in Tobago, she thought she'd reached her maximum limit on friendship. And until she met Roman … no – she wouldn't go there. Not yet. Exploring the world was one thing, but Samantha wasn't quite ready to explore the shadowy places of her heart.

CHAPTER THIRTY-SEVEN

Roman sat slouched in the terminal lounge, legs propped up on his carry-on luggage. All around him, travellers were dozing off, snoring softly, scrolling their phones, sipping hot beverages from Styrofoam cups, or simply staring ahead. He was at Heathrow, 3 a.m., biding time until his 6 a.m. flight. There was no chance he'd get any sleep.

His phone buzzed in his hand. The late-night call didn't faze him. He was accustomed to getting calls at odd hours. It was the name on the screen that threw him for a loop. When he answered, his voice was rougher than intended. 'Yes?'

'Uh … rude!' Tara snapped.

'Sorry. It's three in the morning.'

'In what world? It's 10 p.m. my time. You're one hour ahead.'

He pulled himself upright. 'I'm not in Tobago anymore.'

'You mean you've come out of hiding?'

'I mean my hiatus is over.'

'Well, where in the world are you?'

'Do you need to know that?'

'If you think I'm going to show up at your door, get over yourself,' she said. 'I've moved on.'

'I may need that in writing.'

'Fine. You're *not* perfect for me. Better?'

Her choice of words filled him with unease. 'I hope you pulled that out of thin air.'

'Not a chance,' she said dryly. 'I'm quoting your sweet little love note.'

'What?'

His outcry earned him a few dirty looks.

'You don't have any right to be upset,' Tara said. 'The only note you ever left me in six years was a grocery list.'

He'd never had to clear out of her apartment because an ex had turned up out of the blue, either. As far as he was concerned, he and Tara were even. But Samantha was another story. The quickly drawn note left on her pillow had been pitiful. Every time he thought of it, his chest went tight. 'How did you see it?'

'Don't you know?'

'Know what?' Roman got up, grabbed the handle of his carry-on, and went to stand by a window. He needed the freedom to shout if it came to that.

'She didn't tell you?' Tara said.

'What's there to tell?'

'Wait … Roman … Is it possible you haven't spoken to Samantha since the wedding? Please tell me that's not true.'

'And you have?'

'You really don't know? Pour yourself a drink, old friend. I have a story for you.'

All he had was a bottle of water, and it would have to do. 'I'm listening.'

After Tara had finished relating the run-in with Samantha, she said, 'Do with that information what you like.'

What was there to do? Samantha had handled herself

extremely well under crappy circumstances. It only made him love her more, but she still hated him.

Three weeks had passed since she'd dunked him in a pool and walked away. It didn't get any less subtle than that. She didn't want anything to do with him. He lived with the pain of it every day. Some nights he chased it with whisky or whatever was stocked in the hotel mini bar in Dubai, where he'd gone for work. This short layover in London didn't make it easier.

'I got the sense that she really liked you.'

'She did until you showed up.'

'That's not fair. How was I to know you were having "an affair to remember"?'

'It doesn't matter. It's too late.'

He could kick himself for every stupid mistake he'd made. By refusing to talk openly about his past, he'd tainted the little trust she'd had in him.

'You know it isn't up to me to fix your life,' Tara said. 'I'm learning boundaries.'

'Is that why you're calling? To test boundaries.'

'To share some news, smart ass.'

'OK. Let's hear it.'

'I took that promotion you passed on – and the office, too.'

'Oh, shit!' If he knew Tara, she was in heaven. 'How did you celebrate? Did you roll around that office floor?'

'Shut your mouth!'

Roman let out a soundless laugh and stumbled backwards onto the nearest seat. 'Congratulations.'

'They wanted you.'

'They got the better person,' he said. 'Don't doubt that. How do you feel about it?'

This woman who was so bold, so fierce, who'd taught him so much, he didn't want her ever to second-guess herself – certainly not because of him.

'Incredibly proud.'

A silence passed between them. Roman shifted from under the weight of all the ways he'd come up short, ultimately disappointing her. She didn't deserve a less than honest love. He wished he'd had the courage to tell her how he felt, or no longer felt, instead of dragging them both down.

'Will you be OK?' she asked.

'I'll be fine.'

'So, where are you really?'

Adrift, that's where he was. Newly employed and focused, but adrift nonetheless. He was on his way to New York for no other reason than to clear out his storage space. Next month, he was headed to Morocco. That's when his job started in earnest. He'd volunteered for this quick trip to Dubai under the guise of 'hitting the ground running' only because he couldn't stay in Tobago after Samantha had left. Roman wasn't sure what he'd do from now until he left for Morocco, but he kept his angst to himself. 'On my way back from Dubai.'

'Fancy. What were you doing there?'

'I'm consulting for Trident Data Corp.'

'You *dog*!' Tara's cry pierced his eardrum. 'All this time I thought—'

'You thought I was asleep at the wheel.'

'That's exactly what I thought!'

'I think you know me better than that.'

'I see …' She was breathless. 'Tell me everything. Where are you based? West Coast?'

'I'm not based anywhere,' he said. 'That was part of the deal. I go where needed and camp out where I want and take on new clients so long as there's no conflict.'

'A true digital nomad.'

'I like how that sounds.'

'I should go,' she said. 'It's late here, too. I have a coffee date in the morning.'

'Oh, yeah?'

'Yeah,' she said. 'The world keeps spinning even though you and I are no longer dance partners.'

'I like how that sounds, too.'

'Maybe we could keep in touch, share info, be partners in tech.'

'Be friends?' he suggested.

'I'd like that,' she said. 'Love you, Ro. Safe travels.'

'Love you, T. Goodnight.'

Roman clutched his phone to his chest. Outside the wide windows, the views were blurred from a wash of silent, steady rain. The night was a blur anyway. He tried to picture Samantha on that fateful flight. She must have been out of sorts, dropping her passport and all her things like that. But … she'd kept his stupid note. She hadn't ripped it to confetti or flushed it down the toilet. Instead, she'd kept it with her important papers. That was valuable information worth acting on.

Roman tapped on the phone's search engine and entered her name. She lived in Manchester, that much he knew. Yet there was so much he didn't know about her. This brief layover in England was especially triggering. He was on her turf and saw her everywhere, heard her laugh over the steady drum of mundane airport conversation. He wondered how she dressed for the cooler climate, how she took her tea, what her routines were, which pubs she preferred and how she liked her beer. More than that, he wanted to know how she was doing. Was she OK? Sleeping OK? Eating OK? Getting back into her routines OK? Did she regret as he did, increasingly with each passing day, the chance they'd squandered? He'd never known happiness like that – easy, uncomplicated happiness. No matter where he was or with whom, a part of him wished he was back in the little house in Tobago with her.

He got his answers in a most unexpected way. He'd been offline for a little bit and, apparently, had missed a whole lot.

RESULTS FOR SAMANTHA ROBERTS: TRENDING NOW

A new candid blog touches a chord with readers. An excerpt.

THE HIDDEN PATH by SAMANTHA ROBERTS

POST #1: LOST?

Somehow I've veered off the path to happiness. I've retraced my steps, checked my inner compass, asked the universe for direction, and nothing. I'm lost and, frankly, confused. What frustrates me most is that I was doing so well. For once I was on the right track, reconnecting with all the things that bring me joy. And then I met someone. It wasn't perfect, nothing is. The timing was off. The setting could make any girl believe in dreams and fairy tales. Yet deep inside, I knew it was right. It felt right. Quite unexpectedly, everything changed. I must have taken a wrong turn somewhere because now I'm lost. Has this ever happened to you? How do you find your way back?

COMMENTS (1,034):

@Cora579: Same, girl. Same.

@_LeslieLeo: I feel lost ALL THE TIME

@FUN&FASHION: It's the worst feeling. Sending you love.

@Iheartbooksandcandy: Ugh! The worst!

@BFFFFFF_: You got this! Stay focused on you!

Samantha had finally posted her blog ... and it was a hit.

Roman read and reread the one and only blog entry posted to the site. Too wired to sit still, too petrified to move, he set the phone down and stared out the window and the black glossy night stared back.

Sam was lost, and so was he. Worst of all, he'd made her feel that way.

If they could talk one last time, maybe together they could find their way. Calling or texting wouldn't work. He'd left her a note and sent her a message through Naomi and heard nothing back. He had to take action.

Before he knew what he was doing, Roman reached for his phone and typed a text message.

CHAPTER THIRTY-EIGHT

7 August, 3.45 a.m.

New Message to Naomi, Hugo, Jas, Jen

Roman: Hey. I'm in London.

Jen: Nice! Need restaurant recs?

Roman: No, thanks. What if I wanted to reach out to Samantha?

Jen: What if? You're not sure?

Roman: I'm sure.

Jasmine: It's roughly 4 in the morning London time. How sure can you be?

Hugo: She's right, my man. Get some rest and get back to us when you're thinking clearly.

Naomi: ...

Roman: Just asking for an address, guys. I'll skip the advice, if you don't mind.

Jen: You're new here. When you come to the group chat, you get what you get.

Roman: Just found out Tara was on Sam's flight. Would have been nice to hear it from you.

Hugo: We talked of nothing else for days!

Jen: Hello! He's new here.

Jasmine: Someone add Roman to the chat. Well ... no. Let's see how serious he is about Sam first.

Roman: I'm very serious.

Jasmine: You're going to see her. That's the plan?

Roman: Yes. Do you think she'll see me?

Hugo: She might. Or she might push you into the Thames. Who knows?

Jasmine: Take your chances.

Jen: I say yes. Have you read her blog? It's practically a love letter.

Hugo: *1 Attachment. Photo of Roman stretched out on the edge of a pool in a dripping wet wool suit.*

Roman: Thanks for the memories.

Hugo: Anytime, man.

Jen: LOL

Naomi: …

Jasmine: Seriously, though. Your intention has to be clear.

Hugo: Don't mess with her head.

Roman: I won't. I've got something important to ask her.

Jen: Chris says to MAN UP!

Hugo: Like he's got skills?

Jasmine: Tell the Player of the Year to calm down.

Naomi: Roman Carver! I'm pregnant with your godchild. Are you trying to raise my blood pressure?

Roman: Jesus … Go lay down. Anthony would kill me if anything happened to you.

Naomi: Don't tell me what to do. I've been waiting WEEKS for you to come to your senses. Now, where exactly in London are you? If I have to draw you a map, I'll draw you a bloody map.

Jasmine: Too funny.

Jen: LMFAO

Hugo: I need a drink for this …

CHAPTER THIRTY-NINE

After turning in the last assignment of the week, after yoga at the gym, a slow walk home and a quick stop at her favourite spot to pick up an order of chicken tikka masala, Samantha was ready to shut it down for the night. She dimmed the lights, lit a candle, chose a show, and set up dinner on her coffee table. She hadn't yet unpacked from her trip. An open suitcase lay on the living-room floor. She likely wouldn't get to it until Sunday and that was just fine. Now it was time to chill.

The buzzer rang.

The buzzer *never* rang, not without some advance warning in text form. It had to be a mistake.

She hit the intercom button. 'Sorry. Not expecting anyone.'

The voice that answered was rich like honey. 'I know you're not expecting me. Can I come up anyway?'

A tingling sensation spread from the tip of the finger pressing the button to her whole body. 'Roman?'

'Hey.'

'What are you doing in England? How did you find me?'

'Naomi drew me a map.'

'What?'

'It's a long story.'

Her heart was racing now. All she was doing was stalling for time to recover from the shock.

'I have something to ask you,' he said. 'I'd rather not do this from the steps of your building.'

She wanted to let him in; that was the problem. She wanted to throw open the door, rush down the three flights of stairs, grab him and not let him go. His voice had switched on the lights. Everything went from dull to dynamic when he said her name. That was his power over her. To keep from disclosing all this, she kept her answer short. 'Sure. Whatever.'

Roman Carver showed up at her door in a grey jumper, grey slacks and a light trench coat. The shock of seeing him in anything other than a rumpled T-shirt blew her over. 'Who the hell are you?'

He shoved his hands in his coat pockets, a gesture she knew well. 'I clean up OK.'

He sounded almost sheepish. She would have bought it if his wolfish grin hadn't betrayed him.

'I've got a job now. Thought I'd give the shorts a rest.'

Samantha felt the sting of disappointment. 'So you're back at your firm? You took the promotion.'

He looked at her a while, connecting all the dots. 'Tara got that promotion. I'm with Trident Data, consulting.'

'You work with Chris? Lucky you!'

'Lucky *him*.'

Samantha clapped slowly and reverently. 'Well played. But you're back in tech.'

'Tech wasn't the problem,' he said. 'It's what you do with it. Chris is smart about that.'

'Chris is just plain smart.' Samantha was suddenly conscious of her own attire. She was dressed in grey, too, but everything was 90 per cent Spandex. 'I just came back from yoga … no multi-million-dollar deals to speak of.'

He leaned against the doorframe. 'You look pretty.'

Frizzy hair, shiny skin, beat-up trainers and mismatched athletic wear, it didn't matter. He could always make her feel beautiful.

'I hate how we left things,' he said. '*You* left me high and dry.'

'If memory serves, I left you soaking wet.'

'Wet like a dog.' He let out a low laugh. 'I still have night-mares. Who knew you were so strong?'

'Well, now you know.'

She moved aside, allowing Roman Carver to step into her world.

'I was about to have dinner. There's enough for two if you like.'

'Thanks,' he said. 'I checked into a hotel, but haven't eaten all day. I'm surviving on coffee.'

'Take your coat off and drop it anywhere.' She went to the kitchen to retrieve another plate and upgrade the takeaway disposable utensils to the gold-toned ones her mother had bought her. Her heart was still racing. Naomi could have warned her that he intended to stop by. She was going to rip into her as soon as he left for bluer skies, as she was certain he would.

Roman called out to her. 'Hey. Where are you off to?'

Samantha took a deep cleansing yoga breath, pasted a smile on her face, and marched out of the kitchen. 'What did you say?'

He pointed at the open suitcase on the rug. 'Going on a trip?'

'Just got back from Rome, actually,' she said. 'Contrary to what you see in films, the Eternal City is therapeutic for everyone, not just for American divorcées.'

'More people need to know about that.' He took the plate from her. 'What great insight did Rome provide?'

'I learned that travelling is well and good, but home is fine. This is my home and I like it.'

Roman looked around. 'I like it, too. And I'm glad you got to travel.'

'It's easier now. My office went virtual and I can work from anywhere, even a plaza in Rome.'

His fingers tightened on the plate. 'You can work from anywhere?'

'And I get to blog like I've always wanted to. Tonight I'll edit the photos I took in Rome.' She swivelled on her heels and returned to the kitchen for proper drinking glasses. She'd been drinking from a sports water bottle. 'Hope you like chicken masala as much as I do.'

When she returned, he was standing pretty much in the same spot, still gripping the plate as if he intended to send it flying like a Frisbee. It was clear they would not be able to enjoy a meal without first clearing the air. She set the glasses on the coffee table and took the plate from him. Dinner could wait. Reheated masala was just as good.

'You said you wanted to ask me something. What is it?'

His expression softened. 'You're direct. I love that about you.'

Samantha took another deep breath, hoping to clear her fogged brain. She had to establish a few ground rules. 'I'm not playing any more guessing games, Roman. If you have something to say, spit it out.'

Holding things in had not served her, not in her love life or even in friendships. Going forward she would speak up and be as honest as possible. Samantha would expect no less from the people she let into her life.

Roman moved closer. 'All right, let's start there. You never answered my question, the one in my last text. If anyone was left guessing, it's me.'

Oh, damn … She knew exactly which text he was referring to. It wasn't as if she hadn't read it a thousand times, deleted it then went insane trying to get it back from oblivion.

For the sake of clarity, he repeated the question. 'Would you want that kind of intense love from me, Samantha? The kind of love I didn't think possible until I met you? Because if you do, nothing stands in my way.'

Samantha hadn't answered his question the first time around because her emotions were too big to squeeze into a text. She couldn't answer it now because there were no words for how she felt. Instead, she did what she'd wanted to do since his voice had spilled out of the intercom. She touched him just to make sure he was real, not a product of a fever dream.

Roman drew her to him and wrapped his arms around her, enveloping her in his warmth and strength. Her hurt and anger melted away. She was close to tears. She never thought she'd make it back to this place.

'Sam,' he whispered in her hair. 'How did I survive three weeks without you? I hated every minute of it.'

'Well, I hated you. So there's that.'

'Can you love me now?'

She pulled back and smiled up at him. 'Depends. How long are you staying for?'

'I'm headed to Morocco next. Think you could work from there?'

'I'll think about it.'

He kissed the corner of her lips as her smile grew wider. 'What can I do to convince you?'

'I'm all for Morocco, but where do we go from there?'

He slipped the tie out of her hair and let her curls spring free. 'Spending time at home would be nice.'

'And where's home for you lately?'

He stroked her cheek with his thumb. 'It's where you say it is.'

There went Samantha's heart. It may never return to her, and she was fine with that. She rose onto her tiptoes and kissed him. 'Welcome home, love.'

THE HIDDEN PATH

LIFE & TRAVEL BLOG

INTRODUCTION

Hello, everyone! Thanks for dropping into The Group Chat where we discuss all the things that make life in our twenties both wonderful and dreadful. Come with me as I travel the world with my partner, all the while staying connected with family and an exceptional group of friends. Love, life goals, money issues, and marriage – no subject is off the table. Don't forget to sound off in the comments and feel free to drop a meme or two. More later.

XO,

Sam

ACKNOWLEDGEMENTS

Wow. I can't believe we are here.

First of all, thank you for the support and belief in me so far. I hope this book makes you proud.

To have the opportunity to do this book is fantastic. It means so much more to me than just a romance. For me, this book represents a lot more, like diversity and representation. I have always been interested in books, mainly non-fiction growing up as a young girl. At the time, I didn't realise how vital seeing representation was for young people or how it probably shaped and impacted my life. And now, to bring this book out with characters who look and sound like me and characters who remind me of my friends from different backgrounds is very rewarding and humbling.

To Nadine, thank you a million times for seeing my exact vision and bringing Samantha and Roman to life in ways I could only have dreamed of. You are incredibly talented, and I am grateful that I could work with you.

Thank you to the Harper Collins and the Mills & Boon teams for all the passion and positivity you injected into this massive project. I must extend a special mention to Becky Slorach for the long zoom calls of me trying to explain every last detail of each chapter. You listened to me intently and understood everything and, in doing so, helped me fall back in love with the romance genre.

Thank you to my friends and family, who helped me create and set the scene from the reader's perspective and were genuinely excited to read the samples and gave me great advice and feedback. To all the people who inspire me daily, you know who you are, and my team for constantly pushing me to strive for more.

Finally, thank you enormously to all my supporters for being there and believing in me. Without you, I wouldn't be able to complete these kinds of things so close to my heart. I truly hope you enjoy Samantha's trip to Tobago.

Amber